S

S

# OVER 100
# GREAT NOVELS
OF
# EROTIC DOMINATION

If you like one you will probably like the rest

NEW TITLES EVERY MONTH

If you want to be on our confidential mailing list for our Readers' Club Magazine (with extracts from past and forthcoming titles) write to:

SILVER MOON READER SERVICES

Shadowline Publishing Ltd
Box 101
City Business Centre
Station Rise
York
YO1 6HT
United Kingdom

telephone: 01904 525729
Fax: 01904 522338

NEW AUTHORS WELCOME

Please send submissions to
Silver Moon Books
Box 101
City Business Centre
Station Rise
York
YO1 6HT

Silver Moon is an imprint of Shadowline Publishing Ltd
the print publishing division of the Convecto Media Group
First published 2007 Silver Moon Books
ISBN 9781-903687-94-9

# AFRICANUS II

# RITUAL OF PAIN

BY

## GEOFFREY ALLEN

ALSO BY GEOFFREY ALLEN

(THE AFRICANUS SERIES)
ARENA OF TORMENT
RITUAL OF PAIN
TEMPLE OF DARKNESS
SISTERS IN CHAINS (DUE OCT 2008)

# CHAPTER ONE

She was tall, shapely and naked, seemingly walking in a daze, her head twisting from side to side and occasionally looking over her shoulder as if she feared some unseen predator. At a rock pool she halted, bending low to splash its captured water over her bruised shoulders. Suddenly she stood up and looked swiftly at the black, towering rocks, but then realizing the sound was nothing more threatening than the beating wings of a seagull, she knelt again at the pool and continued washing her sand-caked limbs. All along the shore, shattered remnants of a ship lay scattered and broken. A few lifeless bodies, mostly female drifted aimlessly on the surface, disturbed only by the gentle motion of the waves. Above, the sky was clearing as the dark thunder clouds that had caused the storm began to disperse. On the cliff top a small group of men from the Dumnonii tribe watched in silence as their women folk collected driftwood and searched through the wreckage. There was little worth salvaging.

Africanus, as yet unnoticed by either the Celtic men or women, made her way to a cave in the cliff side and laid herself out on a large, flat rock. It had all happened so quickly, a storm that seemed to come from nowhere, the seas, one minute calm and serene and the next boiling with fury. The ship, rowed by female slaves destined for the slave markets of Londoninium, had been tossed like a cork, its terrified passengers, crew and slaves shrieking and swearing in terror as it drifted helplessly onto the rocks. All sense of discipline was lost and the rowers who might have propelled the vessel to safety scrambled onto the upper deck praying for deliverance. Even the whip lashing onto their bare backs failed to restore order. Above the sound of splintering wood came the command to abandon ship. Then, in an instant, the vessel keeled over. It took only one gigantic wave to wash its occupants overboard and cast them to the mercy of the raging sea.

Dimly, Africanus recalled seeing Circo swimming desperately towards her, and then he was lost from sight in the heaving swell. She never saw what happened to either Quintus or Nydia. All of them drowned, she assumed. And she was alone; it was as if the entire population of the world had suddenly vanished.

But gradually as her sense regained authority, she realized that could not be true. She was alone in a land occupied by people. But where? The ship had been heading for a country called Britannia; Circo's homeland. The ship had been wrecked on a wild and barren shore; a landscape as dark and foreboding as the storm clouds that had sunk her. She wished she had planned her escape from Rome with all its cruel perversions and uncertainty with more thought. It would have been better if they had set off overland instead of trusting to the sea. But that was irrational, for the Emperor's Praetorian Guard would soon have overtaken them and put them all to the sword, or worse.

She sat up and rubbed her naked thighs. The blood was flowing more freely through her veins now she had rested. Quickly, she inspected her body. No broken bones or gashed skin. Only a few aching bruises that would soon heal. Her grumbling stomach rumbled like an angry volcano reminding her she must eat and restore her strength. Somewhere there was a city called Londoninium and she must head for it. But in which direction? And clothes. She needed clothes to cover her nakedness. The short skirt she had been wearing when the ship struck had been ripped from her when she was washed overboard. If this strange dark land really was inhabited by savages, a naked woman would be like fresh meat to a tiger. She stood up flexing her limbs and walked out of the cave and along the deserted beach. She could see the corpses of the drowned bobbing in the surf; perhaps one or two might still have clothes upon them. As she drew closer to the water's edge, she hoped that none of her friends would be there.

The nearest body was one of the slave girls who had plied the oars. She was naked, except for the iron manacles still attached to her cold, lifeless wrists. Another floating close by was one of the female passengers. Remnants of a robe floated around her shoulders, badly torn but suffice to make a skirt that would just cover a naked rump. Africanus bent low to ease the cloth from its owner and then turned so quickly she almost lost her balance.

Out of the corner of her eye she had seen someone or something move behind one the rocks. Her eyes did a quick tour of the cliffs and beach and satisfied it was nothing more than the shadow of a passing cloud, she ripped the robe free from the dead woman. Deftly, she wrapped it around her hips, and feeling a lot less vulnerable set off along the sand.

She walked about a hundred yards then halted, turned full circle, her gaze slowly sweeping the bay, a vast amphitheatre of high rugged cliffs slowly descending to the sands. Again that uncertain and eerie feeling that she was being followed crept over her. The sand beneath her feet trembled as if by an approaching earthquake. The sound grew louder and closer and she recognized the sound of wheels and beating of horses hooves. A pair of chariots came thundering from behind the rocks and quickly divided; one heading along the surf, the other along the sand sweeping in a wide arc to cut off her retreat. Africanus broke into a run, her long bare legs carrying her swiftly towards the cliffs' end where boulders littered the beach. Get amongst them and she was safe, the rocks would break the chariot wheels and hurl the driver to his death. But the drivers knew the landscape well and skilfully avoided the jagged obstacles, steering their chariots clear and closing the gap between them and the fleeing woman.

She tripped, rolling over and over, tearing her skirt and

baring her buttocks to the driver. But she was on her feet in an instant and heading for a break in the cliffs. The nearest chariot, a light springy, wickerwork affair thundered past and began a long turn, coming back straight at her. She dodged the horses and leapt into a thicket of scrub. The chariot could not follow her there amid the deep gullies and ravines. Ahead lay a wood and she ran full pelt towards the trees, taking great leaps over the ravines, not caring that her heart was close to bursting and her soles cut and bleeding. The second chariot had disappeared somewhere in front of her, but the first was still hard behind, bouncing and bounding over the gullies and small protruding rocks. The driver, with a superb display of horsemanship, ran along the shafts and leapt onto the horses' backs. But Africanus was still ahead and entering the fringes of the wood. The driver stood upright on the horse and made a flying leap missing her legs by only a foot. She heard a deep throated groan as he hit the ground and ran on into the trees, not stopping until she found herself in a clearing. Her heart and lungs could stand it no longer and she crashed against a tree trunk gasping for air, her magnificent naked breasts heaving from exertion. The acrid smell of sweat filled the air around her and she closed her eyes; exhausted.

She opened them again and saw him standing directly in front of her, a tall burly man with long wild masses of hair reaching below his shoulders. His beard was long but well brushed it seemed. He looked at her with a curious mixture of surprise and intrigue as if trying to fathom who she was. She moved slightly, unnerved by his penetrating gaze and in a flash his sword was drawn and at her throat, the point just touching into the well. One false move and he'd pin her to the tree. The bushes rustled and his companion emerged, a younger man whose long hair was tied in a pony tail and his beard not so pronounced or luxurious. The point of the sword pressed deeper and she was up on tiptoe, her calves and thighs straining from her recent flight. She was still breathing hard, her tongue parched and her throat so dry it hurt.

"What have we here, father?" the younger man asked, taking a step closer.

He too looked at her with curiosity, but was still on his guard, one hand, she saw was on the hilt of his sword.

"A woman from that Roman ship we saw dashed on the rocks," he suggested, bringing the point of his sword slowly down her chest.

Africanus froze while the point travelled through her breast cleft and under her right breast.

The younger man moved closer still and reached out placing his hand on her breast and lightly squeezing it. There was more than just lust in his eyes, but a fascination both with the texture and colour of her skin. He left off fondling her breasts and reached for her braided hair, running the tightly woven braids through his fingers, seemingly admiring the skill that had woven them. Some of his own hair had been formed into plaits but not as artfully as her own.

The older man took away his sword and sheathed it. She knew it was useless to run now, she was their prisoner and they knew it.

The older man took her wrists and lifted them above her head. With surprising tenderness coming from a man of such rough mien he placed them gently on top of her scalp.

"She is tall and has a fine body," the younger man acknowledged, admiring her figure. "But why is her skin so dark?"

"Maybe she is one of the traders from over the water," his father remarked, placing a hand under her left breast.

He lifted it, wondering at its size and weight. None of the village women had breasts of that size, or such full and ripe nipples. Fear and a sense of hopelessness made the teats hard and erect, and they throbbed when his thumb passed lightly over the spreading pimpled disc. He gave her breasts a squeeze, harder this time, sinking his fingers into the ample mound of soft, sensuous flesh. Then he placed both hands on the sides of her breasts and pushed them together marvelling at the deep crease forming between them. His son, emboldened from his father's groping ran the flat of his hand over her ribs and belly, patting it and smiling at the hollow sound it made. Africanus stood rigid, not daring to move, suffering in silence the humiliation of having her naked body explored by these barbarians. The son's hand travelled over the swell of her hips and down her thighs, then slowly back up again and into the perfect vee of her tightly knitted pubic curls. She could see both men had large erections bulging against their trousers. She guessed that soon they would both have her and there was nothing she could do about it but submit to whatever they chose to do.

The older man placed his hands on her shoulders and turned her facing the tree trunk. Her head turned sideways staring at the dense undergrowth. A fine bead of sweat trickled down the side of her face as she awaited the next assault.

A pair of hands lighted on her buttocks, smoothing the skin in circles, pressing and poking each buttock.

"A strong arse," she heard the older man remark.

And he gave each half a hard slap, hard enough to make her jolt against the tree. Her breasts flattened on the rough bark forcing the nipples to rub hard into the trunk and she winced with pain.

"A good back, too," the son admired, running his hands over her shoulders and down the sides of her indented spine.

The older man knelt behind her and felt her legs, pinching the flesh of her thighs and tight muscles of her calves. At an unspoken command, the son took hold of her ankle and eased it over the earth, spreading her legs open as far as he could. She knew what was coming next and held her breath. It was not long in coming. A hand went under her legs and rubbed the soft sex lips, going back and forth until she felt her sex juice creaming over his fingers.

"Wherever she is from, she must have had many men in her cunt. Feel the size of it. Even a mare would be hard pressed to match that."

His father placed his palm over the mound of her sex and squeezed hard. The son stood up and placed his hand on the small of her back, holding her still against the tree.

"Have all the men from your tribe fucked you?" the older man asked, taking his hand from her sex and running his fingers through her arse crease.

She nodded thinking it wise to go along with whatever they wanted. She wished Circo would come crashing through the bushes, armed to the teeth, his sword flashing, or even Fortuna wielding her deadly whip. They'd soon show these barbarians how not to insult a gladiatrix. But that was just fantasy. Both of them were miles away, and Circo was probably making that fateful journey into the underworld. If only she had her sword and was free. These barbarians would have the biggest shock of their lives.

A hard slap landed on her rump and she was spun round, her back pressing on the tree. Without warning the older man bent his face to her breasts and sucked on the erect nipples, drawing each teat into his mouth, sucking as if she were a wet nurse suckling a thirsty babe. She bucked when his teeth bit on the nipple, her hands flying to his head to pull it away. But his son moved fast and unsheathed his sword, aiming the point at her throat. Even though she was a woman and naked, they were taking no chances. Secretly she admired the speed at which he moved and his accuracy in delivery. Gradually she was forming the opinion that they were not so stupid after all. It took a good deal of skilful training to handle a sword like that.

The older man lifted his head and slapped her breast, bringing his hand down in a fast swoop, landing the flat of his hand directly on the bouncing globe. The nipple rose with pain, but inwardly she felt a sensation of pleasure, a

11

cold stirring in her belly and hoped they wouldn't notice it. It wouldn't do letting them know that pain, particularly sexual pain, brought on an overwhelming desire to have a stiff cock pounding inside her soaking cunt. But they didn't seem to notice the fleeting look of desire in her moistened eyes. The older man hit her again, slapping each breast in turn while his son went wide eyed at the way her breasts swung and wobbled to and fro, each enormous mound colliding with the other, and the nipples! Now they were as hard and stiff as young acorns and he couldn't resist taking them in his fingers and rolling each teat so hard her eyes watered. But still she did not cry out. All those many months of hard, arduous training as a gladiatrix had instilled marvellous self-discipline and it would take a lot more than a couple of groping savages to make her scream.

The son started slapping her thighs, delighting in beating the hard, solid fleshy pillars that quivered with every blow.

"The girl shows strength," his father acknowledged, standing back to get a better look at her tight-lipped face.

"Let's see how strong she rides," his son leered, taking a fistful of hair and twisting her head.

"You can ride her all in good time. But now we'll take her to the village and she can join the others. Bring her to the chariot."

Muttering curses, the younger man dragged her by the hair through the thicket, not letting go until they reached the place where they had left the chariots.

"You run fast," the father told her with begrudging admiration. "Now we'll see if you can run a lot faster. Tie the bitch to the horse. If she falls, we'll drag her the whole length of the beach. See how she likes that."

The younger man baulked at not having the opportunity to ride her magnificent arse, wasted no time in carrying out his father's instructions. He took off his belt and fastened one end to her wrist. The other he secured to the horse's collar.

He gave her arse a final hard slap before mounting the chariot. The older man had mounted his own equipage and was heading out of the thicket onto the beach. His son followed behind at a slow walk with Africanus walking in long strides beside the horse.

"Now we'll see your tits shake," he laughed, steering the chariot further onto the broad expanse of sand.

Africanus stared into the distance. The sea had ebbed and the beach looked a lot longer than when she had first made her escape. She took a deep breath and broke into a steady trot as the chariot gathered speed, keeping her eyes on the sand directly in front of her. If she stumbled and fell before they reached the rocks she'd be dashed to pieces. Suddenly a whip lashed over her shoulders and back, not exactly painful, but the humiliation of being driven like an animal was real enough.

"Heyaa, heyaa," the younger man's voice barked, urging his horse to greater efforts.

The pounding hooves increased in speed and Africanus ran beside it, taking longer and longer strides, trying desperately to keep up and above all, not lose her balance.

"Look at her tits, father," the younger man shouted. "See how they bounce!"

The older man slowed his vehicle and came alongside, leaning over to see Africanus' magnificent orbs bouncing and jiggling with every leap. Her nipples were stiff with fear and he could plainly see the pointed teats rising and falling on her swaying breast. He could also see her long, gleaming thighs and calves taking ever greater strides, jumping over a small outcrop of rock and pebbles. His son whistled at the sight of her buttocks and hips doing the most cock hardening dance he'd ever witnessed.

"Keep your mind on your horse boy! Instead of between that woman's legs," his father shouted, steering his chariot towards the piles of wreckage still littering the beach.

"Aye, aye, father," he responded, but couldn't resist lashing his whip into her beautiful arse.

The sudden pain made her leap high and her bouncing breasts went in circles, jiggling and wobbling with every renewed stride. She was sweating like a mare now, her back, bottom and legs gleaming in the sun like polished jet. It was almost possible to smell the heat rising from her soaking skin. If ever there was a sight calculated to give a man a rock hard cock it was a naked women drenched in her own sweat, especially a tall black one with a figure that any other woman would have gladly killed for.

She was beginning to tire now, her legs were drained of strength and she was panting like a race horse, catching her breath in great gulps.

"Please," she wailed, "I can't go on. I'm finished."

The driver reined in the horse and slowed to a steady trot, letting the exhausted woman regain her breath. He steered the chariot across the beach to where the water had receded and the sand was as hard as stucco. Here the going was easier, at least her feet found a surer footing and the pace had mercifully slowed. He tugged on the reins and the chariot wheels splashed through the surf. The horses' hooves pounded through the water throwing up great lumps of sand and pebbles. When it hit Africanus' naked skin it was like being pricked with red hot needles. With her free hand she shielded her eyes from the gritty spray threatening to blind her. From somewhere under her feet the sand suddenly gave way. The chariot lurched dangerously and spun round throwing her off balance. In a trice she was being dragged through the shallows, her arm almost wrenched from its socket. She twisted and turned, her legs only a whisper away from the animal's pounding hooves. One false move now and she would be crippled for life. Then the belt snapped and she fell flat on her face. The chariot wheel rushed past, missing her body by an inch. She rolled over and over and lay curled in a ball, hugging her knees and sobbing bitterly. The chariot made a sharp turn and came thundering back to where she lay.

"She's had enough," the older man remarked, bringing his own chariot to a halt. "She can ride the rest of the way."

The younger man jumped into the sea and hauled her roughly onto her feet.

"That taught you a lesson, eh?" he smirked, running his lascivious eyes over her sand-caked skin.

Africanus was still breathing hard, drawing his attention to her heaving breasts. He couldn't resist reaching out and grabbing the sweating globe. Africanus stood still, not looking directly into his gloating eyes, but at the chariot. It was only a couple of feet away. If she could mount it, she stood a good chance of reaching the distant cliffs and woods. The older man would surely chase her but once she was clear of the beach and heading over the moor land there would be little he could do to stop her. It was worth a try, anything to escape these savages.

The younger man let out a groan and collapsed like a dead weight into the sand, his hand clutching his balls. The older man watched stunned as the black girl leapt into the chariot and seized the reins. Then he broke into a wild peal of laughter. Now matter how hard she lashed the horses the stupid beasts never lifted a hoof.

"Just shows how much you know about horses," he snorted. "Now get out of that chariot."

Feeling very foolish, she climbed from the footboard and stood on the sand looking at the younger man struggling painfully to his feet. In his eyes she saw murder and took a step backwards.

"Put her over the stallion, bottom up," his father said drily, his lips creasing into an infuriating grin. "And next time try not to let a mere woman get the better of you."

He was livid with anger. No woman had ever dared to

15

humiliate him in such a way. If the rest of the tribe got to hear of it he would have lost all respect and would probably be cast out. He seized her arm and, with a dexterity and speed that surprised her, threw Africanus over the back of the horse, her bottom baring its splendid curves to the sky. He was in no hurry to make it back to the village, but set off at a slow trot, lashing her naked rump with the reins. It hurt far worse than any whip or cane she had endured, the thin leather straps cut onto the fat of her buttocks like tongues of fire. She knew she would receive no mercy and, as the lash whipped into her bottom and thighs, had a horrible feeling this wasn't the only punishment she going to receive from his outraged pride.

Africanus clung to the shaft between the horses, her head upside down and buried under her cascading braids. Beneath her the earth passed by with increasing speed and she could feel her body slowly slipping over the beast's back. She took her weight on her arms, now as straight as arrows. A dull ache started to spread through her shoulders and back as her whole bodyweight bore down on the shaft. But that was nothing compared to the fiery pain going through her upturned bottom. The young Celt was lashing her rump with increasing fury, striking each buttock in quick succession and loving every moment. He heard her cry out and sent the reins whistling across her bare back, striking where he knew the pain would be fiercest, at the base of her spine and crease of her arse. He left off beating her for a few moments and Africanus almost plunged to her death as the horses swung in a wide arc, deftly missing a protruding rock. They were gathering speed now and again the hooves threw up a deadly hail of sand and pebbles. She turned her face away from the hail and fell forward bumping her head on the shaft. She was so far over the horse's back that her legs were horizontal and opening wider to help keep her balance. Underneath her chest, her breasts flattened against the hot hide of the horse, her nipples erect and throbbing as they rubbed hard into its coarse hair. Why did this have to happen now? Her naked body upside down and being aroused both from the renewed lashing and the thrilling sensation of her nipples and buttocks whipped and teased. She knew that the older man was riding alongside her, gazing enraptured into her open sex. She wondered if he could see the first signs of her orgasm trickling between her legs. The Celts were superb horsemen and knew the effect that horse riding had on a woman. Many a village girl had reached her first orgasm riding bareback on a pony only to lose her virginity to the first man that happened to come along. Now the older man was sure this splendid piece of fucking flesh he saw naked and jolting over the beast was no exception.

He drew his chariot alongside the spreading legs and saw at a glance the bitch was already in heat.

"Pull up, boy," he yelled, and Africanus felt the chariot grind to a halt.

She heard the older man dismount and come behind her, hauling her quickly from the horse. Her eyelids were heavy and dolorous with longing and sexual arousal when she stared him in the face.

"Stay where you are, boy," he commanded. "And guard the horses."

His son watched sullenly as the black girl was dragged by the hair into the nearest thicket. The old man could display an amazing strength when needs must, and in a flash Africanus was on her back, legs wide spread watching him releasing his trouser belt. She knew what was coming and it was useless to pretend otherwise. She would just have to submit to the rampant throbbing cock she saw springing free from his groin.

He was like an animal with none of the refined ways she had grown used to at the hands of the Romans. He smelt like a bull and probably hadn't washed within weeks. But there was nothing unmanly about the massive cock rearing up at her, or the powerful muscles honed from so much battle. Scars from previous combats lined his rugged face and chest. He was going to take her like a wild animal and a cold, familiar chill went through her stomach. He slapped her hard on her belly and laughed out loud.

"You're a fine mare," he complimented, putting his hairy forearms under her knees.

With no more delicacy than a rutting cock, he threw her legs over his shoulders and penetrated her with a single thrust. Their eyes met and for a couple of seconds they just stared at each other, the barbarian warrior and his captive slave, eyeing their respective bodies, getting the measure of their physique and strength. He moved slowly at first, riding her as he might an untried horse, settling into the saddle of her soft belly, taking care not to drive her too hard. Africanus looked over his shoulder at the trees rustling gently on the breeze, then at his huge weather-beaten face and wild beard. She rested her hands on his hips and rocked in time with his thrusting. He wrinkled his nose, breathing in her hot, earthy smell of sweat. She in turn could feel the sheer power of his muscles rippling with lust.

The hot reek of their unwashed bodies threw them both into a wild frenzy. Her skin was hot and slippery with a texture that was entirely new, and he wondered at it as he thrust violently into her sex. She grunted and flung her arms tightly around his back. Her legs slipped from his shoulders and locked over his buttocks. There was nothing soft about them when they flexed with every renewed thrust. For a savage and primitive barbarian he certainly knew how to pleasure a woman. Grunting aloud like a boar, he rammed his pelvis hard into the join of her legs, keeping her shoulders pinned to the earth with his outstretched hands. His pace slowed while he lowered his shaggy head to her quivering breasts and gorged himself on her throbbing nipples. He knew a few women from his village that had large teats but none compared to this dark beauty. Neither did they have such splendid, long shapely legs. He glanced over his shoulder at the shimmering pillars of her thighs, the way they went hard when he thrust and softened again as her belly relaxed.

Africanus thrilled to the primitive ambience of it all. She was being fucked hard on the bare earth, her body naked and writhing under her captor, snorting and grunting, treating her like an animal, or some loose whore he'd bought with no thoughts of love other than raw, unbridled sex. She wondered what he would do with her when he had finished. Let her go, beat her for the pleasure of punishing her beautiful bottom, or make her his concubine. She just hoped he wouldn't do anything worse like slit her throat. Circo had told her that the more savage of the Celts killed and ate women on their feast days, or was that just a story he made up to frighten her? But it was that fear that made her feel so horny; a dark, unexplained inner feeling that sent quivers through her belly and made it tense and her sex tight around his grinding cock.

But the feeling was short lived. She started moaning, the beginning of her climax. Pinioned to the earth, she could do nothing but gyrate her hips and thighs. He was right over her, blasting his hot breath over her face, growling like a hungry wolf and slamming harder and harder into her dripping sex. Her heels fell from his buttocks and dug into the soil, lifting them both into an arc. His eyes widened at the power hidden in her legs and hips. Suddenly she was all muscle; her stomach flattened and sucked inwards, her thighs were like iron as she bore his full weight and the splendid length of maleness pounding inside her. Their climax did not last long, maybe no more than a few minutes, and they collapsed panting like mare and stallion at stud. Her fingers had raked the earth and she clutched fistfuls of black, crumbling soil in her palms. She smiled with sexual exhaustion and closed her eyes. He grunted his satisfaction at her performance and lay inert on the soft mound of her body. He eased himself up and rolled off her and, with his cock still hard and throbbing, reached for his trousers.

The black girl was sitting up rubbing her aching thighs and calves, looking at him with a languorous level gaze. Her eyes were so dark he could hardly discern the pupils from the irises that seemed extraordinarily large. Between her open legs he saw the glistening traces of her love juice clinging to her tight nest of pubic curls. He would have sucked her dry, but a cry from the other side of the copse had him on his feet in a trice. Roughly, he hauled her to her feet and dragged her to where the chariots were waiting.

"Was she a good fuck, father?" the younger man asked with a note of hostility in his voice.

"She fucks like a stoat," the older man replied on a note of celebration.

Without another word he lifted Africanus into the chariot and whipped up the horses.

The tide was coming in fast and if they didn't get a move on they would be stranded on the beach.

"Hold tight!" he yelled, lashing the horses.

And the beasts broke into a gallop heading towards a break in the cliff and the road that led to the village beyond.

# CHAPTER TWO

A cluster of circular huts made of wicker and thatch lay within a stockade of pointed stakes, and over the entrance recently decapitated heads grinned horribly at passers by. The chariots slowed to a crawl and Africanus stared agog at the cows and pigs shitting and snorting in their pens. All in all it reminded her of the banished outcasts expelled from Rome who lived in poverty and filth. For a moment she had the fleeting sensation of going insane, it just didn't seem credible that people could actually live in such primitive conditions. But then the villagers emerged from the huts and gathered in a fascinated group around the naked black woman in their midst. She stepped down from the chariot and covered her breasts with her forearms. It was bad enough that she was naked let alone be stared at by these savages.

"Wanda," the older man called to a young woman. "Take the new girl to the slave hut and see she is tightly chained."

The young woman bowed and led Africanus to a solitary hut standing amid pools of black, stagnant water.

"Sit down," the girl said almost apologetically. "I have to do our chieftain's bidding so put up your hands."

Africanus obeyed and the girl smiled while she fastened iron shackles to her wrists linked with a short stout chain. She fitted more shackles to her ankles and an iron collar around her neck. A length of chain was fastened to the collar and secured to the centre post of the hut. Feeling more like a tethered animal than a human being, Africanus watched her fill a beaker with water and place it in her manacled hands. She was not unattractive with a kindly oval, sunburned face. Her long flaxen hair was parted at the middle and gathered into two long plaits reaching to her waist. She wore a tight fitting woollen vest which showed off her ample breasts. Her bright blue skirt reached to her ankles and around one of them she sported a finely crafted silver ring. Bracelets of magnificently wrought gold and silver adorned her arms. Whoever made them possessed a skill equal to any Roman goldsmith. Africanus was beginning to wonder if they were not so primitive after all.

"Are you from that wrecked ship?" the girl asked, refilling the beaker. "Because if you are, we've got a load more slaves like you, but they're in the nets waiting for the men to have them. It's our custom. We always give new slave girls to the men." She looked curiously at the chained black girl, her head on one side like a bird. "What's your name?"

"Africanus," she said, looking up at her and noticing how her nipples poked provocatively through the thin vest. "And I am from that ship. Do you know if anyone else survived? Any men?" she added softly.

The girl shrugged. "I didn't see any. We found only women. Are you hungry?"

Africanus nodded. She had forgotten her hunger until the girl brought it to her attention. The girl went off, closing the door behind her and plunging the hut into darkness. It seemed impossible to believe that only a few days ago she was living in Rome, a great city of marble palaces and buildings that reached to the sky and where bath houses and paved streets were common place. Now here she was chained in a hut that the Romans wouldn't have used as a dog kennel. She tugged on the chain but it was too well fastened to rip from the post. Whatever plans her captors had in store, Africanus had no intentions of remaining amongst these savages longer than was possible.

The door opened and Wanda brought in a plate of meat and vegetables. Through the open door Africanus watched the villagers going about their business. Most of the women were engaged in weaving and spinning, working their looms with consummate skill, and all dressed in brightly coloured skirts and tunics. The men wore loose baggy trousers and

22

tartan tunics and worked in their narrow fields tilling the earth. But for all their seemingly peaceful domesticity, Africanus came to the conclusion they would be dangerous people to cross.

"Why are all those heads over the entrance to your village?" she asked, chewing.

"Oh, those," Wanda replied casually. "They're the heads of our enemies in the next village. We had a battle a few days ago and brought them back as trophies. Serves 'em right for taking our women and our cows."

Africanus stopped chewing and spat out a lump of gristle. "Are you always fighting?"

Wanda shrugged her slim shoulders. "Pretty much. If there isn't a war on, we'll soon start one." And she burst out laughing. "I think there's another battle coming soon with the Bear clan on the other side of the hill. Caractus wants to prove himself."

"Who is Caractus?"

"The son of Prasutagus, our chief who took you prisoner." She smiled slyly. "I think the chief will be visiting you later."

"He's visited me already," Africanus retorted, putting aside the plate. "Am I going to get any clothes?"

"The slaves usually go naked, except in winter. But I'll see if I can find you a skirt."

Africanus thanked her and the girl left but the door remained open, and one or two curious women poked their heads in, anxious to get a closer view of the tall black woman captured on the beach. Men passed by and glanced at her, but none dared to enter the hut. It was more than their lives were worth to tamper with the chieftain's chosen slave.

At nightfall a huge bonfire was lighted in the centre of the village and an ox roasted in celebration of capturing so many slave women from the wrecked ship. It wasn't often that such valuable booty washed upon their shore. They would fetch good prices when the time was ripe.

Prasutagus, looking resplendent in a long tartan robe and his hair now in plaits, strode into the centre of the assembly.

"Bring forward the slaves," he commanded.

Africanus shuffled on her knees, getting as close to the doorway as the chain would allow. The women rowers were slung from the trees in nets, their naked bodies struggling against the mesh. The men released the ropes that suspended them and with a painful thud the slaves fell to earth. The nets were speedily untangled and the women processed in single file towards the blazing fire. Africanus strained at the chain to see if Nydia was amongst them, but there was no one there she recognized.

The first slave girl was brought to Prasutagus. Naked and trembling, she hid her face in her hands. Africanus could see her head shaking and knew she was crying with fear and shame.

"Open your legs, girl," he commanded.

The girl dumbly obeyed and stood with her slim legs wide apart. She was still hiding her face and weeping.

"Take your hands from your face!" he snapped.

Her arms fell limply at her sides and he reached forward and took a tuft of her hair, lifting her head and nodding at her beauty. His other hand went under her legs and, with one powerful heave of his arm, raised her clear off the ground. Africanus let out a whistle. For an elderly man he was in good shape and had kept himself fit. The girl seemed weightless in his grasp as his hand closed around her sex. His hand clenched into a fist crushing her mound and Africanus heard a sharp cry of pain.

"Who wiill have her?" Prasutagus asked.

A dozen voices yelled out at once. A tall, burly Celt stepped out of the crowd and came boldly to his chieftain. The chief nodded his assent and tossed the girl into his arms.

"You fought well, Brinorth, do with her as you wish."

"I salute our great chief," the warrior acknowledged,

throwing the girl over his shoulder and giving her bare rump a hefty slap.

He strode off to his hut and another trembling girl was brought forward. But this time Prasutagus didn't lift her, but ordered her to bend over and spread her cheeks. Blushing with shame, she placed her hands on her buttocks and stretched them open. One of the village women knew what he had in mind and stepped up to the girl and, using a small brush, dipped it into a pot of wode and painted a circle around her bottom hole.

Africanus squinted in the flickering light and saw one of the warriors approach the painted girl. He filled his mouth with wine and sent a fast jet hissing over her buttocks. The liquid missed the circle and splashed off her left buttock. A roar of laughter had the onlookers in convulsions. From her place in the darkened hut Africanus permitted herself a wry smile. At least the chief had a sense of humour.

Cursing wildly, the warrior rejoined the crowd and another came forward. He missed the circle and sent a stream of wine cascading over her back and hair.

"Can none of my fine warriors hit her arse," Prasutagus taunted jocularly.

A tall warrior with a dark brooding face raised the jug to his lips, took careful aim and sent the liquid squirting into her bottom hole. She jolted from the shock and toppled over falling into a crumpled heap. He was there at once and grabbed her wrists. Africanus watched her naked body dragged through the crowd and into his hut.

The next girl was ordered to her knees. She did exactly as she was told, thrusting out her breasts and throwing back her head. More logs were hurled onto the fire and through the leaping flames Africanus saw the woman paint huge circles over the girl's nipples.

"The first man to squirt his own juice over her tits can have her for as long as he pleases," Prasutagus announced.

The warriors came closer and dropped their trousers. The roar from the crowd was deafening as they started rubbing their cocks to erection. The first to come aimed badly and sent a hot jet of sperm over the girl's chest. She shuddered as it ran in a stream through her breast cleft. The next angled his cock to her nipples and rubbed his cock fast and furious. The girl grunted when his juice sailed over her chest and splashed all over her face. A warrior, small and stocky, took more careful aim and sent his sperm directly into the circles. The girl winced and came upright looking at the juice dripping from her breasts.

"She's yours, Eldred. See that she is well fucked before sunrise."

He too, grabbed her hair and dragged her screaming across the earth. Africanus watched closely as the proceedings continued. She had seen many acts of depravity but none so cruelly humiliating. But there was worse to come.

"Get on your back, girl," Prasutagus barked, but chuckling at the sight of the next terrified slave. "Open your legs and point your toes to the moon."

The girl was sobbing as she obeyed, opening her legs wide and lifting them high in the air, toes pointing to the starlit sky.

"Look at the size of her cunt. She must've had more cock than all the stakes in the stockade," a warrior guffawed.

"Even a bull couldn't satisfy that hole," another rejoined.

She was still on her back, legs frozen in terror as each warrior took turns to do nothing more harmful than squirt wine into her open sex. The successful warrior lifted her with surprising gentility and carried her into the darkness.

The rest of the slaves were quickly dispersed amongst the remaining warriors and Africanus shuffled away from the doorway and sat leaning against the pole. The Celtic warriors were fine men, courageous and strong, but she reasoned that given the right circumstances, she could defeat them in open combat, for as yet none of them had any idea of how well-trained and ferocious she could be.

A shadow moved across the doorway and she looked up suddenly. A man stood in the shadows eyeing her nakedness. She heard him move stealthily outside the frail walls of the hut, standing still and breathing heavily. She was chained and fettered and could do nothing against him if he chose to slit her throat. But at the approach of another man the figure scurried quickly into the darkness. Africanus wasn't easily frightened but a cold, clammy sweat broke out under her arms and she breathed a sigh of relief when Prasutagus strode through the door.

"How long are you going to keep me chained?" she asked bitterly. "I'm not a dog."

"No you aren't," he agreed. "You're a splendid looking bitch."

She looked at the growing bulge in his trousers and the lustful glint in his eyes. "Are you going to shoot your spunk over my tits?" she said.

Something of a smile flickered across his lips. "You saw that, did you?"

"Yes, and the way you frightened that poor girl."

She was about to say that she would have given them something to think about if she'd been armed, but thought better of it and sat patiently while he unshackled her chains.

"I see you've been fed and watered," he observed. "A woman's all the better when her belly's full."

He undressed and sat beside her stroking her thighs. His hand roamed over her belly and breasts. In the half light of the tallow lamp he had lighted she saw an undisguised look of admiration for the body he was inspecting.

"You're a strong woman," he murmured. "Someone has been working on your body strength, building up these muscles, but now we'll see just how strong you are. Fetch me that pole."

She went over to a pile of discarded poles and rafters and brought over the one he indicated, as long and as straight as a spear shaft.

"Kneel up," he ordered, sliding the shaft through his hands and testing its smoothness. "And spread your thighs."

Africanus got up on her knees and he slid the shaft behind them. A gentle push on her chest sent her tumbling backwards and the cry of pain shrieking from her lips echoed across the slumbering village. Her thighs and calves felt as if they'd been pierced with red hot needles. Her back arched and she was sure she heard her spine crack. While she lay writhing in agony, he selected another pole and placed it under her neck. It took only a few moments to stretch her arms along the pole and bind her wrists. Crucified, she lay still feeling the pain creeping up her thighs. His erection was enormous as he knelt between her open legs, and even in that dim light she could see it throbbing. He held the lamp closer to her quivering sex and stroked the fat, blubbery lips. She gasped when he thrust his fingers inside her; pushing them in as far as they could reach. She felt the bony ridges of his knuckles revolve against her sex lips, forcing them open, and all the while the burning pain in her legs and belly grew hotter. He fingered her for several minutes and when they were slicked with juice, took his hand away and thrust them into her mouth. He moved them slowly in and out of her lips until she had sucked them clean. Her breathing came in slow, deep inhalations and he watched her magnificent breasts rise and fall. He was in no hurry. He had all night to do whatever he chose. But the pain increasing in her legs and back was unbearable.

"Please," she gasped, "take that pole from under my knees."

"It stays there until I've fucked you," he said sternly.

He was about to penetrate her but something held him back. He reached for his trousers and, gathering up one of the legs, tied it around her head, making sure she was firmly gagged.

28

It wouldn't do, having her screams waking up the whole village in the dead of night.

His hand closed around his cock, stroking it to an even greater erection. She could see his balls moving with anticipation. Her stomach churned when he lay over her, guiding his cock into her gaping sex tunnel. He made some crude joke about her being able to take a stallion, but it was lost on her. The pain was going through her buttocks and back, stabbing with excruciating persistence. Her head rolled from side to side as his cock slowly filled her, going in an inch at a time until his balls slapped against her sex. Thoughtfully, he took his weight on his elbows and let his chest ride gently over her breasts, just enough to feel her hardened nipples graze against his skin.

"It's an old tribal custom," he told her. "To test the strength of a woman's legs. If you can walk after being fucked with the pole under your knees, you will have proved your worth and will be rewarded."

She would have loved to have told him to bury his head in a pile of shit, but all she could utter was a series of agonising grunts. Her thighs had turned to iron hard pillars of black, sweating flesh. The muscles in her calves bulged and strained. Her outstretched arms threatened to wrench from her shoulders. Only the delicious feeling of his massive erection pumping her sex offered any relief.

Through the slits in the wicker walls of the hut she saw a full moon rising above the dark scudding clouds. It seemed to mock her with its silvery rays, gentle and dreamlike as they lighted on the village roofs. Her eyes were ablaze with pain and frustrated anger, impotent against the rope that bound her wrists to the shaft. The more he pumped her, the greater her muscles ached. But Prasutagus had no thoughts of pity. His mind was filled with the pleasure of fucking the magnificent woman straining beneath him. Her sex had closed around his cock like a soft glove. He could feel the tender petals of her vaginal walls caressing his cock, especially over the swollen tip. A tickling sensation went right to the root of his manhood and filled his balls with an overwhelming desire to shoot his load deep into her belly. He stopped riding her and took time to gorge on her breasts. Her nipples had swelled to the size of ripe blackberries, large, round and wondrously dimpled. The dark discs around the throbbing teats had spread over half her breasts and he sucked hard, drawing all of the sweating mounds into his mouth. His teeth nibbled on the teats, rolling each bud back and forth while his tongue flicked fast over the indented skin.

A warbling started in her throat and he saw her teeth cutting into the cloth that gagged her. Her blazing eyes stared wide with pain and the thrill of being fucked defenceless and in so much agony. It was coming from everywhere at once, but it was her thighs and back which suffered most. Prasutagus rose on one arm, and with his free hand, slapped the sides of her thighs. He liked women with strong, hard thighs, good for pulling ploughs and fucking, particularly when they were straining like the pair heaving either side of his hips. He stopped slapping them and ran the flat of his hand up their full length. From her knees to her hips was one long length of hard, silky skin that was wet with sweat. He reached under the arch of her back and wriggled his hand around the globes of her buttocks. Her arse was firm and solid under his palm, a striking contrast he noticed to the soft, wobbling arses of the village women. Again he wondered how a female body could be so well honed to perfection. There was not an ounce of excess fat on her anywhere. She was all woman; shapely, curvaceous and, he decided, the best fuck he'd had in living memory. Only a captured, olive-skinned slave approached her beauty. But that had been a long time ago when he was a young warrior. Now, in middle age he was proving to himself and the writhing, grunting woman beneath him that he could fuck as well as any young Celt in his clan. He recalled an old tribal motto, 'when a man's balls are full, his mind is empty,' but his mind was full of the black woman, and now he couldn't get enough of her. He'd had several slaves and free born women crucified and with the pole under their knees. None had lasted long. But this bitch was still snaking her hips as he again resumed his manic pumping.

He fumbled with his trouser belt and drew out a small dagger. Ignoring the terrified look in her eyes, he reached out and cut the ropes binding her wrists. He put his finger to his lips and she nodded, understanding not to make a sound as he fumbled with the trouser leg and tore it from her head. He didn't give her a chance to breathe before crushing her voluptuous lips under his open mouth. Their hot tongues met in a frenzy of wriggling and poking. Her freed arms flew to his back and raked the skin with her sharp, broken nails. The pain in her racked limbs and buttocks had reached the point where it had turned to numbness, and the only thing she felt now was the sensation of his cock slamming brutally into her sex, and the crushing and squeezing of her breasts under his mauling hands.

"You can really fuck," she breathed, punching the sides of his ribs.

He took hold of her braids and forced her head backwards. He was still keeping his weight on his arms. If he had rested his chest on her, even though the temptation to feel her soft breasts flattening under him was irresistible, her spine would have snapped. He rode her with long, powerful thrusts, giving her his whole length while she writhed in painful ecstasy beneath his rippling frame.

He let go of her hair and raised himself up, gathering strength in his loins for the final strokes that would fill her with his hot, squirting juice.

Africanus' face took on the mask of rising orgasm; her eyelids drooped and through her parted lips he could hear her breathing in short jerky pants. Her breasts rose and fell and he paused, watching the splendid black globes wobbling and quivering.

Her head rolled to one side and she suddenly stopped moving. The full moon had disappeared, but only for a second as the silhouette of a man passed stealthily by. She could see the figure outside the hut and knew instinctively they were being watched.

"There's someone outside," she whispered, holding his shoulders tightly.

But he didn't hear her, or if he did, took no notice. He was coming fast and in those few brief seconds the world had stopped while his organ trembled inside her. Africanus hugged him close regardless of the numbing pain shooting through her thighs and back, and he came with one massive pelvic thrust. Her bottom jerked and slammed her sex mound hard into his pumping cock. Her orgasm suddenly erupted and she let out a deafening shriek. Quickly, he clamped his hand over her mouth, stifling her orgasmic cries. Then it was all over and he slid his sweating torso from her quaking belly. His arms went under her shoulders, lifting her off the ground and, with one fast sweep, the pole was whisked away. She was on her knees, slumped against his chest, all passion spent.

"You did well, my beautiful slave," he croaked. "And you shall be rewarded."

"I need a drink," she rasped, hardly able to mouth the words.

Prasutagus left her and in his brief absence Africanus experienced a chill of fear, the first she had felt in living memory. Instinctively, she reached for the pole ready to fell anyone who crept into the hut. An owl hooted and she almost wet herself. It was fear of the unknown that had her on edge, the strangeness of unfamiliar surroundings amongst a people who were wild and barbarous. More than ever she longed for Circo, or Fortuna, but most of all she missed Rome with its sun baked streets and olive groves, and the glory of the Colosseum.

"Wine," Prasutagus offered, shoving a pitcher into her belly. "It is your reward for fucking so well."

She drank deeply, letting the wine trickle over her chin and chest. "We were being watched," she said darkly. "Someone was outside looking through those sticks."

"The wine's gone to your head," he dismissed, looking briefly over his shoulder. "Now let me see you walk."

She got painfully to her feet and stretched her aching limbs, then bent over rubbing life back into her thighs. He watched in silence at her breasts shaking from side to side, the nipples erect and pointing to the floor.

"Bend over and touch your toes," he said, getting up and going to the pile of discarded wood.

"Are you going to beat me?" she asked, seeing him come back with a rod.

"You fucked well," he grated. "Now let's see you hold up having this across your bare arse."

"Do you people always treat your slaves this way?" she asked, backing away at the sight of the rod bending in his hands.

"We have a saying, 'a woman is all the better for a good beating, like a walnut tree, the more you beat them, the better they be. Now bend over!"

"Wouldn't you rather I sucked your cock instead," she whispered, placing her hand under his balls and giving them a squeeze.

He looked into her smouldering eyes and his cock went as hard as the rod he wielded.

"Your mother mated with a serpent," he muttered, feeling her hand stroking his shaft.

And your mother mated with a hyena, she thought, but didn't say so. She dropped to her knees and placed the tip of his cock on her lower lip. Her tongue licked over the plum, and the rod fell from his hand. Somewhere on the other side of the village a woman shrieked breaking the silence. A dog

33

barked and everything was quiet. So quiet the silence hung over the landscape like a brooding cloud.

"You like me sucking your cock?" she whispered softly.

There was no answer to that. He inhaled a deep breath as her mouth slithered down his shaft and nibbled at the root. Her head came up again, lips sucking so softly it was like being immersed deep in her cunt.

"It's as hard as a rock," she purred, squeezing his erection between finger and thumb.

He knew just what the artful bitch was doing and why she was doing it, but there was nothing he could do to stop her, not with her mouth swallowing his whole length, and her hand fondling and tickling his balls. Her voluptuous lips stretched all the way around his cock and licked greedily at the throbbing shaft. Most women close their eyes when they suck, but this one kept her eyes open, and he watched the changing expressions on her face, fascinated at the way her cheeks went into deep hollows then puffed out again as her hot breath blasted over his wetted meat.

Prasutagus never pretended to understand women. On the whole he preferred the company of his own warriors, but women had their uses, especially during the long, dark winter nights. There was no finer sight than the shape of a woman's arse by lamplight, it's rounded curves and deep split between the globes, the tuft of hair sprouting beneath, particularly if she was well oiled. He had fucked many women and girls; slaves and those captured in battle mostly, or abducted from neighbouring clans. They didn't differ very much; generally blonde or auburn haired, pale skinned with pink nipples and soft of limb. But the one whose lips were slapping against his balls was different. It wasn't so much the colour of her skin, or the size of her generous breasts and splendid legs, but her eyes. When they went into slits she looked like a predatory cat, not only dark, but mysterious, something he couldn't quite put into words. And that both fascinated and intrigued him. And there was another thing; the shape and strength of her body. She fucked like a stoat, but had the endurance of a mare. She was no stranger to cock, he was sure of that.

Her lips popped his cock from her mouth and her head bent lower, going under his legs engulfing both of his balls, sucked into her mouth and rolled around on her tongue. Only a seasoned whore knew those sorts of tricks, yet he was sure that whoring was not her profession. But one thing he had made up his mind about; no one was going to get so much as a sniff of her cunt while she remained under his command.

She left off sucking his balls and played the tip of his cock around her nipples, now erect and succulent. She placed his length between her breasts and rolled them against it, letting the purple head rest gently on her chest, and all the while her thumbs flicked her nipples driving him wild at the sight of the enormous teats. His cock suddenly went hotter and harder and she knew he was coming. Her hand gripped the shaft and rubbed it slowly, keeping the tip close by her nipples. When he erupted he came over both nipples, covering the teats with a stream of creamy juice. He thought it was all over, but she placed her hands under her breasts, cupping and lifting them until her tongue lapped at the creamy fluid, and a wide, loving smile broadened her mouth revealing rows of perfect teeth and a tongue dripping with sperm.

"No woman has ever sucked me like that," he admitted honestly.

"I've never sucked a cock like that," she lied. "You must've satisfied many a woman in your time."

She was still on her knees, smoothing his organ against her cheeks and lips.

"Stand up," he said, helping her to her feet. "And pick up that rod."

"You're not going to beat me after I've sucked you?" she asked agog.

35

A wry smile creased his lips. "You thought by having me in your mouth I'd forget giving your bare arse a good beating. You're not the first who thought she could get away with that. Now touch your toes."

"You bastard," she muttered, bending over.

"Not good enough," he rasped. "Lift your arse higher."

She grunted and placed her hands flat on the ground, raising her bottom and thrusting the glistening halves at the whistling rod.

She howled as it hissed into her bottom.

Her knees bent and straightened again, just in time to receive the next lash. He smacked it hard in the centre of her buttocks leaving a long, dark weal.

"You are my slave," he told her, swinging back his arm. "And slaves must be taught obedience."

A hollow smack of wood on naked flesh reverberated around the hut followed by a loud shriek. One of the warriors from a neighbouring hut had come outside to relieve himself and smiled at the sound. It wasn't very often a slave woman escaped a beating at the hands of his chieftain.

Africanus snorted and blasted through dilated nostrils like a charging bull. A peculiar hissing came from between her grinding teeth. Her head bobbed violently every time the rod struck her darkening cheeks. The goose-bumped skin was crossed with wide, livid lines and he could smell the strong, earthy aroma of her sex.

"I should've beaten you before I fucked you," he observed, noticing her pubic hair sticky with juice.

Africanus silently cursed. It was always the same. Every time a rod or whip lashed her bare buttocks she felt like having sex. It wouldn't be long before this bearded savage left off bruising her defenceless bottom and stood behind her, slamming his cock hard into her cunt. Bare, hot and tingling, her bottom took another ten strokes before the rod was tossed to the ground.

36

His foot thumped into the middle of her arse and she went head over heels, crashing her legs against the wicker wall.

"Now you can sleep," he told her.

And he put on his trousers and went across the village without as much as a backward glance.

# CHAPTER THREE

"Oh, not again," Africanus protested, turning over in her sleep. "Haven't you fucked me enough already. My arse still…hurghs…"

A hand stifled her mouth, and in the darkness she heard clothes coming off. She sat up still in the confused state, neither asleep nor awake. A hand pressed gently on her chest forced her down again. Her thighs were eased apart and he lay between them, fumbling with his cock. Africanus reached down and guided it into her sex. She heard a growl of satisfaction, and then with a couple of pelvic thrusts she was fully penetrated. She lifted her legs and wrapped them over the small of his back, hugging him tight.

"I didn't think you'd come back for me so soon," she laughed, throwing her arms round his shoulders.

"I couldn't resist you," he muttered, easing backwards and letting her legs fall from his back.

His arms went under her knees and lifted them over his shoulders, and kept on lifting until her thighs crushed her breasts. Bent double, she reached up and grabbed her ankles, holding them tight. He started riding her with long, slow strokes, taking his cock to the very portals of her sex, playing the tip around her labia before ramming hard into her, so hard she caught her breath.

"By the Gods, you're so big," she breathed.

He muttered a reply, deep and indistinct. A waft of strong wine blasted into her face and he rammed so hard her whole body shuddered. It was like being impaled with one of the stakes surrounding the village. She knew from memory that when a man dreams of a woman his erection throbs larger than in the waking hours, which is why few women deny their men in the dead of night.

She certainly couldn't deny the man riding her now. His

hand was smoothing her thighs along their silky length, and going under the globes of her buttocks. Her body rocked in unison and he slowed his long penetrations and left his cock embedded deep in her sex, contenting himself by lying full weight on her body, barely moving his hips, but feeling every bit of her that his hands could reach.

"I suppose you're going to beat me again afterwards," she muttered, groaning from his weight and the effort of clinging to her ankles.

He made no reply, but took hold of her left leg, wrapping his arms around the sturdy thigh, as if clinging to the mast of a ship in a storm. Africanus lowered her right leg and draped it over his shoulder. The palms of his hands smoothed her skin and she heard him mutter approval.

"You're a good fuck," he mumbled, but the words sounded distant, as if mouthed in a dream.

"You keep a good hard on," she returned, but he didn't seem to hear her, but rocked on his heels, returning again to the long, hard penetrations.

Her eyes had rown used to the gloom and she lay back enjoying his studied thrusting. It made a pleasant change not being fucked like an animal. He was taking his time, savouring her, angling his cock into the walls, going deep, then pulling right back and teasing her sex lips. When he touched her clitoris and heard her gasp, he lingered and gently rubbed his shaft against the tingling bud.

She swallowed hard and returned his cock thrusting with splendid movements of her hips, moving them in slow serpentine motions, lifting her bottom to let him penetrate deeper, and all the while he gripped the length of her leg, caressing it lovingly.

"You're a good lover," she whispered, then something which had been missing suddenly hit her.

Whoever was fucking her was not Prasutagus.

Oh, well, she thought, it was quite natural that any red

blooded male with an enormous hard on would want to fuck a slave in no position to argue. By morning it wouldn't surprise her if most of the village warriors had been through her, taking it in turns to fuck her any way they chose.

The shadowy figure between her thighs withdrew and slipped her leg from his grasp.

"Straddle me," he muttered, tumbling onto his back and dragging her after him.

Africanus squatted over his middle ready to impale herself on his rigid organ, but he spun her around facing the opposite side of the hut. She balanced on the soles of her feet, knees bent, her open cunt hovering over his cock. His hands were on her hips, guiding them downwards. She reached under her legs and placed his shaft neatly in her soaking sex. Then, in one sudden movement, she dropped her whole weight, engulfing him to the root.

"Phew!" he breathed, feeling the soft globes of her arse spreading over his hips.

Africanus knew how to make the most of her hips and buttocks. While she sat upright on his cock, her hips began to roll up and down, side to side and he knew at once that she was riding him as if on a saddle.

He slapped her sides and thighs, encouraging her to ride faster and she broke into a trot, bouncing her bottom higher and jerking her hips, twisting them from the waist. His hands went to the length of her back, slapping her shoulders and digging his thumb nails into her spine. She jolted as he ran them hard and fast down the bony ridges, not stopping until he reached the place where the spine softened into her arse crease.

"Faster," he grunted. "Ride faster."

And this time his hands landed with full force on her flanks. He hit her again, lashing her hips and ribs with his bare hands. Africanus began cantering over his middle, lifting her hips higher and plunging down again, feeling his hardened length

40

spearing her sex. She leaned forward and rested her hands on his knees and, even in the darkness, he could see his cock going in and out of her, could smell the rich aroma of cunt juice, and hear his cock squelching against her sucking lips.

They fucked each other in silence, not speaking, but revelling in the sheer enjoyment of sex. He stopped slapping her and laid flat on his back, watching the silhouette of her bottom and hips writhing over his still body. She rode faster and harder, breaking into a sweat, working her arse with strong, backward thrusts. Only the sound of muted grunts escaped her lips. It had been a long time since she had fucked like this. She sat upright, wanting his cock as deep as she could get it. When she felt it tremble and knew it would not be long before he came, she squeezed her vaginal walls, using them to bring him off while her body remained still. She heard him gasp as the quivering petals inside her moved around his cock. It was like being inside her mouth, a sensation of warm, wet juice and the softness of a tongue licking over the glans. But most of all was the feeling of her magnificent arse wobbling over his thighs, and the wetness of her cunt against his balls.

It was too much to resist, the unseen beauty of her sex and the nocturnal sounds it made coming from within her hot and perspiring body. His hands moved to her buttocks, fingers wide spread, exploring every pore of the voluptuous halves, bouncing and splitting with every move. Then his fingers sank with slippery ease into the hot folds of wet, fleshy lips. Africanus suddenly straightened, her heart pounding at the fingers teasing her sex bud. She reached for her own breasts and cupped them, feeling their weight in her hands. Her nipples were so hard they ached. Quickly, her thumbs started brushing over the throbbing teats. She was masturbating her breasts, using her hands to stimulate the rising orgasm his hands were producing. Unseen by her strange lover, she lifted the globes of black, shining flesh and fed both nipples between her pursing lips. If he could have seen the look on her face, the rolling eyes, the fullness of her lips, the creasing of her brow as she sucked the whole areolae into her mouth, he would have erupted there and then. As it was he could only hear her sucking on her tits, but knew what she was doing. The flow of juice coming from her sex became a river and her skin was hot, so hot it almost burned at the touch. They both knew it wouldn't be long before they climaxed and suddenly they broke into a wild orgy of thrashing legs, arms, fingers and tongues. Her whole body shuddered under the fierceness of his thrusting cock. Using all his strength, his buttocks lifted from the bare earth and left her balancing over his pelvis, her cunt filled with throbbing male meat.

"Phew!" she breathed, as her belly trembled. "You've got a long cock."

It was true; his erection had gained in length, and he joyfully bounced her bottom on it. Her hips gyrated from the onslaught and, moaning helplessly, she released her breasts and spread her legs, trying to hold the position. His hands went out and grabbed her hips, lifting her in time with his own body, and then slammed her back down with full force. Africanus caught her breath at the quivering going on inside her ravaged cunt. But with each upward thrust of his pelvis and cock the quivering rose to a shudder and she cried out a babble of words he could not understand. Neither did he need to. The only thing on his mind was the delicious sensation of her soaking pussy and the soft touch of her skin. Her hands went into clenched fists as she punched the air. Her hips were working so fast her whole bottom quivered and shook. Now, in the first light of dawn, he could see just how magnificent she looked naked.

But then, in a moment of wild ecstasy, she climaxed.

A long, tortured groan filled the hut. From bottom to breasts her entire torso spasmed and she threw back her head, gasping for air. Her pelvis went into convulsions, and he felt her vaginal muscles tighten around his shaft. One final heave of his loins filled her with hot male juice and she slumped forward; gasping. A few moments later when they had both regained their breath, he eased her off him and she rolled over in a ball, hugging her knees.

She heard him moving about, gathering his clothes and putting them on. Unlike Prasutagus, he didn't beat her or send his foot flying into her rump, but planted a kiss on her tear-streaked face and quietly left.

Gradually the hut filled with the light of morning, and through the open door she saw Wanda making her way towards her carrying a bundle and an earthenware bowl. For a confused moment Africanus wondered if she had dreamt it all, but her aching pussy and the wet patch of earth beneath her bottom dispelled that idle thought.

"I've brought you some porridge," Wanda smiled, placing the bowl beside the squatting black woman. "And I managed to get you some clothes." Her nose wrinkled. "What's that smell?"

"Just stale sweat," Africanus replied casually, holding up a red linen skirt.

Wanda shrugged and looked at a trail of footprints leading out of the hut. She recognised the imprints of warriors' skin shoes and smiled.

Africanus slipped the skirt up her thighs, but when it came to swell of her hips it wouldn't go over them. Clearly, the garment was made for a woman half her size. She wriggled and twisted until it reached her waist, then looked down. It barely covered her bottom let alone reached her knees. If she bent over it would ride right over her buttocks. The vest was little better. She put it over head and rolled it over her breasts, tugging at the hem.

"Red suits you," Wanda acknowledged.

The colour might but the size certainly didn't. It clung to her breasts like a skin and she swallowed at the sight of her nipples poking at the thin linen. No matter how hard she tugged, the hem wouldn't drop further than her navel, and a large expanse of black skin showed between the bottom of the vest and top of the skirt. For all the good it did, she might as well have been naked. Gingerly, she bent her knees and picked up the bowl.

"This is good," she said, surprised at the taste, a sort of almond and spice mixture. "What's happening out there?"

Wanda looked through the door at the gathering clan. "The Druids have summoned the clans to the ceremony of Epona, the Goddess of Fruitfulness. It is a long journey to the Circle of Stones, so we must be away soon."

"Am I to go too?" Africanus asked, shovelling porridge into her mouth.

Wanda shot her a curious look and merely nodded.

"Who are the Druids, anyway?" Africanus enquired, but Wanda could not have heard, because she went out of the hut to join the throng.

Coming out into the sunshine, Africanus saw footprints where she was sure someone had been spying on her. So she had not imagined it after all. Someone had been watching her fucking Prasutagus, and it seemed, judging from the prints leaving the hut, it was the same man who had been her second lover. She shivered at the thought, but had no time to dwell on it, because a warrior seized her arm and dragged her to where the chieftain was waiting.

He looked regal with his hair freshly washed and combed, the intricately woven plaits hanging over his breast. His gleaming war helmet was domed with two long horns projecting from either side. Over his tunic he wore a long woollen cloak fastened with a golden broach. His burnished shield was embossed with entwining serpents and scrolls decorated with red and blue enamel studs that twinkled in the sun. The Gods knew how long it must have taken to make. A sword hung at his side, much longer and broader than the gladius used by the Romans. The women had put on their finest dresses and tunics of colourful linen and had fitted bands around their hair. All of them wore gold and silver bracelets and broaches. They all stared at Africanus looking ridiculous in clothes that were too small.

It took one sweep of her escort's hand to rip the vest and skirt from her back and buttocks.

"Slaves are not permitted to wear clothes," Prasutagus told her. "Aelfred, have her chained with the others, and make haste, the sun has far risen."

The warrior bowed and led Africanus to where the other slave women stood in a frightened huddle. Most already bore livid welts from the whips and rods laid cruelly across their backs and rumps.

"Form a line," the warrior barked, prodding their flanks with the end of his spear shaft.

Like cattle they dumbly obeyed their master, standing one behind the other, staring over their shoulders, past caring what lay in store. From a basket, the village women selected iron collars and fastened them around the necks of the slaves. Chains of equal length were fitted to the front and back of each collar and fastened to the woman either in front or behind. Beside them were more baskets containing food for the journey. On the word of command the fettered slaves knelt in unison and lifted the baskets, onto their heads. They stood up and dutifully awaited the next command. A plaited leather whip flicked the haunches of the leader and they set off, heading through the gate of the stockade and out across the barren moors. Prasutagus rode in his chariot with his favourite concubine, a pretty flaxen-haired girl who could not have been much more than eighteen. Her fine clothes made an unsettling contrast with the nakedness of the slaves who trudged at their side. Most of the village women rode in carts pulled by oxen and chatted cheerfully amongst themselves. The warriors rode on horseback proudly displaying their armour and shields. Wanda rode behind a young warrior, her arms lovingly around his waist. They had not gone but a quarter of a mile when a minstrel struck up a tune on a harp whose plucked strings were punctuated only by the loud crack of a whip sailing over the backs of the slaves.

Humiliated in her nakedness, Africanus brought up the rear, her bare bottom a prime target for the whip. Her buttocks were more rounded and firm than those of the other slaves and the mounted warrior wasted no time in lashing them. It was part of a slave's duty to provide sexual comfort to the accompanying warriors, and already he was determined to have her. He reined his horse in close and sent the whip cracking over the crown of her bottom. Balancing the heavy basket on her head and chained to the woman in front, there was nothing she could do but endure the pain blazing through her buttocks and thighs. In between lashing her, the warrior marvelled at the shape of her arse, the way her hips rose and fell with every step, and her long legs, he particularly liked her legs, especially her thighs. There was no doubting their strength, let alone their shimmering beauty. Idly he wondered if his chieftain would allow him to buy her, but that would depend upon the Druids. Even Prasutagus was powerless to defy theim.

His train of thought was rudely interrupted when Prasutagus ordered a halt. The sun had reached its zenith and it was time to rest.

Africanus surveyed the landscape; seemingly endless moorland stretched as far as the eye could see. In the distance, blurred by the haze, was a line of low hills, with dense woodlands and towering rocks. The road on which they had travelled was little better than a goat track which ahead dropped abruptly into a deep wooded valley. She guessed that they must have travelled eight or ten miles since leaving the village, and there was none to be seen anywhere else, nothing but an empty moor with windswept trees blasted into fantastic shapes. Wherever they were going, Africanus had an uneasy feeling that she would be better off far away from it.

They set off again, but not before Prasutagus had the slaves more securely chained. Now they were approaching the meeting place he was taking no chances and had evidently come prepared. A long length of chain was wrapped around the waist of the leading slave and locked in place with an iron hasp. Then it passed to the woman behind her and locked over the small of her back, and so on until all the women were secured. A whip lashed into the buttocks of the leading woman and the line filed off, their chains rattling and clinking with every step.

The entourage descended into the wooded valley and all laughing and singing stopped. It was as if some mysterious unseen force had taken control. Even the rider who had so joyfully whipped Africanus' buttocks grew silent and stared sullenly ahead. The deeper they descended, the denser the woods became until the track was no more than a chariot's width passing through impenetrable undergrowth. At the base of the trees the earth was bare, so little light penetrated that nothing except briars and fungi flourished.

"What a fucking awful place," Africanus shivered, shifting the basket onto the centre of her head.

She could see that the other slaves were beginning to tire under their loads and the pace had noticeably slackened.

"Whip them faster!" Prasutagus' voice commanded. "Will we never reach the Stones before nightfall?"

The mounted warrior needed no second telling and sent his whip smacking over Africanus' shoulders. Another warrior lashed the leading woman and her cries of pain echoed through the forest. But above her cries Africanus caught the unmistakable sound of babbling water and, as they rounded a bend, a wide shallow river came into view.

Prasutagus' chariot crossed first, followed by the carts of women which halted on a wide expanse of green sward. They had evidently neared their destination, for further along the bank other clans had camped, erecting tents and lighting fires.

"Get the slaves across," Prasutagus called, and one by one the manacled slaves stepped into the freezing water.

It reached no higher than mid thigh, but was cold enough to chill the blood and by the time she had reached the opposite bank Africanus was shuddering. The sight of her erect nipples was not lost on the warriors who had gathered to watch the naked women pick their way through the river.

"That one likes her cock," a warrior gesticulated, nodding at Africanus. "Just look at the way her arse wobbles."

"No one is allowed to touch her until the priestesses have made their choice," another reminded him, and reluctantly he watched the naked, shivering woman herded into the centre of the camp.

It was only after the tents had been erected and cooking fires lit that Prasutagus had their chains removed. But he had second thoughts about Africanus. Ever since their encounter on the beach he had come to the conclusion that she was no ordinary woman. Her body was not only superb, but extraordinarily fit, the sort of fitness that only derives from rigorous training. But most of all he was struck by her flashing, gleaming eyes and vigorous intelligence. He didn't trust her not to bolt at the first opportunity.

"Have the black slave shouldered," he said grimly, and went into his tent to enjoy his young concubine.

"Fuck," muttered Africanus, as two virile young warriors seized her arms.

She had already made a survey of the land and the possibility of escape. It wouldn't take much to steal the clothes she needed and maybe a weapon. By morning she would have been far away, but now she dumbly held out her arms, fully stretched either side of her body like a scarecrow. A stout log was fetched and she knelt, bowing her head as the log was placed on her shoulders. It took only a couple of minutes for the men to bind her wrists to the log and another rope at her elbows for good measure.

"See how you get out of that," they joked, and seated her at the base of a tree.

But they had not yet finished. A long length of rope was passed over her breasts and pulled tight around the trunk. She visibly winced when her breasts squashed and flattened over her ribs. One of her tormentors gave her thighs a hefty parting slap and joined the clan seated around their roaring log fire. Soon the smell of roasting meat wafted across the expanse accompanied by cries of raucous laughter. Now that they had made camp and had neared their destination, the cloud of despondency lifted helped by the bevy of naked slave women scurrying to and fro, waiting upon the throng.

Africanus watched them from the flickering shadows, shifting her bottom and crossing her legs. More than anything else she needed to empty her bladder, but had no intentions of giving these animals the satisfaction of seeing her pissing in public. But as the night wore on, the need increased until her bladder had swelled beyond endurance.

There was nothing for it but to obey the command of nature, and she turned her head quickly from side to side. Her back ached lashed to the trunk and her arms and shoulders had numbed from the weight of the log, but the churning going on inside her belly was unbearable. She hung on until the last of the revellers had gone into their tents and uncrossed her legs. Her water came in a gush, hissing loudly into the soil and she saw, in the chill of the night air, a cloud of steam rising from a pool of piss.

"Ooogh," she breathed, smiling ruefully with relief.

Then she farted.

"That's good," a voice whispered. "A woman is all the better with the wind and water out of her belly."

A hand came from behind the trunk and groped her breasts. Her head turned but saw nothing more tangible than a shadow moving furtively through the bracken.

The hand moved slowly over her belly and slipped between her legs.

"Touch my cunt and I'll scream," she warned, wriggling her shoulders.

The hand was withdrawn and she heard footsteps retreating through the leaves. An animal, perhaps a fox, ventured close, sniffed her cunt and ambled casually into the undergrowth. One of the guards glanced her way and looked back into the dying embers of the fire. Then the hand was back again placing a branch as thick as a baby's arm horizontally into her mouth. Cords attached at both ends were pulled tight and knotted at the side of the trunk.

"Arrurgh," she grunted, gagged so firmly, her face was almost splitting.

A length of cloth was wrapped around her head, covering her eyes so she was now rendered temporarily blind and dumb. She knew what was coming and crossed her legs; locking her ankles and flexing her powerful thighs.

She heard twigs snapping and the shuffling of limbs as the figure seated itself. She braced herself in preparation for the struggle that was to surely follow. She had strong legs and it would take a stronger man to uncross them.

His hand lighted on her thigh and stroked its length. The fingertips went into the hardened hollows and under the straining muscles, went over the splendid curve of her calf, and fondled her knee. A murmur of appreciation escaped his lips, and his hand followed the pelvic crease and lightly brushed the upper fringes of her pubic bush. Through the crushing gag she suddenly caught her breath, and he felt her muscles soften.

"Your legs are the most beautiful in the land," he whispered, smoothing her flanks. "And your arse is worth more than all

50

the gold of the clans."

His hands were under her bottom, groping and squeezing the generous moons. He noticed her breathing was more urgent when his fingertips just touched her sex lips. She wriggled uncomfortably under the weight of the log. She heard him move, shuffling behind her, then the rope around her breasts suddenly slackened and dropped into her lap. Freed from the constraint, her breasts resumed their normal shape and hung from her chest like two enormous bells.

His hands were there at once, weighing the quivering mounds, gently kneading the globes and teasing the nipples.

Saliva trickled from her stretched lips and dribbled down her chin. She was breathing faster now, her breath blasting from dilated nostrils. His hands left her breasts and went under her arms, easing her upright against the tree.

"Pant all you like," he advised. "No one will hear you."

His lips were on her nipples, sucking so hard they lifted from her breasts. His tongue flicked over the teats, fast and furious until tears formed in her eyes. Her legs had softened and he had no difficulty in uncrossing her ankles and spreading them over the earth. Where brute strength would have failed, gentle coercion had succeeded. Her cunt was wet and dripping. The sex lips quivered under the assault of his worming tongue. Sweat had broken out over her silky skin and he licked the whole length of her thighs.

"Spread your legs wider," he said through pursed lips.

Her ankles dragged over the soil, spreading wide.

Her head rolled and she moaned when his fingers dipped inside her, fingering her sex and driving her wild.

He went on fingering her, listening to her muffled grunts and pants, and when she was on the verge of orgasm, withdrew his soaking fingers and whispered in her ear;

"I know you want my cock. You're begging for it. If you promise not to scream, I'll take off the gag."

Her head gave a slight nod and the knife that had freed her

51

breasts, sliced through the gag cords. She coughed and spat, sending the branch flying over his shoulder.

Now her head was free there were no more ropes to bind her body to the trunk.

"On your back," he muttered, taking the weight of her shoulders and dragging her into the open.

He was quickly behind her, holding her outstretched arms and lowering her to the ground. Still crucified, there was nothing she could do to resist his rampant cock, or the urge stirring in her belly.

"Enjoy it," he whispered ominously. "This might be the last fuck you're ever going to get. Now, bend your knees."

Africanus obeyed, lifting her knees to her chest. Her breasts still smarted where the rope had cut into them. A livid line stretched under her nipples where the skin had rubbed raw.

"What do you mean? This is the last fuck I'm going to get," she asked suspiciously, as his cock hovered at her sex lips.

He said nothing, but penetrated her at once, kneeling between her thighs and jerking his pelvis so fast she was robbed of speech. His hands gripped her hips and rode her on and off his throbbing erection. The angle of his cock was perfect and each thrust touched her pulsating clitoris until she gave vent to a long harsh moan.

Her legs thrashed over his sides, heels drumming his ribs like a drum.

"Quiet!" he snapped, forcing his fist into her mouth.

She could see his head twisting towards the guards, and then at the tents. A woman came out and spoke to one of them. He laughed and playfully slapped her arse. For one brief, heart-stopping moment he glanced in their direction, sword drawn. His head cocked; listening. The man between Africanus' thighs froze, and for several seconds she hung there in an agony of unsatisfied arousal, quivering on the very edge of orgasm. She swallowed and turned her head.

The guard was stirring the embers of the fire with his boot and had heard nothing.

"One more sound and they'll cut our throats," Africanus' lover whispered.

It was no idle threat. He meant every word and, she had the distinct impression that he was not supposed to be doing what he was doing with her, probably on the pain of death. She was sure it had something to do with the ceremony at the Circle of Stones, and it was not a pleasant thought.

Her head nodded and he took his fist from her mouth. He was still hard but fear had taken away the throbbing in his cock and his pelvic thrusts soon had him spending into her cunt. Africanus hadn't reached her climax when he withdrew and she panted and heaved, silently begging for sexual release. But he was out of her quickly and dragging her back to the tree, sitting her upright and lashing her breasts to the trunk.

"You might've let me come," she whispered savagely.

"You'll come right enough, when the priestesses have finished with you," he informed, pulling the rope tight.

He was gone as furtively as he came, a shadow melting into the trees. She was sure he was the same man whose footprints she'd seen outside the hut. The same man who had come into the hut and fucked her hard and long. But why didn't he reveal himself? Was it fear of the chieftain who had given strict orders she was not to be touched, or something much more sinister? The Celts were by no means people easily frightened. After all they almost driven the Roman army out of their homeland only a few years ago, but the mention of the priestesses had them in awe of some supernatural power and Africanus knew she was part of it.

She drew up her knees and let her body slump against the rope. Tired and aching, she fell into a disturbed slumber, waking only when the sun rose and the clan emerged from their tents.

It was Prasutagus who came over, a contented smile on his lips. His young concubine had satisfied his lust and he had the look of a man whose balls had been well emptied.

"Free her, and give her food and drink," he ordered, not unkindly. "Then chain her with the other slaves. We move as soon as the tents are struck."

Wanda brought over a bowl of porridge and a beaker of water flavoured with lime leaves.

"I'm sorry you were tied to the tree," she half apologized, helping Africanus rub life into her racked shoulders. "But at least you were spared the warriors. Some of the slave girls were fucked so hard they can hardly walk."

"I know the feeling," Africanus muttered, spooning her porridge.

When she had finished she went over to where the other slave women were being chained, but much more heavily this time. The iron collars were fitted around their necks. Their hands were manacled behind their backs and shackles placed on their ankles. The connecting chain allowed just enough slack to walk at an even pace. All the tents had been gathered into the carts along with the women and children. Prasutagus rode in his chariot, his pretty young concubine walking dutifully beside it. They set off through the woodland swelling the throng of other clans, all heading for the Circle of Stones.

Again Africanus brought up the rear, but the spear point and lash she expected to torment her naked hinds never touched her. That familiar silence had descended once again.

# CHAPTER FOUR

"This is the sacred grove," Prasutagus explained, as the gathering came to a halt. "No one may enter it except for the priests and the sacrifices."

At first sight it looked nothing more sinister than a large clearing in the forest with a circle of stones rising from the earth like rotting teeth. Oak, yew and ash trees grew in profusion, but something was missing. It was the silence that betrayed it. No birds perched in the trees filling the air with song, nor did any beast make its lair in the undergrowth. It seemed even they were afraid of the wooden images of the Gods lurking amongst the trees. Some were just hideously carved heads; others were like totem poles with one head mounted on top of the other. At either side of the heads were long poles with human skulls vacantly staring at the silent onlookers.

The stone circle was no less horrifying. At the centre a huge stone phallus reared upwards, its glans carved and shaped to perfection, but at its base were no testicles but a large polished flat stone decorated with more human skulls. Some wore garlands of mistletoe and yew leaves. Africanus' eyes lifted to a series of trilithons, three upright stones with another resting on the top giving the appearance of a vast three legged stool. She could just make out ropes and chains dangling from the top stone, some fitted with shackles, others tied into huge knots. She was sure that they were not there merely for decoration.

"Bring forward the slave sacrifices."

It was the voice of the old man who had suddenly appeared from nowhere. He stood atop the phallic stone and motioned the slaves to enter the circle. The warriors gently prodded the women's buttocks with the tips of their swords, herding them like animals towards the old man. He was dressed in a long white robe which matched his long white beard. The women entered the circle much like unarmed slaves destined for slaughter at the Colosseum, looking all around them, eyes wide with terror, wondering what terrible fate was in store. They were still fettered by their wrists and necks. No one was allowed to enter the sacred circle unless bound or chained.

The old man nodded his satisfaction at the naked, trembling women.

"The Goddess, Epona accepts your gifts," he announced to the clans now gathered in a huge circle at the edge of the grove. "Have the priestesses prepare them."

"Oh fuck," muttered Africanus, watching a group of priestesses advancing like spectres from the trees.

Their white tunics were partially hidden under cloaks of fine purple linen. Over them, their long wild hair flowed to bronze girdles held in place with enormous silver buckles. Around their necks were twisted golden torques sparkling in the sunlight. The high priestess wore a crown of silver and gold reaching to a point with a half moon glistening at its apex. Her bare feet moved noiselessly as she approached Africanus.

Her long bare arm reached out and stroked the black woman's breast.

"You shall be the first to summon the Goddess," she said. "Epona delights in the sacrifice of women taken in battle or slavery. Your cries will rouse her from her slumber. But first all the sacrifices shall enter the holy pool and be cleansed."

"Thanks," muttered Africanus, heading towards a pool at the edge of the grove.

The water was clear, so clear she could see the pebbles at the bottom. A spring bubbled innocently at its centre, and Africanus let out a howl as the high priestess shoved her into the freezing water. Behind her, another naked slave crashed into the depths, gasping as her head reappeared above the surface.

"Nice of the bastards to give us a bath before slitting our throats," Africanus remarked drily, shaking water from her hair and eyes.

The women stood thigh deep, shivering more from dread than the biting cold. The men at the edge of the grove leaned forward getting a better view of the dripping pubic hair and tightly puckered nipples as the slaves splashed their way to the other side of the pool.

The priestesses were ready for them and flicked their short plaited whips across the goose-bumping buttocks, driving them back into the centre of the stone circle.

One by one, the shackles and iron collars were removed ready for the next stage of the ceremony.

"Paint them," the high priestess commanded, resting her hands on her magnificent hips.

In Quintus' training school she would have made a fine gladiatrix with such splendid thighs and powerful arms, but now she just stood impassive, not a flicker of a smile on her lips as her underlings approached with pots and bowls of paint.

It was all part of the ceremony, painting the slaves naked bodies with bright reds, blues, greens, and yellows, fashioning circles and scrolls all over their bare skin.

Africanus stood upright and still, her eyes riveted on the trees whilst the priestess passed the brush over her breasts.

"Don't tell me red suits me," she hissed sarcastically, as the brush plopped onto her nipples.

It went in a circle, brightening the dark areola and highlighting the throbbing nipple. She painted each breast, covering the whole globe, taking great care not to leave any skin uncovered. Next, she painted a swirl over Africanus' chest, taking the brush in broad sweeps right into her collar bones. She replenished the bristles and liberally applied the colour over the soft stomach mound, going deep into the navel and under the pit of the stomach.

"Open your legs," the priestess said, much as if one at a banquet might ask for more wine.

Africanus shuffled her feet over the earth and stared beyond at the warriors watching the women being painted. Prasutagus was shielding his eyes from the rising sun, but she knew he was looking at her and, at that moment she wondered if he knew all along what fate awaited her. No wonder the bastard fucked her so hard knowing he probably wouldn't get a second chance. Her eyes searched the mob desperately trying to find a break in the circle where she might at least try for escape. But there was none. The clans were densely packed and even if she did make the perimeter the warriors would soon cut her down.

Suddenly she jolted. The brush was working its way around her open sex lips, coating the lips with bright red paint. The priestess was paying particular attention to her sex, soaking the pubic curls and passing the bristles under her legs, gathering a fresh dollop and going all around the joins of her thighs. Then she went behind her and wormed the loaded brush into the deep arse crease, forcing it hard between the muscular halves. Africanus could feel her painting more scrolls over her buttocks and back. She shivered as the brush tickled up her spine and broadened across her naked back. Finally she painted the whole length of her legs turning the ebony skin a gorgeous hue of scarlet. It was the same with the other slaves. All of them had bodies thoroughly covered and decorated, some blue, others green, and one or two a combination of both. Africanus could see that they too had their sex mounds and buttocks covered.

"Epona, Goddess of Fruitfulness and Virility, we call upon you to hear us," the high priestess chanted, lifting her head and addressing the tops of the trees. "Awake from your slumber and accept the sacrifices we offer. Let their cries of pain and ecstasies bring us your favour, and the flowing of their blood your bounteous gifts."

58

It didn't take Africanus long to work that one out.

"Are you going to have us all flogged and fucked?" she asked the nearest priestess.

"Yes," she replied flatly. "And after the Goddess has responded we shall slit your throat and fill the holy skull with your blood."

At least, she thought, I'll have one last fuck before I enter the underworld.

One of the priestesses came over to where Africanus was standing and in her hand she wielded a sheaf of ash twigs freshly cut from the holy tree.

"You will walk around the circle of stones and bare your back and buttocks to the holy ash," she announced, pointing to the edge of the stone circle. From somewhere in the trees came the plaintive notes of a harp and flute accompanied by the soft beating of a drum.

"Music to be whipped by. Now I really know I'm favoured," she hissed bitterly.

"Shut your mouth, slave," the high priestess retorted. "You will keep silent while the Goddess is roused from her slumber."

And a loud crack echoed around the grove as the first blow splintered across Africanus' naked rump.

"The harder you are whipped the greater the chance of virility being bestowed on the warriors," she told her.

They're virile enough without my arse being whipped, Africanus thought, but kept her mouth shut as the second blow cracked across the small of her back.

The circle seemed much larger now she had to walk slowly all the way around it, a fresh blow accompanying every step. But she was not the only one crying to the Goddess with pain. As Africanus drew level with the trilithons she could see now why they were hung with chains and ropes. One of the slaves was hanging by her thumbs, her toes just touching the ground while a priestess flogged her buttocks, sending her swaying back and forth. Another was hanging upside down, while a sheaf of yew twigs lashed over her belly and breasts. As Africanus passed the third trilithon she saw a slave suspended in a girdle of rope artfully passed under her legs and around her hips so that her whole body weight bore down on the rope cutting into her naked sex. Weighted stones tied to her ankles only served to increase the pain going through her sex and belly.

"See. The Goddess has responded," the high priestess acknowledged, following Africanus' painful procession.

It couldn't be denied. The sight of the flogged women was already having its effect. Many of the warriors had bulging erections straining at their trousers. Some were already fondling breasts of the nearest women who responded with groping hands.

The priestess kept up her relentless lashing, cracking and splintering over Africanus' bare and painted rump which by now was criss-crossed with livid welts made more emphatic by the peeling paint. Africanus paused and stared in disbelief at a slave hanging upside down, not by her ankles but with thin rope tied around her big toes. There seemed no end to the pain the priestesses were determined to inflict. But it was nothing compared to what awaited Africanus as she painfully completed the circle, hobbling as the lashes whipped into her swollen buttocks.

"Take her to the sacred stone," the high priestess smirked, her eyes glinting with malice.

At the base of the phallus were carvings of the same design, larger than their real flesh and blood counterparts, about half as long as a man's forearm and almost equally as thick, perfectly capable of entering a woman, providing she was able to take it.

"The pleasuring of a woman will arouse the Goddess to further rewards." the high priestess told her, "Now squat over that stone cock."

There was going to be nothing pleasurable about having that thing rammed inside her cunt.

"Who said it was going there," the high priestess laughed, summoning two of her acolytes.

"You mean I have to have that thing up my bottom?" Africanus asked agog.

"That's exactly where it's going and, judging by the hardness in your buttocks, you shouldn't have much trouble taking it."

"I'd rather have my throat slit," Africanus blurted, eyeing the stone cock.

"That will come later," the high priestess assured her. "But first you have other duties to perform. Now get your cheeks over that stone."

The acolytes grabbed her arms and lifted her over the stone glans, positioning her bottom hole directly over the tip. Instinctively, Africanus reached behind her and placed her hands on her buttocks spreading them as wide as she could. Slowly, her full weight bore down on the stone, the tip eased into her bottom hole pushing open the orifice until she was penetrated. She gulped and swallowed, feeling the coldness of the stone entering her bottom.

"Go on," the high priestess ordered dangerously, "give her the full length."

Africanus clenched her fists in agony as the acolytes lowered her further onto the stone phallus. Her eyes went into slits and she uttered a cry of pain. Her bottom hole was stretched to its full capacity as her buttocks spread over the phallus base. She let out a gush of air and threw back her head, gasping at the unbelievable sensation passing through her belly.

"I knew you could take it." the high priestess said.

Africanus remained frozen over the stone, her anus filled with its rock hard cock. The high priestess went over to Prasutagus.

"Choose your most virile warriors to complete the ritual," she ordered. "And see that they do not disappoint me."

Prasutagus obeyed at once. A group of men filed into the stone circle, not knowing what was expected of them.

"Drop your trousers and fill her belly with your spunk," the high priestess commanded. "And see she wastes not a single drop, or you will join her on the sacrificial stone."

One look into her blazing eyes told them that was no idle threat. The high priestess had full command over them; the least disobedience would be rewarded with death.

They stood around Africanus, loosening their belts and casting off their trousers and displaying their manhoods.

"Hold her head still!"

At her next command, one of the acolytes stood behind Africanus, grabbing the sides of her head holding it rigid.

"Open your mouth and start sucking," the high priestess growled, folding her arms under her breasts.

There was no disguising the tell tale signs of her arousal at the sight of the naked slave impaled on the stone phallus, her mouth wide open, ready and waiting for the first cock to spill its juice deep into Africanus' throat. Her nipples were fully erect and poking at her tunic. A flush spread across her face and her lips parted in anticipation. Through lowered eye lids she watched the first warrior guide his cock over the tongue of the impaled slave.

As Africanus' lips closed around the cock pushing into her throat, the high priestess turned to the slaves hanging from the trilithons. An exhausted priestess was delivering the final lashing to the slave hanging by her thumbs. The face of the high priestess clouded with anger.

"This slave has shit herself!" she shrieked. "You know very well that a slave who fouls her own body also defiles the sacred circle and angers the Gods."

"Yes mistress," the priestess whispered, looking at the slave's fouled bottom and thighs.

"She must be cleansed with the piss from other sacrificial slaves to show the Gods our repentance. Fetch down the other two and bring them hither."

The two slaves still hanging from the trilithons were swiftly brought to earth and dragged to where the besmirched girl lay sobbing in terror. In that mood there was no telling how the high priestess might react. At previous gatherings not only had she executed a dozen slaves but also four of her own priestesses.

"Stand astride this creature and empty your bladders," she commanded. "Cleanse the filthy wretch with your water, and you," she told one the warriors whom Africanus had just sucked off, "can piss down her back."

Astonished at this outburst the female slaves stood astride the sobbing girl, spreading their legs wide and heaving their plump bellies. Soon streams of hot yellow urine hissed over the girl's bottom and thighs. They could barely stand from the merciless flogging that streaked and welted their own backs and buttocks.

"Have them taken to the sacrificial stone," the high priestess ordered, then motioned the warrior forward.

He took his cock in his hand and aimed the tip at the girl's shoulders. A fast jet of urine splashed over her back and hair. But the girl was still not washed clean. Traces of her foulness lingered in her bottom crease.

"Fetch another of the slaves," the high priestess barked, eyeing the fouled slave with utter contempt.

"Lick the shit from her arse," she rasped, pointing to the soiled slave.

Without hesitation, the young girl slave dropped to her knees and bent low, sweeping her tongue through the fouled arse crease. When she thought she'd finished she stood up facing the high priestess, over her shoulder she saw the black slave sucking hard on a warriors cock, her face, chest and breasts glistening with streams of creamy spunk.

63

"Not good enough," the high priestess muttered. "Now lick her again, get your tongue right in her arse, or I'll have you fed to the wolves."

Too terrified to answer, the girl buried her face in the slave's arse crease, licking deep into the cleft, gagging at the smell and foul taste hanging on her tongue. Then without warning a foot landed on the back of her head squashing her face hard into the girl's bottom. It twisted from side to side until the girl almost suffocated.

"Now the Gods will be appeased," the high priestess said softly, anger subsiding from her face.

She turned and went over to where Africanus was still impaled on the stone phallus. Great globules of spunk clung to her face and hair. Her lips and nostrils were almost buried under the warriors' spending.

"How many has she sucked?" the high priestess asked dully.

"About twenty," an acolyte replied.

"Is her belly full?"

"I think she could take a few more," she replied, knowing that was what she wanted to hear.

The high priestess smiled ruefully. "Let her have another twenty. The Goddess must see we are obeying her will."

Africanus' mouth opened in horror. Already her jaws ached and she had swallowed so much spunk her stomach churned. But it was her bottom that hurt most. How ever hard she tried it was impossible to keep still while the men rode into her mouth, forcing her to suck their cocks, some rammed right to the back of her throat.

"If I suck one more cock I'll be sick," she wailed, licking the spunk from her lips.

The high priestess regarded her for a moment, seemingly in deep thought. "In that case you will join the others on the sacrificial stone," she said, and strode over to where the other slaves were already positioned.

"I want to hear them scream," the high priestess said,

looking down at the confused huddle of welted flesh. "I want to hear them scream so loudly that the Goddess herself will appear before us in recognition of our efforts. Have the wretches prepared."

"Kneel," a priestess ordered, flicking her plaited whip over the shoulders of the slaves.

Africanus and the other slaves struggled to their knees forming a semi circle. Much of the paint had flaked and peeled giving the impression their skin was mottled with some horrible disease. Africanus' face, chest and breasts were still covered in spunk, some of which had solidified over her nipples.

"Lick that mess off her," the high priestess said, curling her lips in disgust.

A whip lashed into the shoulders of a pretty red-headed girl who crawled over the polished stone towards Africanus. She squatted on her haunches before the creamy streams now running between the black woman's breasts. For a few moments she seemed entranced watching it flow over the ebony belly and slowly filling the deep indented navel. The high priestess stood behind the squatting slave, her eyes fixed on the large dark areolas and sprouting black nipple bud.

"Suck her nipples first," she grated, fiddling with the bronze girdle.

Africanus watched her wringing hands move closer into her groin, the fingertips stroking the outer fringes of her pubic bush just visible under her tunic. There was no mistaking a dampness spreading between her legs which she made no attempt to hide. At the sight of the cowering slave closing her lips over Africanus' twitching black buds she heaved a deep breath. Her teeth chewed on her lower lip and then suddenly her tunic went into points, her nipples erect and throbbing beneath the white linen.

Africanus straightened her shoulders thrusting out her ample breasts as the girl sucked hard on her nipples. Her tongue went all around the dark pimples of her areola, licking at every drop of spunk, like a lizard flicking at insects. An icy chill went through her belly and she swallowed hard. Much more of this and she'd come there and then. In agonies of frustration she clenched her fists, digging her nail hard into the palms. The high priestess had moved so close to the squatting slave, Africanus could smell her scented perfume.

"Lick her whole breast," she muttered, prodding the girl between the shoulder blades with her whip handle.

The girl obeyed, lashing her pink tongue over the whole of Africanus' spunk-soaked skin. Her head bobbed as she swept each stream clean, angling her head under the breast and going all around the sides. Her face almost disappeared from view when she buried it in the breast cleft, licking upwards over the broader expanse of the gleaming ebony chest. Africanus' eyes went into narrow slits, but all the while she watched the range of emotions passing over the face of the high priestess. A hot flush had coloured her neck and cheeks and her lips were visibly trembling.

"You're on heat," Africanus muttered softly, her lips barely moving. "You dirty, crafty bitch."

Then it hit her. This whole ceremony was no more than an excuse to slake her lust. It didn't take a genius to guess that she must have had all her young priestesses at one time or another. But at the same time she held the tribes in fear and awe, terrorizing them with her mystical power.

As if reading her thoughts, the high priestess lurched forward and grabbed Africanus' braids. Her blazing eyes stared right through her as she whispered, "I shall sacrifice you tomorrow, my fine black slave. You may be sure your death will be slow and painful." Her lips broke into an evil knowing grin. "That is, after you have spent the night in my own sacred chamber."

And she stood back as the squatting redhead wormed her tongue into Africanus' navel, lapping at the pool of spunk.

"That will do," she hissed, her flushed face resuming its normal hue. "Now get up on your knees."

She turned to the other kneeling slaves. "Thumb your nipples. I want to see them fully aroused, and you," she said, turning to one of her priestesses, "fetch over the needles and rings."

Africanus and the other slaves brushed the tips of their thumbs over their nipples, making them tingle and sprout. The teats rose up erect and throbbing and the young priestess knelt before them opening a leather pouch and spreading it over the sacred stone. She selected a long pointed needle and tested its sharpened point with her thumb. Even the slightest prick drew blood. Her left hand reached for Africanus' breast, and using her forefinger and thumb she squeezed the base of the nipple lifting it painfully from the surrounding disc. But the pain was nothing compared with what was to follow. In her right hand she held the needle, rolling it between her fingers as she aimed the glinting point at the erect bud.

"Aaaaagh!" Africanus shrieked, jolting her chest.

It took only one shove of the priestess' wrist to spear the needle right through the base of her nipple. She left the needle in place, adjusting it so an equal length protruded either side of the speared bud. Then she went to the other breast, repeating the procedure, lifting and squeezing the dark black teat and spearing it with the deadly point.

Leaving the black woman writhing in agony, she went to each slave in turn, sending cries of pain reverberating around the grove.

"Now fit the rings," the high priestess commanded, unashamedly delighting in the agony the slaves were suffering.

Another leather pouch was spread over the stone, this time containing huge golden rings, large enough to slip over a wrist or ankle. The priestess selected one and stretched it between her fingers. The ring opened revealing sharpened points in its circumference which tapered back to the thicker golden band. She knelt in front of Africanus, her face emotionless as she positioned the gap in the ring over the speared nipple, forcing it open until the needle fitted between the gaps. Africanus held her breath knowing the pain she was about to endure. The needle was there merely as a guide, opening a hole in her nipple so the rest of the thicker golden ring would pass easier through the soft fleshy teat. She looked up and saw the high priestess watching with detached amusement. She had seen the operation performed many times, but never through such generous teats as were sported by the sweating black slave. Her whole breasts, chest and belly were gleaming with sweat, partly from the heat for the sun now shone directly into the stone circle, but more from the pain she knew was soon to come.

"It's going to hurt," the high priestess assured her, her lips creasing into a wide, voluptuous smile.

Just then a breeze shook the trees, rustling the leaves and branches. The long tunic of the high priestess blew open at the waist revealing for the first time her long, splendid shapely legs.

"Epona has answered our call," she yelled, taking advantage of the unexpected breeze. "See how she watches us from the forest, willing us to sacrifice the slaves."

A murmur rose from the assembled tribes like a distant swarm of bees. Many of the warriors raised their swords in salutation of the high priestess' power to arouse the Goddess. She acknowledged their salute with a haughty bow then turned to her acolyte.

"Ring the slave!" her voice boomed.

Africanus gritted her teeth and waited.

The priestess gave a vigorous shove and the tapered point entered the base of the nipple where it sprouted from its pimpled disc. Africanus sucked her breath and shuddered. It was as if she'd been branded with a red hot iron. The pain spread rapidly through her nipple and breast and beneath her ribs her heart pounded. The priestess took hold of the needle and whirled it round in her fingers enlarging the hole it had pierced, and then her arm gave another shove forcing the tapered end of the ring to go right through the base of the nipple. She slid the ring through the enlarged hole and let go, locking it into place. Air gushed from Africanus' lungs. Now that her nipple had been ringed the pain miraculously abated. She looked down marvelling at how such a huge ring could possibly pass through her skin. The priestess moved to the other breast and repeated the procedure, forcing the needle through the teat, twirling it in her fingers, enlarging the hole and then following it with the tapered point. When she'd finished both rings hung over the swell of Africanus' breasts and so large that the outer circumference rested on her ribs. The priestess gave each ring a gentle tug, making sure they were firmly fastened and moved on to the next slave, again driving the ring mercilessly through the puckered teat, ignoring the scream of pain screeching in her ears.

"Now bind the wretches," the high priestess hissed.

Eager to impress their terrifying mistress, the underlings went to work with a vengeance, seizing the nearest slave and dragging her to the centre of the stone. The strongest grabbed the girl's arms and bent them behind her back, whilst another deftly roped her wrists. A foot thumping between the girl's shoulder blades sent her crashing to the stone. She lay groaning on her belly whilst her legs were bent at the knees, forcing her feet onto her buttocks. These too were swiftly tied. Another stouter rope bound ankles and wrists together so tightly the girl's back threatened to snap. She lay writhing with pain, her back arched and arms straining in their sockets. Bodily, the priestesses carried her to the nearest trilithon, placing her neatly face down under the top stone. It took less than a minute to carry out the next bone wrenching exercise. A long rope had been passed through a massive iron ring set in the underside of the top stone. One end was tied to the rope binding the girl's wrists and ankles. Africanus knew what was going to happen next and winced in sympathy. A gut wrenching shriek followed by an ear piercing scream rose to the heavens as the priestesses hauled the girl into the air. Her body almost bent double as she rose higher and higher. Africanus could see the girl's shoulder blades crunching together and her spine cracking from the strain. She hung, suspended by a single rope, her body swaying from the momentum, arms and legs pinioned behind her, taking her whole body weight. Beneath her chest, her breasts wobbled like ripe melons, the rings now dangling from her nipples. The crowd at the edge of the grove vied with one another to get the best view of what was to follow. They did not have to wait long. The priestesses who had bound and hung the girl quickly fetched two circular stones, fantastically carved with scrolls and serpents. A hook had been let into the top of the stones, large enough to fit through the nipple rings.

Africanus' hand flew to her mouth. She had seen some outrageous and inventive tortures devised by the Romans, which alone beggared belief; women mated with bulls in the arena, others forced to have sex with wolves, but this was beyond her wildest imaginings. The priestesses, ignoring the girl's panic-stricken eyes, lifted the first stone and, groaning under its weight, just managed to slip the hook through the nipple ring. Her face was a mask of agony with rolling eyes and opened mouth, the stone weight tugging at the ringed nipple sent her whole body into convulsive spasms. But this was not the end. The second stone was hooked into place; its weight doubling the strain on the girl's already bent spine and wrenching limbs.

Just then, another breeze shook the trees, and the high priestess, quick as ever, mounted the stone at the base of the phallus, addressing the eye goggling mob.

"See now, how the Goddess has accepted the slave we offer in your name. You, the gathered clans who have come to the sacred circle to pay homage, cast your offerings into the sacred pool."

Golden bangles, bracelets, torques, necklaces and broaches went flying into the water, whilst the high priestess chanted prayers and devotions wishing the clans good fortune and fruitfulness. Africanus had to admire the bitch. The pool was no deeper than her mid thigh, and as soon as the clans had dispersed the priestesses would be wading in recovering all the gold and silver, no doubt dutifully handing it over to their mistress. Africanus guessed rightly that she had amassed quite a tidy fortune during the seasons.

But there was no time to dwell on that. The priestesses came forward and rushed her to the sacrificial stone. She grunted when her belly and breasts hit the cold hard surface, and a lot louder as her arms were pinioned behind her back. She felt her calves bending and skilful hands binding her feet and wrists. They carried her upside down to the next trilithon and soon she too, was swinging in the air, arms and legs racked with pain, her head hanging down, face buried under tumbling braids.

"I want this offering severely punished," the high priestess rasped. "See that her breasts carry the sacred skulls."

They were not real, but carved from solid stone, so heavy that the priestesses could just lift them in place. A bronze hook had been driven into the cranium, and the eye sockets filled with molten lead.

"It is our deep belief that whoever carries the skulls is favoured by the Goddess," the high priestess told her. "And the greater the pain, the more bounteous gifts she bestows."

"I'm going to kill you," Africanus muttered savagely. "By all the Gods of Rome, I'll kill you."

But at that moment there was nothing she could do but endure the agony of the stone skulls tearing at her nipples.

The pain was everywhere, ripping at the sinews of her limbs, burning into her buttocks and spine, but most of all through her pierced nipples which tugged from her breasts.

"She has good breasts," the high priestess complimented. "Just ripe for the lash. Give her twenty on each, and lay them on hard."

The priestesses took their plaited whips and stood either side of Africanus' suspended body. Even though the weights forced her breasts into conical shapes, their sheer size kept them full and globular, an easy target for the whips winging in under her chest. Each lash landed with perfect precision, cutting into the fleshy sides, and sweeping in an undercutting arc, either side of the rings. A hollow, smacking sound echoed under the trilithon and while Africanus uttered shrieks of pain, her suspended body swinging slowly in time to the lashing whips, the high priestess stole quietly away unnoticed by the mob stepping as close as they dared to get a better view of the whipped black woman. Those at the front of the crowd could just make out her magnificent thick pubic bush bristling under her bending thighs. But it was her breasts which held their attention. Stretched beneath her, weighed by the stone skulls, they seemed much larger than they ordinarily were. To Africanus, almost numbed with pain, they seemed to have swelled to three times their size. Her body twitched and spasmed at every lash, her buttocks hollowed at their sides as she clenched her cheeks, trying to ward off the pain. As the final lashes smacked into her swollen flesh she uttered one long cry of surrender and passed out.

At that very moment, a raven flew from under the furthermost trilithon accompanied by a great sigh from the mob. The high priestess suddenly appeared from behind one of the standing stones, her face all aglow. The raven was a sacred bird, the bearer of knowledge, and a messenger of the Gods. Its very appearance had the mob falling to their knees in wonderment and adulation. The high priestess acknowledged their salutations with her customary bow and ordered the rest of the suspended slaves to be well flogged.

It was late afternoon before the flogging was completed and the slaves released from their bonds. Exhausted and racked with pain, there was little they could do in the way of resistance as a group of selected warriors advanced upon them.

It was the final part of the ceremony and there was no doubting the massive erections bulging in their trousers. One by one the slaves were carried to the sacrificial stone in readiness for multiple penetrations.

"The longest and largest of you may take the Black sacrifice," the high priestess offered. "See that she is well fucked and your own women will bear fruit."

Three sturdy Celts came forward, their trousers already discarded. Africanus lay on the stone, her long gleaming legs already open and waiting for the first cock to penetrate her gaping cunt. The rings were still piercing her nipples and would not be removed until after she had been finally sacrificed. But that would be after she had spent the night in the high priestesses' sacred chamber. Now she eyed the three rampant cocks nodding at her sweating thighs.

"All of you are to penetrate her at the same time," the high priestess informed. "One of you will take her belly, the other her bottom, and one her mouth. You may decide amongst yourselves which you prefer."

There was no contest. The boldest of the warriors stepped forward and ordered Africanus to straddle his cock.

"You will be well fucked before you die," he told her, taking hold of his shaft and stroking it.

His hand closed around the throbbing length leaving enough that could have easily accepted the other hand with more to spare. He lay on his back whilst his two companions lifted her under the arms and thighs and carried her to his naked meat. Clumsily, they positioned her over his middle, opening her thighs and aiming his cock directly into her quivering slit. Her breasts still throbbed from the lash but had resumed their shape and remarkably seemed none the worse for her recent sufferings. Only her dark areola and nipples showed any signs of outward change. The black disc had spread over half her breast and the teats had expanded to twice their size. The sight of those deliciously succulent buds sent blood racing through the cock veins of the warriors who wasted no time in obeying the high priestess.

Africanus dutifully knelt over the Celt, his unbridled animal lust filling her nostrils as he reached out and grabbed her hips. She looked down at his manly, bearded face through dolorous heavy-lidded eyes. The chaining and flogging had taken their toll and she submitted to whatever lay in store with dumb servility. He entered her easily, letting his cock slip deep into her sex, smiling broadly as her bottom cheeks spread over his pelvis. Her magnificent ebony thighs rested either side of his middle and he reached out stroking their silky skin. She was in no hurry, and it seemed as if she were in a dream, feeling his length gliding against her clitoris, and his hands caressing her thighs and breasts. He cupped each one in turn delighting in their weight and size. She leaned forward, resting her hands on his chest, rocking her haunches with a slow almost drugged motion. But his companions were growing impatient.

"I'm going to take her arse," the second said crudely, and knocked her hands from his chest.

She fell forward, suddenly alerted to what was going to happen. He knelt behind her, placing his thumbs deep into her arse crease, prising open the splendid dark moons.

"A tight arse hole," he guffawed, pushing his forefinger into her bottom and wiggling it against her anal walls.

Africanus lay flat over the first warrior, squashing her breasts on his chest. Her legs were tight together and resting on those of the man beneath her, but not for long. The third warrior seized her ankles and threw them over the stone, so wide her bones cricked. The halves of her buttocks wobbled and shook and she felt the wiggling finger swiftly withdrawn. Quicker than she could blink, his cock was pressing into her anus, struggling to penetrate her gorgeous bottom. It took one shove of his hips to penetrate her anal hole, and another to send his pelvis smacking against her rump.

"First time I've ever fucked a woman's arse," she heard him laugh.

And he started riding her, resting his weight on the cushions of her soft buttocks, worming his cock inside the cosy warmth of her bottom.

The third merely shrugged at the sight of his two companions fucking both her arse and cunt, although he managed a sloping smile at the black woman sandwiched between two swarthy men, pumping their hips and slapping her flanks and back. He ambled to where her head rested and placed his hand under her chin.

"Open your mouth," he said quietly, putting his fingers on her lower lip and forcing it downwards.

Her mouth opened and he slipped the glazed, purple plum over her lip. He was content to let her suck on the cock head, rather than engulf her throat. That way she would feel his bursting essence filling her mouth instead of jetting it straight down her throat. He always thought it very arousing, watching a woman licking his spunk off her lips, and then lapping at the drops running down her chin.

Africanus didn't know what to think. She could hardly breathe with the weight of one man bearing down on her, thumping like a madman into her bottom, crushed against the other beneath her who jerked his hips and cock with equal savagery. Neither could she inhale, her mouth stuffed full of cock, prodding from one cheek to the other. Out of the corner of her eye she saw a slim young slave being penetrated by three huge, brutish men who had no intentions of treating her gently. Her pert buttocks were almost splitting from the huge cock spearing her virginal arse. Her head was held rigid by the man riding her mouth and he plunged in and out of her, forcing her bruised lips to the root of his cock. Her wiry legs spread over the stone, rigid with pain and trembling from ankle to hip. From a distance, the high priestess watched the suffering girl with a satisfied grin. Giving the warriors a helpless slave to ride always stood her in good stead with the chieftains.

Africanus felt the hardened cock inside her bottom suddenly enlarge. Its throbbing heat seemed to be filling her whole belly, then suddenly she heard him groan and his spunk filled her arse. The man at her head displayed much more control. Her lips sucked on his plum, going into the groove at the base whilst her tongue licked rapidly into the eye. He held her head still, never allowing the shaft to go any deeper into her mouth until he came his whole load. He drew back coming over her lips and chin, covering her upper lip and nostrils. Globules of spunk clung to the corners of her mouth and slowly trickled down the side of her face. Her tongue lapped at the creamy fluid, licking her lips clean. He saw her swallow and smoothed the side of her face with this cock head. He would have complimented her but the groans of the warrior riding her cunt cut him short. His loins jerked and heaved, then with one shudder he erupted flooding her cunt until he lay still, breathing like a wounded bear.

They disengaged and left her lying on the sacrificial stone, her mouth, cunt and arse filled with their juice.

"You have done well," the high priestess said softly. "Now take her to my sacred chamber and see she is well bound."

They carried her through the grove and into a subterranean chamber made remarkably comfortable with warm bedding and a fire already blazing in the hearth. It took only a few minutes to bind her. Chains and manacles already there for the purpose were quickly fastened to her wrists and ankles.

A length of chain was passed through each nipple ring and secured to hasps let into the stone wall.

"It's a pity that such a magnificent piece of fucking meat has to be sacrificed to the Goddess," one her captors remarked sadly.

"It is the will of the high priestess," another rejoined, giving her breasts a final affectionate squeeze.

He couldn't resist gripping his cock and jerking off over her face, splattering her lips and chest. The other two warriors quickly followed suit, coming so close their cock plums were only a whisper from her nipples. They both came simultaneously, piling their spunk on her nipple buds, then leaving her alone in the flickering shadows, still tasting their spending on her tongue.

Outside at the sacrificial stone she heard terrified screams from the slaves as they were dragged to their fate. One by one the screams abated and in the immense silence that followed Africanus knew she was alone, and it was only a matter of time before she joined her already dead companions, after the high priestess had finished with her, of course.

"I knew you'd be trouble the moment I set eyes on your ugly face," the high priestess complained, coming into the chamber.

She seized the hem of her bloodied tunic and threw it over her head. Behind her a cowering acolyte followed at her heels.

"Get that stuff off her and then get out!" she barked, going to a ewer and splashing water over her face.

The acolyte swiftly removed the chains and shackles and fled from the chamber. Glorious in her nakedness, the high priestess closed the door and bolted it.

Stripped of her ceremonial garb and crown, she looked far less terrifying. It was difficult to guess her age, could be anything between twenty five and forty. She had good legs, and firm, pert buttocks. Her breasts were full and well rounded, but it was her face which was most striking. It was broad with a high brow, prominent cheek bones, and pale flawless skin. The dark eyes glinted with quick, domineering intelligence, constantly in motion as she took in the naked black woman.

"Don't even think it," she whispered darkly, following Africanus' gaze at the bolted door. "Do you think I'd be alone in here with you without being able to summon help at the snap of my fingers? Now turn around and put your hands behind your back."

Africanus turned on her heels, clasping her hands over the crown of her buttocks. Something cold and metallic went around her wrists and was locked into place.

"Just a little precaution," the high priestess smiled, spinning her around to face her.

"Are you going to kill me?" she asked softly.

"Not now," the high priestess laughed coldly. "Do you think I had you brought here to slit your throat without first making good use of you? I know you guessed what I was up to out there, all that chanting and fucking, it keeps the peasants happy and under my control. Quite clever don't you think?"

Africanus thought her very clever indeed, but didn't say so.

"I saw you release that raven," she admitted, but avoided mentioning all the gold and silver tossed into the pond.

"It wasn't my idea, actually. One of my acolytes suggested it. Quite innocently as it happens, thinking it would arouse the Goddess. I took up the idea and had the bird tamed to fly off into the woods. At nightfall it'll return to its cage. Naturally I had the acolyte killed before she could give away the secret."

"You're a murdering bitch!" Africanus blurted.

"True. But in my profession it doesn't pay to have too many witnesses, which brings me to you."

She stroked Africanus' face with the backs of her knuckles, then took hold of one of the rings and twisted it in her long,

78

slender fingers, delighting in the wincing pain going across her captive's grimacing face.

"I suppose a whole army has sucked on these gorgeous tits," she remarked crudely. "And not a few have had their cocks inside your cunt."

"You wasted no time in having me fucked," Africanus replied bitterly.

"That was because I knew what you were thinking," she grinned. "I couldn't risk you opening your mouth before I had you sacrificed, which is why I had it stuffed full of cock. Having your cunt and your arse was just something in the way of distraction, and a little pleasure for my loyal henchman. The last sacrificial slave refused to have them, so I forced her to eat her own shit before I slit her throat."

"Am I to eat my own shit?" Africanus asked, sickened at the idea.

"That depends on how obedient you are," she retorted, going behind her.

A kick sent Africanus crashing to her knees. The high priestess stood over her, spreading her legs.

"Now, lick my clit," she rasped, grabbing her by the hair and forcing back her head.

Africanus angled her face into the high priestess' sex. Her tongue went straight into the hot slit, delving around the sex bud, but cunningly avoiding the stimulation her tormentor anticipated. She could hear the high priestess moaning with frustration, and every time she thought the wiggling tongue would bring her to an earth-shattering climax, it missed its target, preferring to lick at the throbbing sex walls.

"What's the matter with you, girl? I know you can do better than that. Now you will eat a plateful of your own shit."

"It's my hands," she wailed, looking tearfully into the astonished reddened face. "I can't keep my balance. If I could just hold your beautiful thighs, I'd bring you off in moments."

There was some sense in that. The slave's hands were

shackled behind her back, and no matter how she tried, she just couldn't kneel up straight.

The high priestesses went behind her and keyed the lock. "Now do as you are told!" she croaked, "or you'll eat my shit into the bargain."

"Yes, mistress," Africanus simpered, placing her hands on the long, ivory thighs.

The high priestess closed her eyes, awaiting the hot worming tongue to do its work. Then suddenly the roof of the hut went into a spin and she hit the floor head first. Africanus was on top of her quicker than she could wink. Now, all her training came to the fore. Her clenched fist smacked into the side of high priestesses' head, temporarily stunning her. It was quickly followed by a hard punch to both breasts, delivered in quick succession.

"You snivelling bitch," the high priestess hissed, bringing up her knee.

A foot thumping into her stomach caught the black woman off guard and she somersaulted head over heels, banging her head against a huge iron pot.

The high priestess was on her feet kicking wildly at anything within reach. Africanus rolled over and threw the contents of the pot over the outraged woman. For a couple of seconds the brawl came to a halt as the high priestess stood naked, her nipples and hair dripping with urine.

"You filthy bitch. I'll have you killed now," she grated.

Her mouth opened to summon the guards, but it never uttered a single sound. Africanus' long legs crossed over the floor in a single stride, her right arm winging in with the fury of a demon. The high priestess' head twisted sideways and again she crashed to the floor. Her legs were wide open and Africanus' foot sailed into her cunt. Her bottom and hips jolted from the force of the blow and she doubled up, but not before another well aimed kick into her jaw rendered her unconscious. It was all over in seconds and, for a few moments, Africanus stared at her lifeless body wondering what to do next.

Like a thief, she stole to the door and quietly slipped the bolt. The door flew open and she tumbled backwards.

"You!" she exclaimed.

The man closed the door and turned to face her, a bloodied sword swinging in his hand.

# CHAPTER FIVE

Caractus looked disdainfully at the unconscious high priestess, the toe of his boot pressing hard onto her breast.

"She had it coming," he muttered, working the sole harder onto her nipple. "I'm in half a mind to slit her throat here and now."

"She threatened to make me eat my own shit," Africanus retorted, picking up the high priestess' discarded robe, and tearing it in half.

Caractus lips broke into a contemptuous sneer. "You can piss over her stupid face if you wish, then we must be away. Time is not on our side."

"I can't thank you enough," Africanus said softly, straddling the unconscious woman.

Her long legs opened and a fast stream of steaming urine gushed over the face of her tormentor whose eyes briefly opened and then closed again as she drifted into deeper unconsciousness.

"Get dressed and follow me," Caractus said, smiling at the yellow pool around the woman's head.

Quickly, Africanus wrapped the torn robe around her shoulders. Two of the guards lay where he had slain them. A wolf cub was already sniffing at their lifeless bodies. It fled as they passed over them and made their way to the edge of the grove.

"There is something I must do," Africanus whispered, wading into the sacred pool.

Caractus watched in amazement as she bent over sweeping her arm under the surface. Whatever she was gathering was thrust into her bosom and when she had filled it she clambered out, water dripping from her skin.

"You're a strange one," Caractus whispered, helping her over the bank.

"There's a fortune lying in there," Africanus replied, hurrying alongside him.

"You've stolen the sacred offerings," he breathed, taking her hand and leading her through the trees.

"Sacred offerings, my arse! Most of that is already in the high priestess' coffers. It's all a huge game to rob you poor bastards."

He didn't hear her, or if he did made no reply for they were moving faster now, heading out of the wood and into open moor land. Caractus led the way, slashing at gorse bushes and thorns, clearing a path so she could follow in his wake. They moved fast, not stopping until the stone circle and all its evil ceremonies were far behind. The sun was just peeping over the distant hills when they halted at a deserted village. Caractus went first, checking each hut, ensuring that no one lingered there.

"We can rest now," he said at length, entering the last hut. "The water in the stream will quench our thirst, and after we have rested, move on into the territory of the Durotriges clans. My people will not follow us there."

"You saved my life," she acknowledged gratefully, stripping off the sweat-soaked robe.

For a moment, Caractus admired her body, six feet of gleaming black skin and splendid muscles shimmering in the dawn. His eyes wandered to her thighs and buttocks, powerful yet so beautiful in their strength and shape.

"You've still got those rings on your tits," he smiled, looking at them dangling from her nipples.

He came close, lifting one of them, and then let it fall gently against her ribs.

She placed her hands on his hips and they fell into a long, lingering embrace.

His hands went behind her, fondling her bottom cheeks.

She reached for his tunic and stripped it from his shoulders, then tugged at his belt, releasing the buckle.

83

On her knees now, she wrestled his trousers to his ankles. He stepped out of them and kicked them away.

"You've got a thick cock," she purred, taking the throbbing length in her mouth, wondering if he could fuck as hard as his father had done.

His hands rested on the back of her head, holding it still as her lips embraced the whole of his pulsating length.

He watched her cheeks fanning in and out, going hollow as she sucked up to the purple head, then blowing out again as her mouth glided into his bristling pubic hair.

"I'm going to fuck you now," he rasped, unable to resist the blood rushing through his cock veins.

She slipped his cock from her wetted lips and rolled gently onto her back, her long legs spreading wide over the floor.

Ripping off his woollen vest, he tumbled between her thighs and entered her at once, gliding easily into her soaking sex.

"Like father, like son." she whispered silently, throwing her legs over his back.

Her thighs flexed hard and he gasped for breath crushed in a vice of hot, eager flesh.

"Fuck me hard," she grated, digging her fingernails into his shoulder blades.

"I'm going to fuck you so hard you'll be walking bow legged for a month," he said, driving his pelvis hard into her groin.

There was no hurry. Their foes were far behind. They could fuck each other rotten.

"Your cunt is tight," he said, considering how many men must have laid between her gorgeous thighs.

"Keep still," she smiled lovingly. "Let me make you come."

He bore his weight on his elbows, just high enough so that his chest lightly grazed her breasts. Her nipples had gone stiff and he looked at the throbbing black buds sprouting as large as the tips of his fingers. The desire to suck them was too much and he angled his head, sucking hard.

"I said, don't move," she chided, punching him playfully on the ribs.

It was going to be an exercise in self-control, not something for which the Celts were renowned. But as soon as her hips began to move he understood and held his body rigid, keeping his legs straight whilst her hands played around his shoulder blades.

Slowly she uncoiled her legs, letting them fall either side of his torso. Her heels dug into the earth, taking the strain as she flexed her rippling thighs. It seemed as if his whole body weight was lifted and he floated above her, borne on her belly and sex. The only movement he made was a soft squeezing of her breasts and thumbing her nipples. Underneath his body her hips and pelvis began a slow snake like motion. Her buttocks, flattened against the earth suddenly grew hard and squeezed tight into the crease. Now he felt his body lift and he was suspended above her but keeping her impaled on his cock gone so hard it hurt.

"Phew!" he breathed, going wide-eyed. "You can fuck."

"You're longer than…" she was about to say 'your father,' but stopped herself just in time, "than anything else I've had inside me," she blurted.

It wasn't false praise. His cock was so long and thick her head swam. Around its throbbing shaft he felt her vaginal walls close in like a hot wet mouth. Her hips were moving faster now, snaking from side to side and then suddenly he caught his breath, the shock so unexpected his hands crushed her breasts.

"I can feel your cunt lips sucking on me," he gasped, almost unable to believe the sensation going on inside her belly.

As the son of a chieftain he'd had many a willing woman; some fucked like wild animals hoping for greater rewards; others lay like dead things; some could fuck comprehensively on top of his tunic; some needed the whole hut to perform; but Africanus was the only woman he'd met who could fuck lying still using only her hips and vaginal muscles to make his juices flow.

Inside her hot tunnel, the delicate petals of her sex caressed his cock like those of flowers, a touch so light he could just feel them. But over his pulsating plum the deeper muscles gripped tighter almost like a hand closing around his cock. At the same time her labia sucked harder and stronger, drawing him in so hard it was almost impossible to withdraw. Her vaginal muscles flexed and now the petals moved like tendons, closing around the shaft seeking out his hardness and moving up and down its entire length. He reached for her thighs and found they had gone as hard and solid as iron. It was the same with her buttocks now lifting higher from the ground. The cheeks were so compressed it was impossible to separate them. He marvelled at the strength in her body. She was all muscle. And at that moment in time he couldn't get enough of her.

"I said, keep still," she reminded him, embedding her heels further into the earth.

Her bottom lifted even higher and suddenly her vaginal muscles sucked so ardently on his cock he heard the peculiar slurping sound coming from between her legs. And she was hot, so hot and wet he could feel the heat of her cunt burning into his naked shaft. Soon the plum with its sensitive skin stretched tight began to tingle. The only movement he could manage was a slight thrust of his pelvis, but it was enough to send tremors through her sex. Now she began to pant, her mouth wide open and clutching at the hot, fetid air filling the hut.

"Slap me!" she shrieked. "Slap my tits! Go on, hurt me!"

It took a couple of seconds for that to sink in. Then he realized that pain at the height of her arousal gave her as much pleasure and satisfaction as actually being fucked. Idly, he wondered how much satisfaction she derived from a whip being soundly laid across her bare arse. But this was not the time for idle thoughts, not with six foot of hot and throbbing woman panting like a galloping mare beneath his rampant cock. Whatever she wanted, she was going to get. He sent his hand winging against her breast.

"Oh, by all the Gods, yes!" she breathed, jerking her hips faster and faster.

He had no thoughts of sparing the pain she so ardently craved and the next slap landed directly on top of her breasts. The wobbling globe flattened under the force of the blow and she cried out for harder slaps. At the same time her back went into a high bridge, supporting his weight while her hips drove harder against the very root of his shaft.

He slapped her breasts at random, just letting the flat of his hand fall where it would, now on her nipples, then on the sides hitting against the quivering flesh, then coming from underneath so that her whole breasts lifted from her chest. Driven on by her wild shrieks and thrusting hips, he lost all caution and took hold of the nipple rings, twisting and turning them, forcing the teat to swell and ache.

She responded by raking her nails all the way down his back, not a mere customary gesture, but raking deep until the flesh seared. There was nothing sensuous or playful in their love making, now it was all pain, as much pain and pleasure as their raking nails and slapping hands could deliver. But the sex going on between them was magic.

"You're just a filthy savage," she hissed, pounding his back with clenched fists.

No one ever dared call him that let alone a mere woman, and a slave.

"You're just a piece of cheap fucking flesh," he snarled, slapping her breasts so hard his hand stung.

Her arms went tight around his shoulders and hugged him close, but his arms were free to go on delivering the slaps she begged.

Now they moved in unison; her snaking hips and slavering

cunt riding with his thrusting thighs. Inside her his cock rammed deep, so deep her eyes rolled.

"Ride me, you pile of worthless monkey spunk," she shrieked, punching his ribs.

His arms shot out pinning her wrists to the ground.

"You need taming you foul-mouthed whore," he rasped, slamming his pelvis between her sweating thighs.

It was running from them both in rivulets, dripping from their faces and chests. They sweated so much their bellies slithered over one another and it was all he could manage to keep his balance on the wild thrashing black mare bucking beneath him.

"Give it to me harder," she taunted, narrowing her eyes into slits.

She looked like a serpent, looking at him with dark, slit eyes, but the effect was immediate.

Who was she, this dark, enigmatic creature, washed upon the sea shore, more beautiful than any of the flaxen-haired Celtic maidens, more mysterious than the workings of the Gods, but somehow as ferocious as any enemy he'd ever had to face.

He returned her taunts with manic thrusts, riding her cunt by twisting and angling his cock against the soaking walls. He could feel her juices dripping from her lips. The heat and smell of her sex was almost overpowering, a smell like nothing he had ever experienced; a rich earthy aroma, thick and sweet.

He released her wrists and slapped the side of her face. Her head swiftly turned and he heard her neck crick from the force of the blow. She came back and he hit her again and again, landing the flat of his hand on her cheeks until her skin turned as black as night. She would've smiled at his strength, but her orgasm suddenly erupted, catching her off guard.

"Ohhhh, ohhhh, ohhh," she groaned.

Then the groans turned to sobs and she surrendered to the juices soaking the earth beneath.

He soon followed, making her belly heave as he emptied into her sex. Suddenly the titanic strength that had sustained them through such a savage and prolonged bout of sex waned, and they collapsed into a panting, tangled heap.

She curled into a ball, resting her head on his chest whilst he put a protective arm around her shoulder, drawing her close. Throughout their frenzied coupling a strange familiarity had troubled her, like visiting a place which she had already seen in a dream. She knew that the man who had spied on her outside the hut, had come there in the dead of night and fucked her, then again when she had been crucified against the tree were all one and the same. Now she lay close to him feeling his warmth, the same man again who had risked all to save her. Instinctively, she kept silent. It was a tribute of his affections that he could only have taken her anonymously, proving his love by keeping watch, having her when he could without endangering her own life.

"Where shall we go?" she asked softly, placing her hand on his now flaccid cock and giving it a tender squeeze.

"The Roman town of Aqua Magna. It's a good place to do business and the Romans pay good prices for wolf and bear skins." He chuckled at the thought of it. "They feel the cold."

She shivered as if reminded that now their wild love making had ended the sweat on her body had turned cold and clammy.

"Is this place far?" she asked, hugging closer.

"If we set off soon, we should reach it before sunset. Then we can eat and sleep at one of the hostelries. I have gold in my purse."

"Not as much as I have," she chortled. "That stuff I got out of that pool is worth a small fortune. You must be mad, tossing all that in there just for that evil bitch."

"It's my father," he muttered bitterly. "He fucks her and I suppose she gets something back in return."

"I should imagine she gets quite a lot in return," she laughed. "A woman like that wouldn't offer her cunt for trifles."

"No woman ever does," he rejoined. "It's a sort of power, a woman's cunt."

"That's why those who know how to use it never go hungry," she mused. "I shall be glad to get to that town. My guts think my throat's been cut."

"It almost was," he muttered, unconsciously reminding her of how much she was in his debt.

But she had at least repaid some of it, and was in no doubt that she would be offering a lot more once they had settled. Perhaps life amongst the savages might not be so bad after all, providing they kept well away from the Druids and those horrible stone circles. She shuddered and hugged tighter. In her hand his cock had slowly hardened and had stood up erect and proud. Slowly she moved her fingers up and down the shaft, admiring its length and girth. He reached between her legs, gently parting her thighs and slipping his palm over her sex mound. Already the slit was warm and wet.

"I could use my mouth," she suggested softly, moving her head towards his rampant cock.

Her mouth opened wide and she swallowed him whole like a python swallowing its prey, but his hands were at her braids, pulling her head away from his cock.

"I'd rather have your cunt," he said seriously.

Without a word she threw a long leg over his middle and guided his throbbing member into her sex. He watched breathless as her bottom broadened over his thighs. She settled comfortably on his cock delighting in its length penetrating far inside her.

"A woman likes a long cock," she smiled widely, and gave her hips a playful wiggle.

"A man likes a deep cunt," he returned, not smiling but relishing the feel of her sex enveloping his shaft.

She closed her eyes and rocked to and fro, feeling his cock rise to its full length, then without warning she drew up her knees, resting the soles of her feet on the hut floor. Slowly her body lifted until his cock almost slipped out. Now she squatted over him, his cock plum resting just inside her lips. He reached out and grabbed her hips, steadying her whilst she bounced up and down, using her calves and thighs to support her weight.

"Phew!" he breathed, having a splendid view of his hardened cock going in and out of her sex.

She kept her balance perfectly, not once allowing his cock to slip from her lips, but keeping it hovering at the entrance to her sex before dropping down to its pubic root. His hands left her hips and went straight to her breasts. How to resist fondling and squeezing those enormous globes whilst she straddled him with her gaping sex. He gave the nipple rings a gentle tug and saw instantly the effect it had. Her mouth opened from the sudden shock of having her nipples tweaked, then her lips compressed into a wide grin. She said nothing but kept up the momentum, letting her bottom rise and fall, gradually increasing the tempo until her orgasm chilled her belly.

"I'd like to come over your tits," he said suddenly, feasting his eyes on her swollen nipples.

"If you do, I'll make you lick it off," she laughed.

He could think of nothing better than sweeping his tongue all over those huge wobbling flesh mounds. Despite their size she wasn't broad-shouldered but beautifully proportioned, no excess fat anywhere that he could see. The harder she rode him, the more he wanted her. He had thought of removing the rings, but seeing the effect even the slightest tug produced, he decided to leave them be.

"I know what you're thinking," she smiled. "And I don't mind. I'm getting quite used to having my tits ringed."

She settled on his cock, sitting astridé him and then leaning

91

forward so he could gorge on her throbbing teats. But her orgasm had already reached its climax, and with one long-throated moan, she came in a flood, pouring her sex juices over his balls. The scream of ecstasy that followed muffled the sounds of approaching feet, marching in unison through the village. Caractus heard nothing but his own groan of ecstasy as he pumped her sex, bouncing her hips and bottom over his middle, delighting in the sight of her shaking breasts.

Outside the marching feet had halted and were dividing around the hut, their owners drawing their swords.

"You didn't let me come over your tits," he laughed, fondling each globe in turn.

"I'd rather your spunk was hot inside my cunt, than wasted over my breasts," she said seriously.

"What would you say if I spunked over your face instead?" he suggested.

"You wouldn't be the first," she told him drily.

"You mean you've let men jerk over your face?" he asked with mock anger.

"I had no choice at the time."

"I ought to beat you for that," he said, trying to keep a straight face.

She was off him quickly and laughing as she gathered up her robe. "Only if you can catch me."

Playfully she ran around the hut, leaping over him, her long legs flying as she ran out into the sunshine. Caractus was barely on his feet before she came flying in again hotly pursued by six Roman legionaries. It took one swift thrust of flashing metal and the Celt crashed against the hut wall, his chest sliced by the blade. Africanus made a grab for his sword, but something heavy cracked across the back of her skull and the world went dark and silent.

"What have we here?" the centurion asked, slinging his helmet to the floor.

Africanus lay on her back, dazed from the blow that had stretched her senseless. Her legs were open and the legionaries crowding the hut fought to gaze enraptured into her naked sex.

"At a guess, I should say either a whore, or a thief. Look at all that booty."

The treasure that she had retrieved lay in a heap beside her tattered robe. It was worth more than the soldiers' earned in a twelve month. One of them gave a low whistle and stirred the glittering heap with his boot.

At their leader's command, one of the men fetched a helmet full of water from the stream and threw it in her face. Slowly she stirred into life and sat up, rubbing the bump on her head.

"Who are you, girl?" the centurion demanded, looking more closely into her smouldering eyes.

She told him who she was and related something of her experiences, omitting how she had fucked with Prasutagus and his son, but greatly embellished the shipwreck and how she had narrowly escaped death at the hands of the high priestess.

"A likely story, if ever I heard one," the centurion dismissed. "On your way from Rome, indeed. I should say you're a wandering whore, having it away with this savage, and this," he said, curling his lip, "is your payment from previous cock fights. I can smell the spunk in your cunt from here."

"It's not true!" she protested, snatching at the robe and covering her breasts. "I found all that stuff at the bottom of a pond where the barbarians make their offerings. Come with me and I'll show you a gold mine."

"A clever trick to lead us into an ambush, no doubt. My, you're a smart one."

And he whipped away the robe, baring her breasts to the crowding soldiers.

"What are those rings in your tits?" the standard bearer inquired.

She related in minute detail how her nipples had come to be pierced.

"Another lie!" the centurion exclaimed. "This whore dreams them up by the minute. I should say they are your badge of office. The whores in Londoninium are required by law to have their tits pierced and ringed, except in your case the rings are extraordinarily large."

"Goes to prove she's mistress of her trade," one of the men agreed.

"Probably served a whole garrison," another broke in, eyeing her gleaming legs.

"I don't like it," a sergeant said darkly. "I shouldn't be surprised if this miserable hut is where she plies her trade and at this very moment a whole tribe of these barbarians is on its way here to dip their cocks in her willing cunt." He gave Caractus a kick. He was not dead but stunned by the ferocity of the blow.

The centurion nodded thoughtfully. More than one good Roman soldier had been enticed to his death by a beautiful slave or whore lurking in dark alleyways or offering her services in lonely places. This deserted village would be hard to defend if it were suddenly attacked.

"Put that booty in my knapsack and bring her along. I think we'll get a good price for her in the slave market at Aqua Magna."

"I want to see the consul." she protested. "I'm the legal property of Quintus, a trained gladiatrix. I fought at the Colo...uurrgh..."

One of the soldiers stuffed a handful of earth into her mouth. "Now bite on that and shut your trap," he barked. "Everyone's had about as much of your tongue as they can stomach."

They formed up in column and marched quickly out of the deserted village, heading across the moor land and onto the high road that led to the city. The mounted centurion watched her mobile buttocks with growing interest. The girl was no ordinary slave that was certain. She was unused to hard manual labour and her limbs were well-honed. He began to wonder whether there might be some truth in her story after all. But the name Quintus meant nothing to him. It was a common enough name, but it wasn't too difficult imagining her swinging a sword in the arena.

At a wayside inn they halted and the men fell out, sheltering from the heat under a nearby oak tree. The centurion generously paid for their bread and wine, and a room for the girl and himself. There were things he needed to know.

"I want the exact location of this stone circle you described," he said, discarding his armour. "Take your time."

"If I tell you, will you let me go?" she asked, knowing what he was really after.

"Depends on how accurate you are," he hedged, dropping into a chair.

She knelt before him, sitting on her haunches, resting her elbows on his knees. She rendered a detailed description of the sacred grove, the paths that led to it and, most importantly, the whereabouts of the sacred pool. The centurion listened intently, not interrupting once, but taking in everything she described. He guessed it would take a couple of cohorts, say about a thousand well armed men to destroy the neighbouring Celts and their Druid priests. Information such as she had given was priceless in a barbaric country like this.

"You should've been a man," he complimented, leaning forward and grabbing her shoulders, pulling her between his open knees. "You would've made a resourceful leader. A good commander always makes sure of his ground before he attacks."

She smiled at the compliment. "Does this mean I'm free?"

"Of course and as a bonus I will allow you to keep some of that booty, providing you obey my next order."

She didn't need to be told what that was and dropped her head to his groin.

Tired from a long day's march, he relaxed in the chair while she sucked him, bobbing her head up and down his length, using her tongue to tease the juices from his erection. His cock was deep in her throat when he came and she swallowed his whole load, licking the drops from her lips afterwards.

It was over and done with quicker than she anticipated and she sat back on her haunches, smiling a devastatingly sexy smile.

The centurion was not one for wasting time and he ordered her up on her feet helping him to get dressed.

"I know some people in the city who will be of great assistance to you," he offered, making his way out into the daylight. "They could use an intelligent woman like you."

"I'm in your debt," she acknowledged, falling in between the lines of soldiers.

She walked with long assertive strides, feeling much more content now that she was heading back into civilisation. She was still naked and assumed her new friends would provide her with suitable clothes. Soon they were passing through the city gate and along a broad cobbled street. At the barracks the men filed through the arch, leaving the centurion to show her to the House of the Grapes, a well known hostelry.

He spoke only a few words of introduction and handed her over to the owner, explaining that she was to be fed and watered and given a good bed until his friends came to fetch her in the morning. Then he left.

"You've forgotten my share of the treasure," she called after him.

But the door to the hostelry was bolted.

"Don't worry," the keeper assured, "Julius Sentus always keeps his word. Now please, drink and eat your fill."

The meal was plentiful; freshly killed venison, newly baked bread and all the wine her stomach could take.

"Your room," the man said, showing her into a comfortable chamber.

Then he too left her alone and locked the door from the outside.

Trust Julius Sentus to come up with the goods.

And he walked away; grinning like a happy drunk.

Africanus slept soundly, thankful that Caractus had been spared. She hoped he would live and know that he would ever be in her thoughts.

# CHAPTER SIX

"There must be some mistake," Africanus protested, standing naked in the hostelry courtyard.

The friend of Julius Sentus was a heavily-built man with a shaven head shaped like an egg. Crudely rendered tattoos discoloured his thick, hairy arms and calves.

"The only mistake is you opening your gob," he said rudely, pushing her face against the wall.

His stubby fingers squeezed her bottom cheeks and thighs, he paid particular attention to them, pressing her muscles and testing their strength. He lifted her feet, checking the soles for ring worm. He ran the flat of his hand up and down her back, slapping her sides and hips, muttering satisfaction, every other word a disgusting oath. He spun her round and slapped her belly, murmuring it was nice and flat without any flab. He squeezed her breasts and pinched her nipples, but strangely, passed no comment on the rings. He manipulated her biceps and shoulders, nodding at their shape.

Africanus wasn't the only naked woman sweating in the hot sunshine. More than a dozen stood against the wall, sweat running from their writhing bodies. There was an emphatic uniformity in their physique that left her disturbed. It seemed that they had all been carefully selected for their strength and height. Each woman had powerful limbs and sturdy hips, not a slim, girlish figure to be seen. The thought flashed across her mind that she just might be returning to the arena after all.

"Bend over and touch your toes," the creature barked, squinting at her through porcine eyes.

She obeyed, touching the ground with her fingertips whilst he prised open her buttocks, seemingly studying her bottom hole.

"Have you ever had the shits?" he asked.

"Not until I met you," she muttered.

His hearing was a great deal more acute than she anticipated. A second later a short leather whip cracked across her bottom, the pain so severe and unexpected she toppled over and rolled into a ball. His foot sailed into her rump with a loud smack.

"Get up and answer my question, slave!"

"I've never had the shits," she murmured meekly, struggling to her feet.

"What about the clap, ever had a dose of that?"

"The what?" she asked, wondering where all this was leading.

He didn't bother repeating the question, but put his hand under her legs and rubbed it back and forth until his palm was slicked with juice.

"I think you're clean," he observed, sniffing her cream.

He turned to the other women and told them to form two lines, opposite each other and about ten feet apart.

"You," he spoke to Africanus, "pick up that boulder and throw it to the first slave."

It was so heavy it took all her strength to lift it from the ground. Grunting, she raised it to chest height and hurled it at the nearest woman who only just caught it. Staggering under its weight, she threw it to the woman standing opposite. And so it went all the way along the line, each woman groaning from the exertion as she threw it to the next.

The creature smiled satisfactorily at their efforts, his eyes squinting so much they were mere slits in his hideous face.

"A good batch this time," he observed, slapping the nearest woman on the shoulder and herding them all through the gate.

"What the hell's going on?" Africanus hissed to her neighbour, a tall, dark-eyed Celtic woman.

"What does it matter," she muttered scornfully. "Slaves just do their master's bidding."

Then it hit her. A slave! She had been sold into slavery! That bastard of a centurion had sold her, penniless and naked!

"I want to see that fucking centurion!" she shrieked, opening her mouth without first engaging her brain.

"You'll see no one," the creature bellowed, slapping her jaw.

"He stole my treasure!" she bellowed back.

He would've hit her again, but his hand stopped in mid air.

"Treasure?" he whispered. "What treasure. He never mentioned anything about that."

"Shows what a shit he is," she returned, rubbing her aching face.

He made a mental note to question Julius Sentus. Anything that belonged to a slave was supposed to be shared equally amongst them. After all, they were partners. It seemed one couldn't trust anybody these days.

"Never mind about your treasure," he said dangerously, shoving her forward. "Just get your backside into that waggon before I whip it raw."

It stood at the courtyard gate, a lumbering conveyance, closed in on all sides with heavy boards punctured at intervals with narrow slits to let in the air. A sturdy door armed with bolts and chains creaked open and the slave women were driven inside, one at a time. The first took her place at the far end, seated on her bottom, knees drawn up to her chest whilst the creature's assistant chained her to the wall. Both wrists were positioned above her head and locked into iron manacles. Her ankles were fitted snugly into rings fastened to the floor boards. When he was sure she was well secured he beckoned to the next who dumbly took her place opposite the first. The waggon was narrower than its outside dimensions betrayed and there was barely enough room to sit. The knees of the woman opposite Africanus rubbed against her own as she sat shoulder to shoulder with her suffering neighbours. The door slammed shut and they were plunged into darkness apart from narrow shafts of light beaming through the slits. The waggon gave a lurch and set off along the cobbled street leading out of the city and into the open countryside.

It wasn't long before the air became fetid from their breath and so hot they were bathed in sweat. Their hair turned lank and clung to their skulls like dirty rags. Try as they might it was impossible avoiding the numbness creeping through their chained limbs.

"Anyone know where we're headed?" the dark Celt croaked, shifting her bottom over the uneven boards.

"If I know that bastard, Dragorn, we'll probably end up pulling ploughs, or slaving in one of the villas," her neighbour muttered savagely.

"The last batch he sold ended up as sword bait in the arena at Londoninium," another broke in, twisting her shoulders against the wall.

"Or one of the brothels in Celdorum," a voice suggested. "It's right next to the barracks, that's why they need women like us. You need to be strong having thirty men a day grinding away at your cunt."

Africanus listened with a sinking heart. It seemed now that the rest of her life was going to be spent dragging a plough or on her back wearing out her cunt.

"It might not be so bad," a pale-skinned blonde beauty cut in. "The women from the Regni tribe were sold to a rich Roman merchant and were shipped to Rome as concubines. It wasn't so terrible, I mean locked up in a harem and only fucked once or twice a day."

Africanus suddenly looked up. "Are many slaves shipped to Rome?" she asked, galvanised into life.

"Hundreds," the blonde responded. "Celtic women are prized by the Romans. They think we make good house slaves."

"And fuck hard as well," the dark one added ruefully.

101

It was a crumb of comfort at least, the possibility of going back to Rome. Perhaps Quintus might have survived and returned home, or even Circo might be at that moment battling in the arena. Anything was preferable to being harnessed to a plough and whipped over the fields like an animal.

She would like to have questioned the blonde further, but her mouth had gone dry and her tongue stuck to the roof of her mouth. She blinked continuously at the sweat stinging her eyes and more had run down her back and trickled through her bottom crease, forming a sticky pool under her buttocks. Her vision had become blurred, but she could see the shaft of light lighting up the woman opposite whose breasts shone with perspiration. Their whole bodies were slippery and smelling of feminine odour. Most of them had passed out from the heat when the waggon rumbled to a halt.

The bars and locks were shot and keyed, and the door creaked open admitting a delicious blast of fresh air.

The shaven-headed creature was nowhere to be seen, but his henchman, equally repulsive with a leering squint and a noticeable dent in the side of his bald head, peered cautiously through the opening, grinning like a lunatic.

"This cart stinks of cunt," he sniffed, wrinkling his hairy nostrils.

He disappeared and they heard the sound of water splashing from a bucket. "This'll cool yor steamin' cracks," he grunted, tossing the contents through the doorway and over the nearest women.

They shuddered at the sudden coldness hitting their hot skin like ice. He went off laughing and came back with another bucketful, hurling it at random over anyone within reach.

"That made your teats go hard, eh?" he observed gaily, looking at the erect nipples sprouting from the shock.

Then he noticed the rings hanging from Africanus nipples and eyed them suspiciously.

"Bless me, if they ain't made o' gold," he noticed, his eyes glinting with avarice.

His arm was through the doorway in a shot and tugging hard at the rings.

"Aaaoow!" Africanus shrieked as her nipples were pulled from her breasts.

He ignored that and twisted and pulled, trying to wrench the rings free.

"Can't move 'em," he muttered, reaching under his tunic.

Africanus almost soiled the boards beneath her sweating bottom as the knife blade twinkled in the sun light.

He would have cut them free had it not been for a rider drawing up alongside the waggon. The captive slaves heard him dismount and he looked into the gloom at the ranks of naked women now drenched in water.

"What's this?" he asked, scrutinizing the cargo.

"Slaves for up yonder," the driver grumbled, piqued at the interruption.

The man, dark and handsome, well-built and smelling of hot leather, cocked his head at the raised arms and lifted breasts. He took time to survey the raised knees and bare expanse of naked thighs. Then, after taking his fill, slammed the door shut and shot a bolt into place.

"You're lucky," a full-breasted slave informed. "If he hadn't come, that brute would've sliced off your tits to get the rings."

"Fuck him," Africanus snarled, heaving on the shackles.

The waggon lurched forward sending its miserable passengers jolting painfully in their chains. Outside they heard a horse walking beside it, the rider admonishing the driver for stopping in the first place.

They journeyed on, half conscious from racked limbs and fatigue. The shafts of light grew weaker and soon they were in complete darkness. Now the sun had set the air in the waggon cooled a little, but the heads of the women dropped onto their chests as they fell into exhausted slumber.

It was well after midnight when the waggon halted.

The rider dismounted and the door groaned open.

"Get these cows out of here," he ordered.

With sullen ferocity, the driver unlocked Africanus' shackles and chains, grabbed her by the hair and hurled her to the ground. He moved fast, dragging each captive after him, piling them on top of one another.

The rider looked disdainfully at the heap of naked, grimy flesh, a pile of bare arms, legs, breasts and buttocks, now stirring slowly into life.

"Take them to the cells," he said drily.

"'Tis too late, master. They're locked for the night."

The rider sighed with exasperation. "No matter. Have them netted, and then bring me some food."

"What about them?" the driver asked, shoving his boot onto the nearest bare rump.

"Nothing for them," he replied. "They can eat in the morning. Now move!"

The driver wasted no time in lashing the naked flesh into obedience, herding them under a grove of trees. Other men joined him, disgruntled at being woken in the dead of night to deal with a pack of women. They worked fast, lashing at their buttocks and forcing them to lie in huge nets, already spread over the ground. Ropes with hooks on the end were thrown over the branches and the middle of the nets passed over the hooks. One by one, the enmeshed women were hauled upwards, wriggling and writhing as their bodies bent double. Africanus struggled inside the net, trying to adjust her body as it swung under the branch.

"They won't get out of that in a hurry," the driver observed, poking his whip through the mesh and into the bottom of the dark Celt. It seemed that having women netted and strung was something of a custom in this barbaric land.

Still grumbling, the men went off into the darkness leaving the women suspended like carcasses of meat in an abattoir, and with good reason. It was impossible to get out of that, hanging like a dead weight, their naked bodies pressing down on the mesh made it impossible to escape. Every time they moved the net further entangled their limbs and Africanus, hanging on her stomach gazed disconsolately at the ground. Once or twice she managed to twist her shoulders, but could make out nothing more than the sheer face of a cliff towering overhead. There were some buildings nearby but the windows were unlit as the occupants slumbered. A full moon breaking through the clouds briefly illuminated a long line of carts and waggons, apart from that there was nothing to indicate what sort of place this was.

Not until morning anyway, when the first rays of sunshine lighted on the cliff face.

Africanus was asleep, worn to the bone when her body crashed to earth.

"Get up," a voice mumbled, kicking her bottom.

"How the fuck can I, tangled in this," she returned irritably, struggling against the mesh.

That problem was solved with a knife slashing at the cords. Disentangled, she and the other women were coming awake, looking bemused at the men standing around them some armed, some merely regarding them with idle curiosity. Thankfully, the hideous driver and his stinking conveyance were no where in sight.

The rider, who had unwittingly saved her from being horribly disfigured and robbed, appeared from one of the buildings, looking refreshed and well-groomed.

"Get in line," he said, not with any untoward severity.

The women shuffled into a straggling line, looking at the ground, ashamed of their nakedness.

With the bearing of a soldier, he walked along the line, lifting their chins with his whip handle, carefully studying their faces and limbs.

He tapped the dark Celt on the shoulder. "Rock face," he

remarked strangely, then passing to the next, "Hammer and tap," then to the next, "Carrier," and all the way along, making incomprehensible suggestions.

When he'd finished he told one of the men to fetch the slaves a bowl of porridge and a jug of fresh water. He waited until they'd finished eating before completing his speech.

"Work well and hard and you will suffer less than you deserve. Slack and you can expect no mercy from me or any of my guards."

To emphasize the point he cracked his whip expertly across the buttocks of the dark Celt, and again on the flanks of the pretty blonde, who both yelped with pain.

"All right. Take them away," he ordered, and marched off back into the building.

Africanus knew at once that she and the others were destined for hard labour, she didn't know how hard until they entered the tunnel in the cliff face.

Africanus stood in wonderment, partly from shock, but mostly in sheer disbelief. The tunnel had terminated into a gigantic cavern where dim figures moved through the gloom illuminated only by candlelight. Naked men and women, chained in pairs worked at the rock face swinging pick axes into the stone. Others piled the hewn rock into sledges dragged away by more slaves. A rope around their waists passed under their legs where it was connected to a chain, in turn hooked to the front of the sledge. They crawled on all fours, sweating under the heavy loads. In places a woman held a long iron bar into the rock face, whilst her companion smacked the end with a hammer, splitting the rock in twain. All around the continuing sound of clanking chains and metallic clashes of hammers and bars echoed through the chamber, punctuated by sharp cracks of whips on naked flesh quickly followed by the agonising shriek of the victim. The guards, dressed in light armour carried three-tailed whips which they used with alarming frequency on the bare buttocks and backs of the toilers. The roof of the chamber was supported by columns of stone left in place as supports, and between them men and women passed like grim shadows.

The slave women were quickly separated into their allotted tasks, and now the meaning of the rider's words became clear. The dark Celt was sent to the nearest rock face and chained to an awaiting companion wielding a pick axe. The pretty blonde was despatched to hold an iron bar ready to be tapped. Some of the carriers were roped and chained to sledges, whilst others carried the loads on their bare backs. Africanus, the last to be chained was led up a steep stairway cut into the rock. At a wide ledge she was fitted with an iron band passing around her waist. A chain linked her to a man, naked and powerfully built. A leather thong covered his groin, and she could see he was already bulging at the sight of her.

"The men are allowed to fuck their women companions," the guard kindly informed her. "If they fulfil their quota. Those who fail are flogged. The women who fail are either whipped or allocated special duties," and he laughed and handed her a pick axe.

"What is this place," she whispered, positioning herself alongside the man.

He introduced himself as Gallus and told her they were in a silver mine. Then he swung his pick into the rock and Africanus followed suit. It wasn't easy, angling the point of the pick where it should fall and several times she narrowly missed taking off his head. Neither was it easy being chained to him. Every time she leaned backwards to swing her arms she dragged him from the face. It soon became clear that if she carried on like that they would never fill the days' quota.

"If you get me a flogging," he warned darkly. "I'll see you're fucked from here to the next full moon."

Africanus picked up the tool and swung it savagely into the rock face, sending shards of rock flying into the side of his head. She made up her mind there and then that as soon as she found a way out of this hell she would track down the centurion and strangle him.

Surprisingly, she began to get the measure of swinging her pick and rock tumbled from the face in ever increasing amounts. Gallus, quickly learnt how to avoid her flailing arms and continued hacking at the rock and by the end of the day their quota was fulfilled, but only just. Women chained to the sledges dragged the pile away, crawling slowly along the ledge, their unfettered breasts swinging ponderously beneath them. The ropes were clearly embedded deep in their sex slits and they winced at the pain as it rubbed against their vaginal lips.

A whistle echoed around the vaulted chamber and all the clanking and groaning abruptly ceased.

"We eat now," Gallus told her, dropping his pick.

"Where do we sleep?" she wondered, accepting a bowl of thin, watery soup from a passing slave.

"Right here," he said, spooning the liquid. "Unless they want you for special duties. New slaves are always selected, especially those with big tits, so I reckon you'll be on your back ere nightfall."

"Oh, thanks," she muttered, grimacing at the foul-tasting soup.

Gallus was right. As soon as the meal was finished a guard arrived and unshackled her. She followed him along the ledge and down the steps and into a smaller cavern set apart from the main vault. A group of men, naked except for their leather thongs sat around the wall covered in sweat-streaked dust.

"She's yours 'til morning," the guard offered, shoving her forward.

"Don't I get any sleep?" she protested.

"Not with that much cock going in and out of your cunt, you won't," he smirked.

"I want that one ringed," she said, looking at the man who had already cast aside his thong.

108

"You'll take it all, or have forty lashes on your bare arse," the guard calmly informed.

"She could share it," one of the grimy men suggested hopefully.

The guard shrugged as if to say, he couldn't care less either way, and he marched off into the flickering gloom. It was the dark Celtic woman who came trudging behind him, her face a mask of racked exhaustion.

"You can have this thing as a bonus," he said, smacking her rump with his whip. "But mind that both of them are back at work before sunrise, or you'll take their place at the whipping post."

"We call him the mule," one of the men said, indicating the slave with the enormous organ. "Make up your minds which one of you is going to be first."

Both women stared at the throbbing organ, hoping the other would offer to take the lead.

"Why not have them both," another man suggested. "Put them bottom up over the sledge. We can wager on which one screams the loudest."

"I'll take it," the Celt said suddenly, closing her hand around its length.

"You don't have to on my account," Africanus retorted.

The Celt shot her a sly sideways glance, and then flashed her eyes in the direction of the men busy removing their thongs.

"This is our way out of here," she whispered. "Look at the state of them. One good fuck and they'll be finished."

Africanus nodded. Whatever she had in mind was worth a try. The Celt bent over the sledge, throwing her legs wide.

The sight of her gaping cunt had the men hard as iron, but Africanus wasn't looking at their cocks. Their faces were haggard and worn, exhausted from years of hard labour. Despite all their bravado, it wouldn't take much to leave them wasted. She glanced through the cavern into the main vault. An eerie silence pervaded the gloom broken only by exhausted snoring. If they could make it to the entrance tunnel they stood a good chance of escape.

The Mule dropped to his knees, aiming his cock into the Celt. She braced herself for the length she so courageously offered to take. Her bottom cheeks flexed and twitched in anticipation. Her hands gripped tightly on the sledge and she let out a grunt as his enormous length began to penetrate her belly.

Another of the men had his arm around Africanus' waist, steering her to the sledge.

"Why don't we go over there," she volunteered, indicating a long smooth ledge. It was much darker and away from the rest of the horde. "I'll fuck you rotten and pull tricks you never imagined, but why let the rest of them watch us. I want to fuck you in private. It's not often I come across such a real man."

His tired eyes made a quick tour of her body with all its voluptuous curves and shining skin. It wasn't often he came across such a real woman, so why share her with the rest. He was a gang master and they wouldn't argue. Let them have the Celt now already fully penetrated.

"I'm keeping this bitch for myself," he grated, walking her to the ledge.

The gang knew not to argue and lined up behind the Mule. The Celtic woman had broken into a cold sweat and was trying hard to accommodate the length of throbbing meat pounding away at her cunt. One of the gang, desperate to empty his balls, had gone to the front of the sledge and rammed his cock into her gasping mouth, forcing it to the back of her throat. Africanus couldn't help but admire her courage and quick thinking.

"Get on your knees," the gang master croaked, putting his hands on her shoulders and dropping her to the ledge.

Africanus opened her mouth and slowly swallowed his

length, taking her time, letting his climax rise as she cupped and fondled his balls. Somewhere behind her she heard the stuttering groans of the Mule as he came into the Celt. He slapped her rump and sides, then withdrew, wiping his cock in her hair. Another took his place and erupted before she was even fully engulfed. Africanus saw the last drops of his spunk spatter over the girl's back and he staggered away into the shadows, barely able to stand.

"Suck harder," the gang master commanded, interrupting her thoughts.

He cuffed the back of her head by way of encouragement, and then grabbed her shoulders, slamming them into his belly.

"Urrgh," she grunted, feeling the sudden thrust of his cock plum gagging her mouth.

She eased gently back sucking so hard her cheeks hollowed and touched the sides of his cock. He looked down at her head; mouth fully stretched around what was still showing of his length. The bitch had taken the whole shaft; even his balls tickled her chin.

"I'm having you in my gang," he breathed, swaying on his feet and clutching her head. "In the morning you'll be chained with me."

Africanus popped his cock from her mouth and looked up lovingly into his pale eyes.

"You can fuck me to death," she complimented. "I want your cock in my mouth every minute of the day. I'll swallow if you want."

"Swallow now," he rasped. "Get my spunk in your throat."

She turned artfully on her knees, angling his cock into her cheek but looking at how the Celt was getting on. She was taking the last of the gang, sitting astride him, bouncing her arse like there was no tomorrow. The rest of the gang had staggered off to their places of sleep, their energy drained. Africanus sensed panic rising in her belly. If they were to make good their escape she had to finish off the brute stuffing her mouth as quickly as she could. But suck as hard as she liked, he was deliberately holding back displaying more resilience than she anticipated. The dark eyed Celt got off the man she had just satisfied and went behind the brute, squirming her naked body against his back, rubbing her breasts and nipples into his dirty, sweating skin. Her pubic bush brushed into his buttocks as she pressed harder. Her knee went between his legs lifting until it grazed his loaded balls.

"You can have me too," she whispered. "I want your cock in my mouth."

The sensation of Africanus' hot tongue lashing his plum and the soft skin of the Celt was too much. Hard, erect nipples and breasts teased all down his back whilst the black woman's head bobbed so fast her jaw ached. His legs went rigid and he moaned like a wounded bear. Africanus drew quickly back and he squirted his load all over her breasts. The Celt threw her arms around his shoulders, dragging him backwards. But he was too heavy to hold and his head hit the floor with a dull crack.

"The bastard's out cold," she murmured, struggling from under his unconscious body.

"Now what?" Africanus asked, swiftly looking around her.

The Celt didn't answer but made off into the main vault with the black woman running after her. It was the early hours of the morning when the mind is at its most comatose, the slaves were sound asleep thoroughly exhausted from their hard labours and the slave women they'd fucked, the guards nodded drowsily at their posts, waiting to be relieved by the morning shift. It was now or never. Africanus' heart beat so fast she could hardly breathe. But there was no time to think about that. Following the Celt, Africanus darted from column to column, keeping well in the shadows, her long bare legs serving her well when they made the final run for the entrance tunnel. Common sense ought to have warned them that the place was suspiciously unguarded. They could even see the first light of dawn.

Side by side, still wearing their iron waist bands, they hurtled through the tunnel. No one followed, neither did they need to. The trap set close to the entrance sprang into action. Rope nooses laid across the floor tightened around their ankles and in the blink of an eye they were hanging upside down, suspended from the ceiling. It happened so fast neither of them could utter a cry until their bodies were swaying to and fro caught in the sudden momentum. Africanus' body went into a demented spin, the rope gradually tightening around her ankles until she stopped spinning, then returned in the opposite direction. Her breasts hung like distorted melons over her ribs, the rings still in place laid themselves over her belly, twinkling as the dawn illuminated the tunnel and the rider coming casually towards them.

"You disappoint me," he said, angling his head into their upside down bodies. "I credited you with more sense than try and escape from the mine. Now you will be punished, but first, I'll have you both flogged. Guard, summon the slaves to witness punishment. Give these pitiful wretches forty strokes apiece, then have them fitted with the girdle."

The guard advanced and drew a long knife from his belt. For one terrifying moment the women hanging upside down thought he was about to slit their throats.

"Leave them where they are," the rider barked. "Flog them hanging by their ankles."

The assembled slaves gathered to watch the flogging stood in subdued huddles, secretly wishing the two women had made it into the outside world, for many of them had spent years inside the mine without as much glimpsing the sun, or feeling rain on their grimy faces.

The guard tested the suppleness of his whip by bending it in his fists, then releasing one end so that it whistled back into shape. At the sound the buttocks of the hanging women visibly flexed. They knew they would not be spared and that their punishment would be severe as much as a warning to the other slaves as a flogging for its own sake.

"Start with their arses, then all the way up their legs and, if you've still got enough energy, down their backs. You may leave their tits and bellies unmarked. Begin."

He sent the whip sailing into the tight buttocks of the Celt who, unused to being flogged, tensed her bottom muscles allowing the whip to inflict much more pain than if she had tried to relax. But Africanus knew better. No stranger to a whip or cane, she took a deep breath and let her body hang limp. The whip smacked into the crown of her arse, but the ferocity of the blow softened as it embedded in her ample moon. The guard left her swaying and returned to the Celt, delivering six lashes in quick succession. Her shrieks and howls reverberated around the high, vaulted chamber like the cries of tormented souls in purgatory. Her whole body went into a spin and the guard amused himself by lashing at her buttocks as they span by, sending her into an even faster motion. He left her spinning and returned to the black woman whose buttocks were, in his opinion the finest and shapeliest he'd ever had the pleasure to flog. For a moment he surprised the onlookers by going up to her and fondling the strong halves, kneading the taut flesh at the edge of the crease and slapping the hollows at the sides.

"After this, I'm going to ride that fine arse of yours," he promised, standing back and lifting the whip high over his head.

"Get on with it!" the rider ordered sharply. "Finish beating these animals, then we can have them trussed."

Africanus felt like an animal, hanging by her ankles, naked and defenceless against the tormenting whip winging into her bottom. The dust and grit from her previous toil still clung to her skin and her once splendidly woven braids dangled like rats' tails. Blood was slowly going to her head and only the fierce cracking whip prevented her from fainting. She too went into a spin, but much slower giving him time to aim more accurately. Time and time again the whip landed vertically into her arse crease, spreading the buttock halves wider until he could send the whip almost straight into her sex slit. He left her throbbing arse and went to the Celt. Her face was streaked with tears and mucus pouring from her nostrils. Her mouth hung open and slack. Whatever she was saying came only in incoherent mumbles.

"It's about time you savages learnt who's master around here," he said, knowing the rider was still watching and listening. "Maybe a couple of dozen on the backs of your legs will help you decide."

"Please…can't..take any..more," she sobbed.

Her words found no sympathy and the whip flew straight onto the backs of her thighs, landing at the crease where they joined her buttocks, then progressing slowly upwards towards the backs of her knees, each lash delivered with expert precision, just above the other leaving only a finger's width between each welt.

"Finish of the black woman and truss them," the rider said, eager to get the rest of the slaves back to work. Even he had his quota to fill and faced penalties if the right amount of ore was not delivered on time.

He went off to his private quarters and was surprised to find an expensive and well equipped carriage waiting on the green. An equally well dressed fellow Roman was alighting from the carriage and raised his hand in formal salute.

"Hail, Heracles," he greeted, seemingly knowing him, even though they had never met. "I bring you gifts and wish to conduct business which you shall find much to your advantage. I'm looking to purchase new slaves for my ludus; a school where I train female gladiators," the stranger informed. "I have it on good authority that you might well fulfil my needs, if the price is right, of course."

115

Heracles had to think about that. The owners of the silver mine had given strict instructions that no slaves were to be sold without their express permission. Strong, well-built female slaves were hard to come by and highly prized. But Heracles was not above selling the odd one or two here and there. If the price was right, of course.

"I think I might have one or two you might be interested in," he replied casually, looking at a case of excellent vintage the Roman's slave was at that moment unloading from an accompanying cart.

They went out of the sun and into the cool of his private apartments just as Africanus was receiving the final lashes on her back and legs.

The dark Celt was hanging motionless and felt nothing when the guard cut the rope sending her crashing to the floor. Africanus managed to put out her arms and tumbled into a somersault, groaning as her welted back rolled over the stone.

"Truss these sows," the guard said, folding his arms over his burly chest.

His underlings raced over and swiftly had both women on all fours. Africanus felt her feet lifted one at a time and some kind of leather breeches were wrestled over her knees and up her thighs. A harder piece of leather, about a finger's length nudged against her sex bud, not long enough to penetrate her completely, but designed to be in constant contact with her most intimate part. Attached to the breeches were iron rings, and these in turn were connected to chains, long enough to reach up to a series of hooks let into the ceiling.

"On your feet, slave," the guard rasped, hauling her upright.

The dark-eyed Celt was ushered beneath the ceiling rings and stood quaking as the chains were passed over the hooks. It took three men to raise her from the floor. Africanus' throat went dry with despair. Now she understood the reason for all this fumbling and cursing that went on at her rear. The woman was suspended by the chains at the sides of the breeches, her full weight bearing down on her groin, and inside her sex tunnel, the leather finger rubbed against her clitoris.

"Now you," the guard motioned, positioning Africanus and tossing the chains over the hooks.

Her chest swelled from a sudden intake of air as her body weight took the strain. Slowly, she lifted from the ground, and with every pull on the chain, the leather finger tightened against her sex bud. Even the slightest movement of her hips or buttocks had the finger doing its evil work.

"Now the weights," the guard said finally, looking up into Africanus' wide-eyed face.

Her ankles were chained together and a lump of iron cast into the shape of an anvil hung beneath her feet. The effect was immediate. Suddenly her whole sex tunnel seemed to split as the leather finger forced its way between her lips, then the hard surface of the breeches rubbed against her pubic bush, preventing any further penetration. To stop herself from toppling, she reached out and grabbed the chains hanging beside her, looking as if she were on a swing.

"You'll stay there until your cunt's sore from so much coming," the guard laughed.

Neither Africanus nor the Celt saw the joke. The flogging had already aroused them almost to the point of orgasmic climax, now they were left hanging by the groin, their clits and sex lips constantly teased to the point of orgasm without being brought off. For hours they would hang there in untold agonies of frustration, desperate to come, always on the brink, but never relieved. It wasn't long before her nipples started throbbing, and it didn't help that the rings fitted through them increased the tingling sensation gradually spreading through her breast. She could see the Celt writhing in her breeches, wriggling her whipped bottom, even risking taking one hand from the chain and pinching her nipples hoping it would bring on an orgasm.

Africanus gritted her teeth, trying to avert her mind from

what was taking place in her sex. She was no stranger to cock, and more often than not welcomed a hard throbbing length deep inside her belly, as any normal highly-sexed, red-blooded woman would do, but she welcomed it most when it happened to be on her terms with the man she loved, now, with her sex tingling and wet, she would have fucked with anyone, even the misshapen beast that had sent her here.

"I'm begging for it," she wept, digging her nails in her palms.

The Celt's agonies were just as acute, and Africanus could see her biting her lips and trying to force her sex harder onto the leather finger. But it was all in vain, the device was superbly designed not to give them the satisfaction they so desperately needed. It didn't help either of their states of mind when a couple of naked young women came through the tunnel, one harnessed to the sledge, grunting as she dragged it forward, the rope and chain straining between her legs, and behind her, another naked girl was on all fours pushing the sledge at the rear, her powerful thighs sweating and hollowing. One of the guards halted them and quickly knelt behind the girl. It wasn't difficult, getting between her legs, ordering her to spread them while he penetrated her to the hilt. She grunted and gripped the top of the sledge, bracing her arms as he pounded hard inside her. The girl came quickly enough, shuddering from head to thigh as her juices flooded over his balls. Even from where she was hanging, Africanus could see the damp pool forming under the sledge. It was all over and finished in a few minutes, and the girl went on her way, pushing and heaving at the load, as if the sexual interruption was just part of her daily routine.

The guard buckled his trousers and would have gone straight back to his duties had he not heard the women moaning and sobbing overhead. Their feet were just above ground level and he could easily reach up and stroke their thighs or fondle their twitching buttocks.

"Fine pieces of fucking flesh," he taunted, stroking the backs of their thighs and pinching the exposed flesh of their buttocks where they were most sensitive.

"And a nice flat belly too," he whispered, slapping the pit of Africanus' stomach.

He put the tips of his fingers just under her navel and pressed hard, aiming them towards her pubic mound. Only a strip of leather prevented his fingers from going into her sex.

"You're on heat," he taunted. "I can smell your cunt juice from here."

"You bastard," Africanus hissed, clenching her fists.

Her nipples were erect and just begging for his teeth to nibble them. He looked at another sledge being dragged through the tunnel and promptly left off humiliating her, and would have taken the slave struggling at its rear were it not for Heracles and the other Roman coming towards him.

"If its good strong thighs and shoulders you're looking for, you've come to the right place," Heracles was saying. "Take these two for example."

He slapped Africanus' flank and, shaken from her sexual coma, she looked down at the stranger.

"Quintus Varus!" she exclaimed.

"Africanus! Is that really you?"

He looked at Heracles, his jaw firmly set, brooking no argument. "I'll take the black woman. Name your price."

# CHAPTER SEVEN

"What the fuck is that?" the legionary swore.

He was one of a centuria sent to build a bridge across the river leading to the moors beyond.

He wasn't the only legionary noticing the strange object drifting on the current. The hammering and sawing ceased as they all downed tools and stared bemused into the distance.

It was getting closer, and once snagged on an overhanging branch, but the current was too strong and it broke free, now they could see it more clearly.

"By all the Gods, it's woman!" a standard bearer announced.

The captain shielded his eyes. "Aye, and a naked one at that. All right, you men, get back to work. You three prepare to rope her in."

She was tied to an X-shaped wooden cross, her arms and legs widely spread. Behind her, long tresses of raven hair floated harmlessly on the surface like reeds. At first sight it appeared that her hands and feet were nailed to the frame, but closer inspection revealed nothing more sinister than tightly bound cords. On her belly and breasts were painted Druidical runes and symbols which meant nothing to the Roman soldiery. Around her brow was a crown of mistletoe and ivy leaves. The cross was almost within reach and more men stopped to witness this strange and unexpected spectacle, but it did make a pleasant distraction, seeing a voluptuous woman whose nipples they could now see painted bright scarlet. A serpent had been expertly painted on her left thigh, its long tongue coiling into her sex.

"She's in good shape for an old one," a soldier remarked, guessing she was in her late thirties, possibly a bit older.

"Don't be too critical," his companion chided, leaning over the parapet. "Some of these older birds can fuck as well as the young 'uns."

"Stop talking and haul her in!" the captain barked, tossing them a rope.

The cross wedged under the stanchions of the bridge, but the water was only knee deep and the men waded in pulling it to the bank.

"She's alive!" a voice rang out and the men scurried to cut the binding ropes.

"Who could do this to a woman?" the sergeant said disgustedly, helping her up.

The captain threw his cloak around her shoulders and escorted her to his tent. It was several minutes before she could speak, her throat sluiced with a goblet of wine.

"Who are you?" he asked, looking at her splendid legs.

She swallowed and cleared her throat. "I am a Roman lady of high birth. My name is Augusta Felix, captured by the barbarians and sacrificed to their Gods. How can I ever repay you for saving me?"

Looking at her half-naked body, he thought of several ways she could repay him, but politely kept them to himself.

"You see that bridge," he indicated through the tent opening. "As soon as it's finished two thousand men will cross over and these barbarians will be beast fodder in the Colosseum."

"The sooner the better," she wept, wiping away a tear.

He sat her down and ordered a dish of baked mutton and oysters. She was a fine looking woman with good legs and breasts. Washed and scrubbed she'd be an asset in any bed.

"You're not related to old General Felix of the Tenth Legion, by any chance?" he asked, looking at the painted tongue licking at her cunt.

"I'm his sister," she said haughtily knifing open an oyster.

"Then I am in august company," he joked. "Please allow me to see to your comforts."

He ordered a bath tub filled with water and gave her a cake of soap from his own locker. He left her scrubbing off the painted scrolls and the tongue lashing between her legs. He had much to do, securing the bridgehead and deploying his men against any possible attack.

The high priestess sank in the cool water, scrubbing madly at the paint and smiling happily. She didn't think for one moment her ruse would have worked against people of more superior intelligence, for only a few hours ago she had been sacrificing slaves at the stone circle, until the high priest arrived. News of Africanus' escape had become legendary. Never had a slave escaped the stone circle and now that she had, misfortune and ill were bound to befall the priests and their followers. Only the sacrifice of the high priestess would appease the Gods and she was swiftly despatched to the holy river, crucified and left to drown in the weir only a few yards down from the bridge. At some point in the future, after the superb discipline of the Roman army had decimated the Druids and neighbouring Celts, she would return and retrieve her golden horde tucked neatly away under the sacrificial stone. She reckoned there was probably enough to purchase a modest villa and a few slaves to run it.

She was still smiling and humming when the captain returned, hot, bothered and irritable. Building bridges was thirsty and exhausting work.

"Let me," she offered, climbing out of the tub and unbuckling his armour.

She was cleansed now and her skin shone with pearly opalescence, pale and unblemished. Her areolas were large, dark circles, perfectly shaped and topped with darker nipples. Her hips were shapely and legs even better. But it was her pubic bush that caught his attention. She had obviously brushed the curls and now they were thick and luxuriant, spreading in a perfect arc under the pit of her stomach and forming a huge triangle at the creases of her thighs.

"I think I should repay your kindness, captain," she grovelled, peeling off his sweat-stained shirt.

"Call me, Octavius," he informed, placing his hands on her hips.

"I shall see that my brother, the general ensures you are rewarded, perhaps he may even promote you to cohort."

"That would be nice," he said, grinning widely and steering her back into the bath.

There was room enough for both of them. She sat at one end with his calves resting on her shoulders whilst she soaped his legs. Her long, sinewy arm reached for his cock and gently stroked it, her slender hand manipulating the beating veins with slippery lathered fingers.

"It must get very lonely up here in the middle of nowhere," she said softly.

"It's even worse without a woman," he added on a note of bitterness.

In the city barracks military brothels abounded, out in the wilds it was but a frustrating dream.

"Then you must allow me to comfort you," she offered, getting up on her knees and bending over, deliberately letting her ample breasts sway tantalisingly over his chest.

She had magnificent tits, he couldn't deny that. And he reached forward, cupping them in his palms.

"I shall see that you are carried in a litter all the way to Londoninium," he said, weighing her breasts.

"With an armed guard, I hope."

"With a whole legion, if you prefer."

"I couldn't take on that many," she teased, reaching under her legs.

Her hand went around his cock and glided the soapy plum head easily into her sex. With one heave of her hips she dropped effortlessly over his middle, filling her cunt in a single gulp.

"The general is highly favoured, being blessed with such a beautiful sister," he complimented, clasping his hands behind his head.

There was little for him to do in the way of sexual exertion. She rode him with magnificent gyrations, moving her hips from side to side, leaning over so far her breasts rested against his stubbled face. He sucked on each nipple, passing from one to the other, flicking his tongue and nibbling the engorged teats.

"You like my tits?" she asked incongruously.

"You have a good pair," he congratulated. "But I think your legs are equally as beautiful. Where in Britannia do you live? I must come and visit your villa."

She hesitated; thinking. "Oh, close to Aqua Magna," she said, mentioning the only Romano-British city she could think of.

Then, just as she felt his cock go hot and hard, she was off him filling her throat and sucking madly. Her head, buried under a cascade of tumbling hair obliterated her view of his searching face. She kept up the momentum, bobbing her head faster and faster, drawing up the sap from his root until he exploded in her mouth. His spunk clung to the sides of her lips and trickled under her chin. In the silence he heard and watched it plopping on her chest and breasts.

"You come well," she said, opening her lips and letting the juice wallow over her tongue.

"I have that reputation," he agreed, getting out of the tub and throwing his cloak around him.

His head poked through the tent flaps and she heard him summon the guard.

"Am I leaving already?" she smiled. "You haven't seen what else I can do."

"Save it for my men," he retorted, as the soldiers entered the tent.

"What!" she exclaimed. "I am the sister of gen…"

A slap across her cheek silenced her.

"You are an impostor. The name, 'General Felix,' was one
. No such general exists. I thought it from the

124

moment I saw you. You have the dark brooding looks of a savage, and I have learnt a little of their ways. The sign of the serpent licking into your cunt is a sign of your incompetence and failure. I should say at a guess you were sacrificed by your own people. Lady Augusta, indeed. I doubt if you can even speak a word of the Roman tongue."

"Fuck you," she said, in perfect Latin.

He saw the joke and laughed. "Take this tramp out of my sight. Give her twenty lashes and as much cock as she can take, then run her out of camp...naked."

"Naked!" she shrieked, struggling against the strong arms hauling her through the tent. "You might at least give me some clothing."

"Try this," a soldier jeered, tossing her a dirty face flannel. "It's enough to cover your cunt."

She struggled like a wild cat, but the soldiers soon had her arms high above her head, tied to the whipping post.

"Open your legs," he commanded. "Ten lashes in your cunt. The rest on your bare arse."

The high priestess gritted her teeth and waited for the whip to lash into her sex slit. The whipper coiled the plaited leather in his hand and took steady aim, delivering the lash smack between her sex lips.

A harsh shriek echoed around the camp followed by a wild gyration of her hips and buttocks, a sight not lost on the assembled soldiery.

"Her arse does a fine dance," a legionary complimented.

"If her rump dances like that when she's being fucked, she'll make a good ride," another observed.

"It's a long time since I had a woman, and looking at that fucking meat, my cocks rampant already."

The high priestess' face turned bright scarlet with anger and shame. No one had ever dared treat her like this, now she was being flogged like a common prostitute, arms roped above her head, her body naked and on full display.

It was the face of Africanus that came into her mind when the second lash whipped under her legs, so hard her feet jumped off the ground. Her knees bumped the post and she swore bitterly, promising dark revenge on the black slave who had brought her to this.

The third lash coiled around the pit of her stomach, carving a line through her luxuriant pubic bush. She was proud of her pubic mound with its thick, bristling curls and carefully shaven shape. Now it looked as if she'd been shaven with a drunken razor. Deep lines etched through the tight curls, and her sex lips felt as if they swollen to the size of her throbbing buttocks.

Each lash had her body twisting and squirming in agony, yet she managed to hold on, not begging for mercy or passing out under the fiery pain spreading through her sex.

"She's some woman," the standard bearer complimented, looking at her whipped cunt.

Octavius couldn't deny that. He'd had quite a few itinerant prostitutes and female thieves whipped, but none had taken the punishment like this raven-haired demon.

"We'll see how she holds up to having the centuria pounding away at her cunt. I'll make a small wager she can't take all of them. Shall we say ten denarii's?"

The standard bearer had to think about that. Fucking a hundred men was no mean feat, even for a seasoned whore, but he did know of one in Rome who had taken two hundred for a bet and won hands down. The woman at the post now being soundly flogged across her buttocks had guts and, more importantly, a large sex and wide enough hips. He reckoned she probably could take on a hundred men.

"Make it fifteen denarii's," he proposed.

They shook hands and watched the woman receiving the final lash over the crown of her arse.

"Now we'll see," Octavius said, as she was laid on her back. "Have her legs shafted."

Two spears were driven into the ground either side of her knees. Swiftly, a couple of legionaries grabbed her ankles and tied them to the top of the shafts.

"A pretty sight to behold," the standard bearer admitted, admiring her long, shapely legs raised high in the air and spread so wide her cunt gaped.

"Form a line," Octavius commanded. "Front line battle soldiers first, sappers' next, weapon carriers last. Fuck her with naked cock."

"What!" she shrieked. "I'm going to have all these men without any protection."

"Serves you right for lying," he said gruffly. A wry grimace crossed his face. "If you're not belly up after this, you'll never be. You, Regarius, get busy while her cunt's clean. By the time she gets to the sappers, her cunt'll be wallowing in spunk."

He wasted no time in dropping his breeches and getting across her belly. She heaved a grunt, bucking her hips as he penetrated her. A hundred men was a lot to take and she put her hands behind her head, resigned to total submission. There was little else she could do, her ankles firmly strapped to the shafts, legs wide open and defenceless. The men stood in a queue, idly chatting awaiting their turn over her splendid mound, their cocks hard and throbbing to a man. Being stationed in this barbarous country, far away from Rome was bad enough, let alone having to build a confounded bridge in the middle of nowhere. Women were as scarce as water in a desert, the opportunity to fuck one for free was even rarer. They didn't take long to come, no more than a dozen jerks of their loins and her cunt was pumped full of foaming spunk.

Octavius retired to his tent to write up his daily reports, ignoring the grunts and curses coming from the woman, and the satisfied groans from the men as they dismounted and went off uttering ribald jokes.

It took five hours before the last weapon carrier finally

shot his load. Her belly and thighs were swimming in spunk and her pubic mound was thickly coated. Many had spattered even after they had withdrawn and her breasts and chest glistened with rivulets. The jokers amongst them had taken great delight in shooting the last drops over her face and hair and it clung like drops of dew all around her lips and chin.

"You owe me fifteen denarii's," the standard bearer announced, coming into Octavius' tent.

"You mean she's taken a hundred men?" he asked incredulously.

"Every one of them, and I'll wager the dirty bitch could probably take on another fifty."

"You speak too freely, Honorius, put your money where your mouth is. Shall we say another ten denarii's?"

"Agreed, but where will you find the extra fifty?"

Chuckling, he went out of the tent. "I want fifty volunteers for riding practice," he announced. "Those who come forward will be excused duties tomorrow."

The men looked bemused at the few horses tethered near the tents. Riding practice was unusual amongst infantry. But there was no shortage of volunteers, anything to get out heaving those heavy timbers around.

"Your mare awaits you," he laughed, pointing at the exhausted high priestess.

"That's cruel," the standard bearer remarked, looking at the sheer horror passing over her ravaged face.

"True, but these savages must learn obedience somehow."

And he went off laughing while the volunteers formed another line, jostling and shoving, hardly able to believe their luck at emptying their balls twice in one evening.

It was dark when Octavius had her released and the last man had joyfully come, pounding her so hard her belly ached.

"You've done well," he complimented honestly. "Even the whores in Rome would be hard pressed to match that record."

She stood up bow legged and clutching her sex. Her eyes

heavy and misted, hardly focused. A thick stream of spunk trickled down the insides of her thighs, and still the face of Africanus haunted her.

"You deserve a reward for giving so much pleasure to my men," he said seriously. "You shall not go naked from here."

And he tossed her an old horse blanket.

A whip across her rump sent her hobbling out of camp.

She reached the high road and kept on walking. She walked all night until she reached Aqua Magna. Instinct told her that was where the black slave would probably have headed, and it wasn't long before a few enquiries brought the information she wanted to know.

"Are you staying long?" the inn keeper asked, hoping that her offer of wild, animal sex in exchange for a bath and a bed just might be extended.

Her face clouded, tuning from pink to red, then a blackened purple.

"Only one night," she hissed. "I have unfinished business with that black slave."

# Chapter Eight

The town of Glevensium was like a miniature Rome complete with its Forum, Baths and magnificent shops and houses, as well as copious amounts of taverns and brothels. Quintus had friends there, amongst them rich merchants and money lenders who were more than willing to get him started in business. The amphitheatre was modelled on the Colosseum, but on a much smaller scale seating only a mere four thousand spectators, as opposed to the Colosseum's fifty thousand. Travelling in Quintus' carriage, Africanus related in detail everything that had befallen her, leaving nothing out. There was no need to lie to a man of his integrity.

"I shall amply reward this man, Caricitus," he said, when her delivery ended.

"Caractus," she corrected, wondering if he was still alive.

He told her his story, of how the tide had carried him and Nydia along the coast where a Roman reconnaissance had rescued them. Of Circo he knew nothing.

They arrived at his villa and were greeted by Nydia, who had noticeably changed during the interim. She was fuller in the figure and her face more mature, but still retained her artful smile. She was now mistress of the household and even had her own slaves, Celts mostly, bought in the local slave market. There was a thriving business in buying and selling slave women mostly captured by warring tribes and sold in the markets of the Roman towns and cities.

"You shall have your own slave," Quintus informed, showing her around the villa.

Again it was modelled on those of Rome, finely decorated rooms with a colonnade built around a fish pond. Her own room overlooked the Ludus he had started, and the combatants were practising and exercising in the courtyard.

"Not bad for the back of beyond," he said, standing beside

her. "Not up to Roman standards I grant you, but good enough for the provinces."

Africanus remained censorious. The gladiatrix were mostly Celtic women, strong and shapely with good legs and torsos, they were willing enough to learn but lacked the dash and speed of their Roman counterparts. More then ever she missed Fortuna with her winning smile and freckles. How could she ever forget those, sprinkled all over her chest and face, the way she expertly went into battle, fearless and laughing at death. She also remembered the torrid night they shared when they had made love with the dildo, and her cunt longed for her.

"I've heard all about her," Quintus said affectionately. "She did well at the Colosseum and now runs her own ludus."

"May the Gods protect her," Africanus said. "Now when do I get back into the arena?"

"As soon as possible. Get yourself honed up, and don't forget to make your devotions to Nemesis. And for Jupiter's sake have those rings taken out of your tits. One pull on those and you be begging for mercy."

"I'll start tomorrow," she said. "But now I need a bath."

"Granted," Quintus conceded, slapping her shoulder. "It's good to have you back, my black beauty. Back where you belong."

They kissed briefly and she made her way to the baths and was introduced to her personal slave, Magda, a young full-breasted Celt now trained in the way of her Roman masters'.

Africanus sank into the water, heated from the furnace beneath. All around were the attributes of civilisation, marble columns and wondrously executed frescos, bowls of burning incense and fruit.

"Wash me first," she ordered, letting the water swirl around her breasts. "Then we shall go to the tepidarium where you can oil me."

"Yes, mistress," she bowed, stepping naked into the bath.

Eager to please, she went enthusiastically about her tasks, scrubbing Africanus' legs with a brush and sponging away the dirt. She could not have been more than eighteen at the most, but open air and a healthy diet had blessed her with a good figure. She had been branded on her left buttock by the tribe that had taken her prisoner, and again on the back of her shoulder by her new master. Around her neck she wore a silver collar proclaiming she was the property of Quintus.

"I want to be thoroughly cleansed," Africanus told her, wishing to rid herself of anything that remotely resembled the barbarians. "That includes my bottom and cunt."

"Yes, mistress," she bowed, sponging Africanus' breasts.

"Where are you from, girl?" she asked, savouring the novel experience at having her own slave, although technically she was still Quintus' property and had not been legally granted her freedom.

From the land of the Belgae," she replied, carefully soaping her new mistress' nipples. "I was taken prisoner by a tribe of the Atrebates and then sold to the Romans."

"It seems you savages are always fighting each other and selling your women," Africanus remarked condescendingly, conveniently forgetting her own similar past.

"It's our downfall," she said sadly. "Now the Romans are our new masters"'

"And I am your new mistress," Africanus reminded her. "Do you like eating oranges, Magda?"

"I've never seen one," she replied.

Africanus pointed to a bowl at the bath's edge, and the girl fetched one.

"The proper way to eat an orange is to peel away the skin, like this and break the fruit into segments, and then eat one at a time," she explained, popping a segment into her mouth. "But the uncivilised way is tear off the skin and take out a whole mouthful. Like this,"

Magda watched intently as her new mistress spat out a

pip. "Do you know that the Romans liken an orange to the female sex?" Africanus informed.

"In my country, we say that a man's cock is like a carrot," she said, smiling innocently.

"You like carrots?"

Magda blushed, grasping where this was leading. "I've eaten some," she evaded.

"Would you like to try an orange?"

She was quicker witted than Africanus assumed. "You want me to suck your cunt?"

Africanus spat out another pip, flying it into Magda's face. She had suffered much at the hands of the Celtic savages, almost slaughtered by the mad priestess, manhandled by the ogre at the hostelry, and then humiliated in the silver mine. Now she decided to take it out on her slave.

"You learn fast for a savage," she taunted. "So start sucking."

"I've never sucked a woman's cunt," she said, paling.

"Do as you're told or I'll beat you!" her mistress snapped, without the slightest twinge of guilt. "Perhaps I should beat you anyway, just to teach you your manners. Go into the garden and fetch me a cane."

Intoxicated from her newly acquired power, Africanus had no thoughts about sparing Magda. See how the little savage felt when she was on the receiving end. Recollections of her former mistress, Octavia came into her mind, the way she had beaten her and forced her to thank her afterwards. That was the way to show who was in charge around here.

"How many lashes do you think you deserve?" Africanus asked, now out of the bath and standing gloriously naked.

She flexed her biceps and saw the girl visibly wince.

"I don't deserve anything," she sobbed. "It's not in my duties to suck your.. your..cunt."

"Your duty is to obey me, whatever I demand," Africanus retorted. "Now hand me that cane, you insolent little heathen."

133

She swished it through the air, her lips firmly set.

"I think you deserve at least a dozen. Now bring over that chair."

Magda fetched it and knelt upon the seat, hands clutching the chair back.

"Thrust out your behind," her mistress told her, admiring the pert buttocks so splendidly offered. "If you want to wet yourself, go ahead. But if you do, I'll make you clean it up afterwards, with your tongue!"

Magda braced herself, thrusting her buttocks at the terrifying black woman, who was now so close she could smell the scented water dripping off her skin.

"One, in remembrance of having to walk naked to the stone circle," she announced, winging the cane hard into Magda's bare rump.

The girl jerked her hips, rocking the chair on its back legs. A sudden rush of hot, throbbing pain shot through her bottom. She wasn't quite sure which hurt most, the slave master's brand, or the cane gathering for a second lash.

"Two, for being threatened to eat my own shit," she added, sending the cane hissing into the side of the girl's left buttock.

"Three, for being sold into that mine," she continued, lashing with full strength across both welted buttocks.

Africanus was laughing now, both at the pain suffered by the girl, and at the enjoyment of beating her own slave.

She paused to look at the livid welts growing more pronounced. Dimly, she was beginning to understand the thrill of beating bare and defenceless buttocks.

"Four, for being strung up by the ankles and flogged," she guffawed, sweeping the cane in an upward cut, landing it beautifully under the buttock and thigh crease.

"Five for…"

"That's enough," Quintus interrupted. "Why are you wasting your strength beating this miserable object when you should be saving it for the arena? Your first combat is tomorrow morning. I've matched you with one of the savages. She's good, so go and get some sleep."

"Yes, master," she bowed, brought back to reality.

Quintus cast Magda a dry glance, looking closely at her hot, twitching bottom.

"She has a fine arse, I'll grant that, but in future, I'll give the order to have her beaten. Such things are not under your jurisdiction."

"Yes, master," Africanus simpered, now put in her place.

She went off to her room, her wrath assuaged and thrilled at being back in combat. She didn't think it would take long to defeat the savage. She hoped Quintus would order a fight to the death.

Magda came to her bedside clutching her blazing bottom, head bowed in total submission.

"I'm sorry, mistress," she said plaintively. "I deserved my punishment."

"You got off lightly," Africanus muttered. "If my master had not come in, you would've got at least twenty. Now, will you do as you are told?"

"I'll do anything you want, mistress," she whispered, getting up onto the bed, ready to do what was expected of her.

"Suck me, and afterwards, oil my body, then you can sleep on the floor."

Africanus raised her knees to her chest and let her thighs fall open. Her calves rested gently over her slave's shoulders.

Like a kitten lapping its cream, Magda put out her tongue and flicked it around Africanus' sex lips.

"Deeper," Africanus muttered. "Suck my clit."

Her calves lifted from Magda's shoulders and she threw her legs wide. Her cunt opened like a yawning cavern the lips stretching into an oval, quivering even before Magda's mouth clamped against them.

"Suck," she heaved, "or I'll beat you from here to Rome."

She wouldn't have, of course, but the young Celt was too frightened to believe otherwise. Feeling her way into a new found exploration, she opened her mouth wide and pressed her lips on Africanus' sex. The taste was unlike anything she imagined, not salty or acrid, but a musky sweetness, seemingly coming from the depths of her belly. Magda, fearful of the cane which had already welted her bottom, started sucking, even managing to draw Africanus' fat, blubbery lips into her mouth.

"You're doing well," she sighed, her tongue involuntarily running over her lower lip. "Now get your face in me."

That wasn't as difficult as she imagined. There seemed no limit as to how far the black woman's cunt lips would stretch. Magda took a deep breath and it seemed that she was engulfed in darkness and the hidden mysteries of feminine sex. Her mouth and pert nose were well inside Africanus' cunt and her flicking tongue easily found the sex bud her mistress so craved to be sucked. It was soft, yet unyielding; about the size of a kidney bean and at the merest touch Africanus went wild.

"Suck it hard, you little shit," she said crudely. "Make me come all over your stupid face."

If Magda had known anything about a woman in orgasm, she would've known that threats, foul language and frantic screams were all part of the psyche. Some women lash out with their fists, others kick like mares, and some can leave a bedroom totally wrecked. Others need at least half a dozen men in quick succession before they're completely satisfied. But Africanus just poured out a torrent of verbal abuse, not lost on her young slave whose tongue licked so fast it tingled.

"Fuck me with your tongue, you heap of crawling vermin," she spat, grabbing the girl's head and forcing it so hard into her groin she thought she would suffocate.

A thick creamy juice began oozing from Africanus' sex lips and over Magda's tongue. She took a deep breath and swallowed, surprised at what she tasted. The juice was a curious combination of musk and almond, not as poisonous as she anticipated.

"Swallow, you little piglet," Africanus urged, raking her nails all the way across Magda's scalp and shoulders.

Magda didn't need to be told that, her mistress' juices were flooding into her mouth and there was nothing else she could do but let it flow down her throat. Then suddenly Africanus' hips and belly broke into wild gyrations, performing beautiful, undulating motions as she rose rapidly towards her climax. Magda sensed she was coming and sucked the throbbing bud between her sharp, pearly teeth. When Africanus started slapping her head Magda bit on the bud, hard enough to bring forth a deafening scream. The pain going through Africanus' sex was exquisite, myriads of tiny tremors tingled all through her sex tunnel, making the petals and walls tremor in return.

"I'm coming!" she wailed, thumping Magda's back.

Magda felt as if she were slowly dying. Her throat was thick with Africanus' love juice, her mouth was dry and her body ached from so much beating. Now the blood was rushing through her veins, the welts on her whipped bottom began throbbing. But she kept her head in place, doing exactly what her mistress wanted, until the screaming and thrashing suddenly ceased as ferociously as it had risen.

"Phew!" You know how to suck a woman's cunt, you little liar. You said you'd never done this before."

Magda came out of Africanus groin, her face flushed and covered in sex cream.

"I've never sucked a woman before in my whole life," she replied truthfully.

"But you have sucked men's carrots."

The girl blushed red. "Not men's, boys," she admitted.

"Did they come in your mouth? Tell me the truth. I shall know if you're lying."

She flushed bright scarlet. "I never let them do that. They just used to shoot over my tits."

"Well, you've got a good pair," Africanus admitted, beginning to like her young slave.

From now on she would only have her beaten if she were disobedient or rude.

"You can forgo oiling me," she said calmly. "Now go to sleep, it's late."


"This is not going to be a fight to the death," Quintus warned. "It's costing me a fortune to train these barbarians. I admit, they fight well, but their methods are different from ours. With us, it's speed, agility and above all, obedience. With the barbarians, it's all hack and stab, just wade in slashing in all directions. But don't underestimate them, they're not lacking in courage, and they don't fear death."

"Neither do I," Africanus retorted, buckling on her armour. "I'll teach these savages a thing or two."

Quintus permitted himself a smile. He could never quite work out what it was about her that always brought on an erection. It seemed that she was now part of his life in a way that no other woman had ever been. Perhaps, because they had been through so much together and he knew that she would willingly lay down her life for him.

"Remember everything you've been taught," he said solemnly, "and make your devotions before you enter the arena."

Africanus summoned Magda who looked at her mistress in awe. She had finished dressing and looked splendid in her gleaming breastplate, perfectly moulded to fit over her enormous breasts, and even sporting huge bronze nipples. It was held in place with leather thongs tied behind her bare back. From her waist trailed broad leather bands weighted at the end with heavy bronze discs, long enough to cover her buttocks, but only just. A leather thong covered her sex, the

138

thin straps going around the swell of her hips and disappearing through her bottom crease. As usual her forearms and calves were protected with thick winding straps and the helmet she had chosen was open-faced, broad-brimmed and high-crested. Her weapon was the gladius, the short sword she always favoured. Magda tied her long braids behind her head and wound them into a knot.

"Good luck, mistress," she beamed lovingly.

"Luck doesn't come into it," her mistress replied. "It's good training and speed that counts, but I thank you anyway."

She made for the alcove wherein stood a statue of Nemesis, Goddess of Fortune, Chance and Revenge.

"Bring me victory," she whispered, placing her fingers on her lips, then at the feet of the Goddess. She turned to go, but then turned again. "May Fortuna watch over me."

Then she went to the Arena gate and waited her turn. The arena was circular, with plain high walls, and at one side, decorated columns supported a covering roof where the local dignitaries were seated. Quintus' rival, Vitellius was already fielding his own gladiatrix, four lightly-armoured women against a host of naked slaves, armed only with short wooden swords, useless against the fearsome horse whips the gladiatrix wielded. But Vitellius was no fool, he knew what the crowd really wanted and had carefully provided it. The naked slaves ran screaming around the arena, their breasts and buttocks tasting the whips at every step. Whenever one of them stumbled and fell she was immediately dragged to a plinth and offered as a present to anyone bold enough to enter the arena and take her. But Quintus also knew what he was doing, apart from naked flesh, the crowd wanted real combat and the most discerning of the audience would be willing to provide the extra cash he needed to stage more fights.

Africanus watched through a grill as one of the gladiatrices picked up a slim, dark-haired Celt and hurled her over her shoulder. She hit the sand with a painful crunch and lay on her back, legs spread and covering her sex with her hands. The gladiatrix lost no time in lashing her belly, breasts and thighs. Her slim legs thrashed in all directions as she rolled over and over, sand clinging to her whipped, sweat-soaked body. The gladiatrix grabbed one ankle and dragged the screaming girl all the way around the perimeter, finally dumping her exhausted body on the plinth. Quintus was right; there was nothing professional in their combat. It was just a brawl between naked women.

Disgusted, she turned away and summoned Magda who was herself almost naked apart from a loin cloth.

"Combat always makes me aroused," she said softly. "After I've finished with my opponent, I shall probably have you."

"I'm here to do your bidding, mistress," she replied, thrilled at the thought of her tall, muscular mistress having sex with her.

Then a trumpet blasted and the audience fell silent. The last of the slaves had been whipped into submission and now the real combat would begin.

"The consul of Britannia is pleased to introduce the most feared gladiatrix from the stable of Quintus," the master of ceremonies announced. "People of Glevensium I give you, Africanus!"

The assembly rose in wild adoration as she walked slowly into the arena, the sun flashing from her breastplate. She raised her sword in salutation and awaited the next announcement and the first view of her combatant.

"Fighting against her is the bravest of all the Celtic warriors. I give you, Gudrun."

She walked casually from the opposite gate, and bowed at the dignitaries; a tall, raven-haired Celtic beauty, whose good looks did nothing to disguise the grim determination on her face. She too had reason for vengeance and it showed in her glowing eyes. She was wearing only a loose-fitting tunic that fluttered around her buttocks. Her legs and arms were bare and her breasts held in place with a single strip of cloth knotted at her back. Her only piece of armour was a peculiar looking shoulder guard strapped to her left upper arm, the armour of the Retarius. The guard came over the top of her shoulder and was high enough to duck behind, her only protection against Africanus' sword. Her long hair was held by a wide bronze headband and tied up behind in a huge bun. She had been branded by her Roman masters and Africanus could see the brand burned into her shoulder, but it was her weapons that made Africanus wary. The net and trident were deadly in capable hands. And she looked very capable indeed.

The umpire stepped up and placed his wand between them. For several seconds they stood staring into each others eyes. The audience had fallen silent, waiting for the first blows to be struck.

"I wouldn't like to bet on the outcome of this," a man remarked turning to his friend. "They're both well matched."

Behind them, a woman half hidden under a blue cloak watched intently as the umpire withdrew his wand.

"My money's on the black woman," the friend said, standing on tip toe.

"So it might be, but the Celt has been well trained. I've seen her in the ludus and believe me, she's fast."

The woman edged forward eavesdropping, carefully noting everything that was being said.

Then the combatants stepped backwards ready to strike the first blows.

During her training, Gudrun had plenty of opportunity to battle with the gladius and kept wisely out of range, gathering her net and balancing the trident under her left arm. Once Africanus was ensnared she would quickly transfer it from one hand to the other and make the killing blow. She too had been warned that this was not a fight to the death, but it wouldn't be difficult faking an accident and leaving her opponent mortally wounded. And it would enhance her own reputation, killing the best Quintus could field.

Africanus kept up her guard, protecting her body with the shield and bending her knees and back, ready to strike. The men in the audience had a superb view of her near naked buttocks thrust out behind, and her splendidly shaped thighs, long and solid but beautiful enough to bring on a thousand erections. Already the men were shuffling uncomfortably on their benches willing their hardened cocks deep in her sweating cunt. Others were concentrating on Gudrun's breasts which, although tied with the strip of cloth, were wobbling deliciously and her nipples were hard and erect. The tunic floating around her bottom was lifted by a breeze and a murmur of approval hummed from the audience as her buttocks were suddenly revealed.

But there was no time to dwell on that because both combatants were now within striking range. The glinting tips of the deadly trident bounced off Africanus' shield as she deftly deflected the blow. She moved in and executed an upward sweep of her sword, but Gudrun knocked it aside and swept her net around Africanus' calves. For a moment it looked as if she were ensnared but a backward leap set her free. Then Africanus moved swiftly, hopping over the net and crashing her gladius into the shoulder guard. Gudrun instantly ducking behind it aimed a blow with the trident narrowly missing her opponent's face. Africanus wished now that she'd worn a full face helmet which would have protected her eyes. She was also beginning to realize that the Celt's intentions were a lot more deadly than just battling her. She too could easily fake an accident by driving her gladius through Gudrun's belly. The shield would cover the killing stroke from prying eyes.

But for the moment, both combatants concentrated on displaying their gladiatorial skills, and both trident and sword thrust and parried with Africanus managing to affect a side swipe at Gudrun's waist. The blade sliced effortlessly through her tunic and it fell in half hanging around her thighs. Another swipe instantly cut through the strip holding her breasts and they fell forward, wobbling from side to side as she leapt out of range. Africanus gave her time to tear away the ripped tunic impeding her stride. Naked now, except for the lower half of her tunic, Gudrun advanced in stages, sweeping the net in broad arcs and keeping her opponent out of range with the trident. Then she did it; Africanus' feet caught in the net and she stumbled over, winding the net around her thighs.

A roar of approval arose from the audience as the black woman lay on the sand desperately struggling to free herself. The woman with the blue cloak urged Gudrun on to finish her, but her encouragements were lost in the rising swell. Africanus lashed out with her gladius, severing the net and keeping the shield well over her head. She heard the trident bounce off it and rolled over and was up on her knees. Gudrun moved in fast, stabbing at Africanus' face with the trident points, but never managing to get close enough. The black gladiatrix deflected every blow and was now up on her feet. The net was hopelessly ripped and useless and Gudrun had only her trident.

"Oh, shit," the cloaked woman swore, but the men in front didn't hear. They were too busy watching the near naked Gudrun's swinging breasts as she leapt back and forth away from the slashing gladius.

Above the sound of clashing metal came the harsh grunts of the gladiatrices as they became more desperate to make the killing blow. With eyes blazing and lips curling in anger, they moved faster, becoming more deadly by the second. Sweat ran from their glistening limbs and backs for now the sun was directly overhead. Quintus could hardly believe what was happening. Soon, one of his best trained fighters would be dead and all that money and effort wasted. But it had

143

gone too far to stop the fight. The audience were on their feet and cheering madly, punching the air with their fists, urging the women on. Gudrun's bare legs and breasts were magnificent to behold, not to mention her buttocks thrusting tantalizingly behind, then she suddenly straightened pointing her throbbing nipples at the cheering men.

Africanus raised her shield in defence but Gudrun was quick and delivered a glancing blow on the side of her helmet. Her head abruptly turned and she lost her balance toppling onto the sand. Gudrun moved in with her trident, aiming the points into the black woman's eyes, but she rolled over and swept her gladius across the backs of Gudrun's knees. With a wild shriek she buckled and fell, and then Africanus was swiftly behind her, grabbing her hair and cutting through the string that held the bun. Gudrun let out a blood curdling scream as Africanus dragged her across the arena almost ripping the hair from her scalp. But Gudrun reached out and grabbed Africanus' ankle and she too fell alongside her. In a moment both women were rolling over and over in a confused welter of bare arms and legs. Africanus swiftly abandoned her shield but kept her sword, managing to jab the point hard into Gudrun's left buttock. Using her free hand, Africanus punched her hard on the breast squashing it flat. The men loved it, watching them kicking and punching, making frantic snatches at each other's hair. Once, Gudrun got to her feet and kicked Africanus hard in the ribs and a lot harder on her bottom. But Africanus got the better of her and knocked her down with the hilt of her sword. Temporarily winded, there was nothing she could do to prevent the black woman from getting between her legs. It was one of Africanus' favourite moves, positioning her body between the open legs of her opponent, placing her hands on one ankle and her feet on the other. No need of the gladius now that she used all her strength to force open Gudrun's legs. They spread so wide it was possible to see the pink of her sex winking at the audience.

"A woman looks her best when her legs are spread," someone joked, hearing a shriek of pain echoing around the arena.

Africanus pushed so hard that Gudrun's long legs were almost at right angles to her hips. Her back bent into an arc and she unwittingly thrust her breasts upwards, the throbbing teats pointing skyward. Africanus' gleaming calves and thighs looked equally magnificent as they went dead straight, straining at Gudrun's ankle. Behind her, she reached out with her arms at the other ankle and heard Gudrun's hips crick as she applied full pressure.

Gudrun raised her right arm signalling defeat. Amid a roar of approval, Africanus relaxed her tormenting arms and legs. Gudrun's legs flew back in place but not before Africanus delivered her final blow. She seized a handful of sand and rubbed it so hard into Gudrun's sex the lips turned red raw. Then she got up and gave her a final kick on her bottom.

The woman in the blue cloak turned red with anger and disappointment, but the men were on their feet chanting her name. Africanus picked up her sword and waved it over her head then did a victory march around the arena, snaking her hips and giving the men a magnificent view of her naked buttocks, made all the more enticing from the sand clinging to the hollows and into her deep crease. Her body was pouring sweat when she passed through the gate of victory and into her private room where Quintus had already arrived.

"You did well," he congratulated, looking admiringly at the now naked gladiatrix stretching out on her bed. "But you both disobeyed me. I told you it was not a fight to the death and you both came close to killing each other. I ought to have you flogged for such arrant disobedience."

"But you won't," she said, smiling a seductive smile.

"Women!" he muttered, still smiling. "I was going to tell you about your next contest, but I'll leave it for later. You need rest. Shall I summon your slave?"

145

Africanus nodded and wiped the sweat from her eyes, turning her head as Magda came into the room.

"Shall I wash you, mistress?" she asked, smelling the heat rising from Africanus burning skin.

"No," Africanus breathed softly. "I want to get started straight away. Now go and open that drawer."

Magda looked at an enormous dildo and swallowed. It seemed very long, larger than anything else she had ever seen, and looked even larger in her tiny hand and frighteningly real. It was made of polished oak and had thin leather straps coming from its base. She carried it gingerly, as if it were a dangerous serpent that might, at any moment turn and bite her.

"You know what that is?" Africanus asked, amused at the shocked look on Magda's face.

"It's a man's thing," she whispered, placing it neatly on the pillow, glad to have it out of her hand.

"I know that, you foolish girl, I meant, what is it for?"

At the gathering of the tribes at Druidical ceremonies she had seen huge stone phalluses where the priests worshipped and men laid gifts at its base so it was logical to assume it served the same purpose.

"Not quite," her mistress replied. "This is used for sex between one woman and another."

Magda went instantly pale and took a step backwards. It would be some woman who could have a thing like that inside her.

"Now, I told you that combat makes me feel hot and horny, so you now understand what I want you to do."

"I think I have to put it inside you," she suggested timidly.

"That is the idea, yes," her mistress said, suddenly realising that the benefits of Roman civilisation had not yet fully bestowed themselves on the native population.

"You have to wear it, and then push it inside me," she explained.

146

That explained the straps, but she still couldn't see how it could be done. It just wasn't natural; a woman wearing a thing like that.

She stood still whilst her mistress went silently to work, placing the base of the dildo carefully over her pubic mound and then passing a thicker strap under her legs, going behind her and pulling it tight through her sex slit and bottom crease. The other thinner straps went swiftly around her boyish hips and were buckled into place.

"You have firm buttocks," Africanus complimented, patting each one in turn.

"Thank you, mistress," she swallowed, looking sideways at herself in a looking glass.

It reared up from her belly and trembled, nodding invitingly at her mistress who in turn admired her.

"Hold it," she said, sliding her arm around her slim waist. "Stroke it and imagine it's been there all your life."

Magda's tiny hand closed around the wooden shaft. Now it seemed even bigger and longer. Both of her hands wouldn't've have covered its whole length.

"Is this what women do in Rome?" she asked, turning face on into the mirror.

She seemed less frightened and now a look of curious fascination crossed her face, not unlike a child discovering for the first time how to open a sack of fruit and steal one without being caught. Her hand went up and down the shaft and the look of fascination changed to one of pride as if she had now discovered a power she never knew existed. Dimly, she began to understand the power that men had over women, and a little more perceptibly, why women longed for a rock hard cock pounding away inside their willing cunts.

While she stood admiring her reflection, Africanus had laid herself on the bed, her legs open and bent at the knees.

"Come over and penetrate me," she whispered. "Fill my cunt with your cock."

147

"Please mistress, I don't think I can," she simpered, suddenly intimidated at the thought of being so intimately close with another of her own kind.

In another situation, Africanus might have exploded with rage, but she merely held out her arms and smiled a devastatingly inviting smile.

Almost in a trance, Magda approached her mistress, getting slowly between her long, silky thighs, smelling the heat rising from the quivering skin.

"What do I do?" she whispered, resting on her bottom and keeping one hand on her cock.

"Lie over me and put the plum head in my sex," Africanus instructed patiently, placing her hands on the girl's hips.

Although Magda was full breasted, she still retained the figure of a young girl; her waist was not much thicker than her mistress' thighs, and her shoulders so slim they hardly seemed capable of supporting the full sized breasts thrusting from her chest. But there was nothing girlish about the tightly puckered nipples spouting from the dark surrounding discs.

"Ever let the boys suck on these?" Africanus asked, rolling the teats between forefingers and thumbs.

Magda inhaled deeply, her face flushing as she whispered in the negative.

"Never, mistress."

"But you tossed them off and let them come over your tits."

She blushed scarlet. "Yes, mistress," she reluctantly admitted.

"But you've never had one inside you?"

Magda sadly shook her head as if being accused of some terrible crime.

Africanus clicked her tongue, yet her desperate longing for a hard cock had not abated. A peculiar feeling stirred in her belly that she had suddenly become more than just a mistress to her slave, but a seducer of the girl's innocence.

"Would you like to change places?" she whispered softly, raising her smouldering eyes to Magda's face.

It took a couple of moments for that to sink in. She blinked and Africanus saw in her eyes that expression that all young women have on the threshold of womanhood, a mixture of confusion, fear, yet longing to be relieved of the burden of their virginity.

"I'll be gentle," her mistress assured.

"Promise?"

"I promise. And afterwards you shall call yourself a real woman."

It would be a real woman who could take that at her first attempt at sex, but she didn't say so. The girl had to have it at some point in her life, so why not now?

Africanus released the dildo straps and deftly tied them around her hips. Magda lay on the bed, her legs wide open and eyes tightly closed as awaiting terrible execution. Africanus lightly kissed her eyelids and her eyes opened.

"You'll never have it if you're so tense," she advised. "Now relax and just let things take their natural course."

"Yes, mistress," she faltered, daring to put her arms around Africanus' shoulders.

"The first thing I have to do is get you all nice and wet," she said, placing the palm of her hand over Magda's sex mound.

There was not the slightest guilt in robbing her slave of her virginity. Her belly and loins thrilled at penetrating her with an outsize organ that would either put her off sex for life, or have her screaming for more. An artful smile creased her lips as she bent her head, avoiding Magda's fixing gaze. She began slowly, rubbing her palm round and round the sex lips, then inserting her forefinger just inside the sweating tunnel. She heard Magda catch her breath and when the girl's sex was wet, inserted another finger, crossing them at the tips and shoving them deeper inside her.

"Oh," Magda breathed, jerking her hips, then she took in a whole lung full of air as Africanus found her clit.

"Nice?" Africanus grinned, teasing the bud with her rapidly wiggling fingers.

"I can't breathe," she gulped, rolling her eyes.

Her nipples were erect and a tingling had started in her belly. Her sex juice began to flow over Africanus' fingers and she slipped them from the quivering lips.

"Mustn't make you come too soon," she said, guiding the head of the dildo between her lips.

She gave a gentle shove of her hips and Magda arched her back in readiness. She threw her legs as wide as she could and reached behind her, grabbing the bed rails. Inside her sex tunnel the muscles suddenly tensed, closing around the cock and holding it still.

"I said, relax," Africanus rasped, leaning over and taking her head in her hands.

Then she kissed her full on the lips, forcing her tongue into her shocked slave's gasping mouth. The weight of Africanus' body bore down on Magda's chest squashing their breasts and forcing the nipples flat. Then, as if struck by lightning, Magda was galvanised into action. Her heels dug hard into the bed posts and her bottom rose from the mattress, bending her spine into a splendid arc. Africanus' hips jerked forward and the dildo slammed into Magda's cunt.

"Aaoow," she grunted, going wide-eyed.

Africanus groaned from the pain of Magda's nails now raking her back. She gave another shove of her hips and felt her slave's sex open under the sheer force of the cock now gliding inexorably deeper.

Quickly, she sucked on Magda's puckered nipples, exciting the buds with her flicking tongue, covering each breast in turn with her hand and squeezing the globes with her fingertips. She risked another thrust and Magda sobbed as she felt her sex fully penetrated. It had all happened so quickly, one minute Africanus fingers were teasing her clit to distraction, and in the next she had the full length of the dildo hard inside her.

"You've taken it all," Africanus complimented, expecting all manner of shrieks and screams.

Magda's bottom hit the mattress and she let out a long sigh. Her eyes rolled and her lips broke into a loving smile, as if to say, 'there, I knew I could do it.'

Africanus rocked gently over her, lifting her weight on her elbows so that her breasts swung ponderously over Magda's chest, the nipples colliding, but only just. Then, taking all her weight on one arm, she slipped her fingers of her free hand in Magda's mouth. Like a child, her slave sucked joyfully on the long, slender fingers, pursing her lips and sucking right to the knuckles.

"You're so beautiful," Africanus whispered, genuinely aroused by her young slave's loving ministrations.

Magda lifted her slim legs and let them fall over Africanus' rump, digging her heels into the soft cushions of her buttocks. Her hands rested lightly on her mistress' shoulders and she rocked in unison, squeezing her sex tightly around the cock and smiling from the sheer ecstasy of its size and length.

But Africanus' own orgasm was stirring in her belly and she rocked faster, whipping her fingers from Magda's mouth and supporting her weight on the palms of her hands. Inside her sex, Magda felt the cock grinding harder and deeper. Tremors of pain quivered her sex lips and soon a sharper pain stabbed her belly like a red hot needle. Instinctively, she knew her mistress was rising to her orgasm and would now ride her hard with all the pent up fury unabated from her recent combat. She unlocked her heels and opened her legs wide, toes pointing at the ceiling, bracing herself for her first volcanic fuck.

"I'm going to ride you hard," Africanus hissed, "I'll make your first fuck one that you'll never forget."

Stuffed full of that thing, Magda didn't think she'd ever forget it, or the sobering fact that she was losing her virginity not to some bold, bearded warrior, but to a woman whose powerful arms now gripped her shoulders.

Africanus withdrew the dildo until the plum hovered at the portals of Magda' sex. She paused, gathering her strength, then plunged back inside her.

"It's so fucking huge!" Magda swore, feeling that her heart had suddenly stopped.

"It's going to feel a lot bigger after I've finished with you," her mistress promised.

But there was nothing vindictive in her tone. From now on Magda would not only be her slave but her own personal property, her lover and confidante. She didn't know how valuable she was going to prove in the coming weeks.

She rode her hard, letting the dildo go in and out of her now deflowered sex with long, deliberate thrusts, and at other times just letting it rest inside her while she jerked her hips, tickling and teasing the vaginal petals with its polished plum head. Magda quickly rose to the occasion, at times lying still with her slim legs wide, reaching forward and grabbing her ankles, holding them while her mistress' magnificent buttocks pounded at her hot, wet tunnel, then she would lie still, just savouring the delicious feeling of having the monstrous weapon thrusting inside her. They took turns to suck and play with each others nipples and breasts, arousing the teats and taking them in their mouths, using their tongues and teeth to stimulate the excited buds, then cupping and squeezing the soft globes, rolling them round and round until they both laughed and kissed until their jaws ached.

Magda came in a flood, suddenly throwing her legs over Africanus' back and clinging like a limpet to the black sweating limbs. Her breath came in a rush of pants and gasps terminating in a long piercing howl. Her whole body went into spasms, jerking and shaking from head to toe until she lay exhausted and wasted, her arm lying across her forehead in that dreamy, timeless aftermath of sex.

"Now you are a real woman," Africanus whispered, lying over her and planting kisses over her forehead.

"But what's it like having a man's naked meat in you?" she mused, brushing falling braids from Africanus' face.

"Getting a taste for it now, are you?" she said with mock severity.

"No, I mean, is it as hard as that wooden cock?"

Africanus laughed and playfully pinched Magda's earlobe. "Well sort of, depends on the man, but of course, it doesn't stay so hard for nearly so long. It goes all soft and wilts inside you, although I admit, the feeling is good having a man's spunk gushing inside your cunt."

"I suppose I ought to try it," she said absently, running her fingertips over her mistress' nipples.

"Not without my permission," Africanus warned. "Don't forget you are my slave."

Magda looked up, her face radiant. "I'm more than that, mistress. Now can we have another go?"

# CHAPTER NINE

"You savages aren't allowed in here," the guard warned, drawing his sword against the hooded woman approaching the Temple of Nemesis.

It had been newly completed and shone resplendent with its painted columns and magnificent statue of the Goddess.

The hooded woman opened her cloak and the guard nearly dropped his sword.

"What if I let you fuck me?" she suggested.

With a body like hers he couldn't refuse. She let the cloak fall back giving him only the briefest glimpse of her splendid body. From what he had seen, he guessed she was probably in her late thirties or early forties, and very pale skinned for a Celtic savage with long, creamy thighs, more than generous breasts and shapely hips.

She looked down at his bulging tunic and slipped a long, sinewy arm under his legs. He gulped as any man would do when her hand closed softly over his balls.

It was late and the temple was deserted at that hour, apart from a solitary priestess refilling the incense bowls and trimming the lamps.

The guard led her into the changing rooms where the priestesses and Gladiatrix' disrobed and put on ceremonial robes prior to entering the temple proper.

"This'll do," he grunted, pulling off his tunic. A button broke free and rolled under a shelf.

"Shit," he muttered. "How am I going to explain that?"

The high priestess wasn't in the slightest bit concerned how he was going to explain anything. She had much more important business in the temple than letting this dimwit fret over a lost button. She discarded her cloak and stood naked in the shadows, watching with growing impatience while the guard tossed aside his breeches.

"I've got to get it in," he said, trembling at the sight of her.

I wish you fucking would, she thought, hoping that the solitary priestess wouldn't come in and catch them.

Without warning he pushed her against the wall and grabbed her left thigh, lifting it to his waist. He was in her at once, juddering hard into her sex and bouncing her bottom cheeks against the stonework. She threw her arms around his shoulders and clung like a limpet, balancing on one leg while he pumped his loins.

Over his shoulder she saw rows of robes hanging on pegs, made from the finest linen, white and trimmed with blue lines at the hem and sleeves.

"You're a great fuck," he complimented, breaking in on her thoughts.

Then he grabbed her breasts, squashing them so hard her eyes tingled. She was up on her toes now, desperately clinging while his organ almost lifted her off the floor. But that didn't stop him from bending his thick neck and biting her nipples. It wasn't very often in his line of work, spending long, lonely hours guarding an empty temple that a stunning woman like this offered sex in exchange for a peek inside the place. But then, these savages were unused to such things, living in huts made from sticks.

"I'm coming," he grunted.

"Me too," she lied, panting like a race horse.

He slammed her against the wall, almost knocking her unconscious. His loins gave a mighty heave and he erupted inside her.

The high priestess looked at the doorway and was sure she heard footsteps, but it was only an echo.

"Will you let me go now, please," she asked politely.

Without thinking, he made a grab for her cloak and wiped the remaining drops from his wilting cock. When he'd finished he kissed her full on the lips.

"You can only stay a few minutes," he warned, taking his

155

tongue from her mouth. "Anyone caught here would be crucified."

He wasn't bluffing. Trespassing inside the sanctum warranted instant execution.

"I only want a quick look," she assured throwing on her cloak, making sure the damp patch was well away from her bare skin.

He went outside and took his place at the entrance while she crept softly into the temple.

It was vast, larger than anything she had seen. The contrast between her temple of crude stones and primitive ceremonies was unsettling. She gazed in awe at the black marble walls, its soaring dome and tiled floor, but mostly at the statue of Nemesis, which was many times taller than her, cast in bronze and red marble and in her right hand a sword, and her left rising in victory. Round the plinth were bowls of burning incense and the remains of devotional offerings: bags of coins, amulets and bracelets, locks of hair and strings of beads. This was the inner sanctum where the gladiatrix would come and pray for victory.

She tiptoed round the sanctum like a thief, keeping a eye on the solitary priestess who was lighting lamps. The flames cast eerie shadows against the statue that now appeared more terrifying, and for one heart-stopping moment it seemed as if the eyes were watching her.

"Get a grip on yourself," she muttered. "It's only a statue."

And she made her way through a small door, exploring every nook and cranny of the place. She went into more changing rooms, a store room where the incense and lamps were kept, a wine cellar with racks of bottles, and finally a chamber full of whips and canes. This she guessed rightly was where the supplicants bared their flesh to the whip, kneeling on the polished floor in prayer while the priestesses flogged their naked backs.

She crept back into the sanctum and saw the priestess

bowing before the statue, lost in her own thoughts. She watched her for as long as she dared, taking careful note of everything she did, the way she chanted her prayers, stood up holding out her arms embracing the presence of the Goddess, lighting incense sticks and waving them back and forth; the way her face had been made up with white chalk and the eyebrows blackened. After she had committed it all to memory, she left, going back into the room where she had fucked the guard and lifted one of the robes from its peg. It was about her size and would fit her well.

She left then, rolling the robe into a tight ball and secreting it under her voluminous cloak. The guard was still there talking to a prostitute, fondling her tits while she groped his balls. He didn't notice the hooded figure making swiftly along the street to the cheap lodging house, her bare feet passing noiselessly over the pavement. She lay on her bed waiting patiently for the dawn, and then as soon as the shops were open, made her way to the herbalist to collect the ingredients she needed. Then she went back to her lodgings and mixed them, too much would result in instant death, too little would have no effect at all. The mixture had to be just right for what she intended. The sun was forcing its rays through her window and she stood naked in front of a cracked looking glass admiring her figure. Not bad for a middle-aged woman. She turned in profile patting her bottom, still pert and round, the cheeks going tightly into their crease. She cupped her breasts and lifted them, pleased with their shape. Her thumbs flicked her nipples and they raised instantly, large, succulent buds rising from splendid dark discs. She turned full frontal and brushed her pubic mound. The hair was still thick and curly. Then she studied her legs looking at her long creamy thighs and undulating calves. No excess fat there either. And she slapped her flanks wondering how much high class tarts charged rich Romans for their services. She thought five or six denarii would be about right. And she made her way to the brothel quarter, selecting the house she thought would pay the highest dividend and went in.

"You can rent by the day or the hour," the brothel keeper told her. "I charge extra for the wash room and if you get the shit beaten out of you, don't complain to me. That's a risk you tarts have to take in your line of work. Ten sestertii. Take it or leave it."

She handed over a week's rent and went upstairs to view the room. It was comfortable enough and surprisingly clean, adequately furnished and overlooking the main thoroughfare where business would be brisk. She reckoned she could easily handle up to twenty men a day, if she got lucky. She locked the room and went off to the nearest eating house. So far everything was going according to plan. She was going to enjoy having that black bitch well and truly punished. But in the meantime she had to make some money and that evening took her place in the brothel where the other whores were already gathered. Catering for upper class Romans, the place was strictly controlled and the clients were introduced to the whores in a waiting room where they made their choice.

They came from all parts of the empire: Gauls, Celts, dark-skinned women from Lusitania, blonde women from Germania and even a few from Rome itself.

"This is Lucia," the brothel keeper introduced, indicating a plump girl from Mauritania. "She's a big girl but gives a comfortable ride. You can stay on her all night, if you're up to it." The client nodded and moved to the next. "This is Amenia from Hispania, foul mouthed and very dirty. She likes it rough and enjoys a good beating." He moved to a slim girl with hair reaching to her buttocks. "This is Maria from Dacia; she's slim but will bounce well over your rod. She takes it up her arse."

"The one on the end. Who is she?" the client asked, indicating the high priestess.

"A new woman in the stable," he informed, moving along

the line. "A Celt called Drusa. She's on the old side, but has fine legs and large tits and a cunt to match. If you have a friend willing to share, she'll happily take both at once."

"Stand up, woman," the client ordered, and the high priestess got to her feet wearing only a transparent dress that did nothing to hide the magnificent body beneath.

"So you can take two men at once?" he asked, intrigued at the idea, and running his eyes over her bottom.

"Your request is my pleasure," she said, wondering if she should double the price if he intended to share her.

"My request is that you get your arse up to your room," he said darkly, handing over a coin to the keeper.

"How do you manage to have two men at once?" he said, settling on her bed.

She stood at the window letting the sun illuminate her body. She had fine proportions; he had to give her that.

"I mount the first sitting astride, and when I lie over him, the second takes my bottom," she smiled professionally, turning to face him.

He was rich; she could tell that at a glance, well manicured nails, and expensive clothes and well fed.

"I meant in your cunt," he said abruptly.

The high priestess turned pale. "I've never done that," she admitted truthfully.

"But you could have two men in your mouth. It's big enough."

"Two men in my mouth," she said aghast, thinking that she could ask at least three times the going rate for the privilege of having her jaw split.

"I'll offer fifteen denarii, if you're willing."

"Done," she said, without thinking, wondering where the second client was hiding.

"You will attend my villa along with those other whores and provide the usual entertainment. The rest will come later in my private apartments. Now get downstairs. Tell no one of what has been discussed here and I shall send word to the keeper when your presence is required, and see that your cunt is well scrubbed before you arrive."

She bowed and joined the whores in the waiting room.

"You weren't long," the plump girl observed.

"I just tossed him off," she excused casually, watching as more clients entered the room making their choice.

She was chosen by a young man who liked older women and could not wait to rip off her clothes. But her mind was elsewhere while she rode him. Offering her services at the villa of a well to do Roman might have additional benefits, if she wasn't too greedy and she bounced her bottom faster over the young man busy fondling her breasts. She also had to keep an eye on that temple when the gladiatrices attended the Goddess prior to combat.

"Now I want your arse," the young man said, rolling her off him.

And she bent over the bed, gritting her teeth while he shoved his cock crudely into her bottom.


"Your next contest is to be held at a banquet," Quintus informed Africanus. "At the villa of Lucius Proximus, an old friend of mine. I've no idea whom you're matched against, but it won't be Gudrun. She's too undisciplined for such an occasion, so I've left it to him to come up with an opponent. Make your devotions at the new temple where the priestesses will call upon the Goddess to favour you."

"I would like Magda to attend me at the temple," she said. "If the priestesses will allow it."

"That is for them to decide. But as long as she keeps out of sight I can't see as her presence would give rise for concern. After all she's only a child."

But growing up fast, Africanus thought, her lips creasing into a smile.

The high priestess, now known by her assumed name of Drusa, kept up her vigil, watching from the shadows, keeping an eye on who came and went in and out of the temple and was well rewarded when Africanus and her young slave approached the precinct. Drusa slipped off her blue woollen cloak and as quickly slipped into the robe she'd lifted from the changing room. It wasn't difficult getting into the temple dressed as a priestess of Nemesis, wearing the white robe decorated with blue lines. Her face had been already made up in preparation for such a moment and she would be impossible to recognize under a thick layer of white chalk and her eyebrows thickened with soot.

Africanus was not the only gladiatrix calling upon the Goddess. Those about to enter the arena as well as those summoned to private functions had gathered there, forming a semi circle in front of the statue, awaiting the appearance of the priestesses. Her young slave was nowhere to be seen and had mysteriously vanished as soon as she had entered the temple.

"Nemesis, Goddess of Fortune and Revenge, hear us in our hour of need," a priestess chanted, lifting her arms in supplication to the statue.

Drusa remembered everything she had seen and followed the ceremony with amazing precision, raising her arms at the right moment, lighting incense sticks and waving them in her hands. It wasn't difficult miming the incantations as she walked around the kneeling gladiatrices, blessing each one in turn who then rose and made her way to the chamber where the whips were stored.

Each gladiatrix stripped off her black ceremonial robe and knelt naked before a small alter lighted only with candles.

Each priestess was handed a whip, some just a plain leather strap, others three tailed and one or two with thick plaited thongs. Drusa accepted a three tailed whip knotted at the ends and took her place behind Africanus.

Now you're for it, she thought, hardly believing her luck. Of all the gladiatrix she might have been chosen to flog it just happened that she was given the one she hated most.

"Twenty lashes on each," a priestess announced, lighting a bowl full of incense.

While the flogging was in progress the priestess would call upon the Goddess to bestow her favours and grant the gladiatrix victory. No one noticed the hardly contained smile struggling at the corners of Drusa's lips as she raised the whip in readiness.

Africanus was on her knees, her hands clasped together, naked except for a garland of laurel leaves adorning her brow. Even Drusa begrudgingly admired how splendid she looked naked and shimmering in the sanctum, her thighs gleaming and breasts full and shapely. The nipples had already gone erect with anticipation of the pain that was to follow. Magda, unseen had crept to an alcove in the sanctum and was lost in shadow as she watched her mistress yielding her bare back and buttocks to the whip. It was the same with the other gladiatrix, their bare backs and thighs quivering in the chill of the sanctum as they too awaited the lash.

"Oh, Nemesis, favour us with your presence as we your humble servants offer up our flesh as a sacrifice in return for victory," the priestess chanted, signalling for the flogging to commence.

"Uurgh!" Africanus grunted, feeling a shock of pain blazing across her back.

The lashes had come fast and furious, biting into her naked skin like a bolt of lightning. Each tail had wrapped around her ribs where the skin was taut and thinly stretched. She had been flogged on previous occasions when she called upon the Goddess, but never with such vehemence as the priestess now lifting her whip for the second blow.

It caught her square across the shoulder blades and her head jolted from the shock. In the shadows Magda watched in terror as her mistress straightened her back for the next lash. Already, dark welted lines were forming on her skin. The tails sailed unexpectedly across her bottom cheeks, striking both buttocks, leaving only the deep arse crease untouched.

Drusa stole a furtive glance at the other priestesses who could, it seemed, order their charges into any position they chose.

"Bend your head to the floor," Drusa commanded, not losing a moment. "And bare your bottom."

Africanus naturally obeyed the priestess at her rear and placed her brow on the tiles, her bottom ready and waiting.

Watching from her place in the alcove, Magda held her breath. She could tell from the angle of the priestess' arm where the whip was going to fall next.

Africanus emitted a grunt as the lash sailed into her bottom crease. Drusa couldn't contain the satisfaction of seeing her victim's buttocks flexing and twitching as the pain spread through each cheek. Biting her lip, Drusa whipped Africanus' buttocks with the fury of a demon. How could anyone in her position resist such splendid buttocks offered up so willingly? Again she couldn't help but admire the shape of Africanus' hips, the way they curved outwards from her slender back, forming into perfectly rounded globes of her arse, the skin so smooth and silky, and the crease deeper than that of any other woman she'd had the pleasure of flogging. Each whipped buttock broke into a dance, the arse muscles squeezing and lifting each half in turn until they collided into the crease, then hollowed and wobbled back into shape.

Drusa gave her six lashes and told her to kneel up and put her hands on the crown of her head. She gathered the whip and stood a little to the left, taking careful aim and sending the knotted tails whistling across her back, but landing them so that the ends whipped around her body. Magda went weak at the knees, but couldn't take her eyes off of what was

163

happening to her mistress. She saw clearly the knotted end curl around Africanus' ribs and over her breast. She heard a high pitched shriek as the knot dug sharply into the nipple. It fell away and the teat rose up so hard and erect the next lash couldn't fail to hit it. Drusa moved from right to left, making sure the nipples were well and truly throbbing before she concentrated on the small of Africanus' back.

Magda knew that something wasn't quite right but couldn't fathom what it was. She could see the other gladiatrix, their backs and buttocks soundly flogged, but the priestesses administering the flogging showed little or no emotion as they sent the whips cracking into their naked flesh. But the priestess flogging her mistress was whipping her with a vengeance and happily smiling to herself as each lash sent her mistress jerking and squirming in pain. Magda was no judge of other women's emotions, but she recognised one on heat when she saw it. Risking life and limb, she crept to the edge of the alcove where she could see the priestess' face, and even though it was buried under thick layers of chalk there was no mistaking the orgasmic expression in her eyes and on the parted lips. Then it struck her; the bitch was having an orgasm right there and then. She was aiming the whip for maximum effect, causing the greatest pain as the tails whistled over the base of Africanus' spine. Her whole back went into spasms, the skin rippling and quivering all the way to her shoulders. Then the whip returned swiftly upwards, coming in diagonal strokes, the tails again lashing into the globes and nipples of each breast. Even in the hands of an amateur it would have impossible to miss breasts of those dimensions. Africanus still had her hands on her head; the arms stretched upwards lifting her breasts and thrusting them outwards from her chest. Magda could see the nipples now hard and throbbing, the knotted tails landing on each excited teat with deadly precision.

Africanus was heroically fighting the pain, gritting her teeth and squinting her eyes as the lash curled around her body and then rapidly withdrew so that the knots tore at each nipple. The final lash struck hard across both buttock cheeks where Africanus least expected it and she fell forward bumping her head on the tiles.

"Get up," Drusa said savagely, and for a moment forgot herself and was about to deliver another round of blows on Africanus' already welted bottom, but the ceremony was over and the priestesses dropped their whips and awaited the next command.

"The Goddess has answered our prayers," a voice assured, and the flogged gladiatrices rose to their feet, the criss-crossed welts burning a livid red in the lamplight.

Magda went back into the shadows but kept her eye on the priestess as the next part of the ceremony proceeded.

The high priestess of Nemesis lifted a huge goblet of wine to the towering statue and asked it to bless the liquid swirling inside. That done she filled the smaller goblets held by the priestesses. The gladiatrices had filed back into the main temple and amid clouds of incense and smouldering pine cones knelt at the statue, lifting their eyes in supplication.

For a moment, Magda's eyes were averted as a priestess slowly beat a gong sending its doleful echoes booming around the walls and dome. But when she looked back it was just in time to see each priestess offering the goblets to the gladiatrix, and in a flash she saw the priestess who had flogged her mistress, reach quickly under her robe, seemingly fumbling with the pin that held it in place. An innocent gesture, but for her hand now passing over the rim of the goblet and the fingers moving as if crushing something in its palm. It happened in the twinkling of an eye and Africanus drained the goblet and then stood up, bowing low to the statue.

The priestesses took hold of the incense burners and processed around the statue, chanting and wailing, then filed off into a vestibule. Magda remained frozen until it was safe to show herself in the now deserted temple. She waited for what seemed an eternity then hurried to join her mistress already preparing for her journey to the villa of Lucius Proximus. At the same time, the whores had been summoned and were making ready, scrubbing themselves and sweetening their skin with cheap perfume. Drusa only just made it to the brothel and quickly sluiced her cunt with rose water before being bundled into a cart and driven off through the streets. Neither had any idea they were heading for the same place.

"Where the hell have you been?" Africanus hissed, tying up her hair.

"Please mistress, I saw something at the temple when you were being flogged by the priestess, I think its import...Ooouch!"

"Don't bother me with that now, you little piglet," Africanus interrupted, slapping her face.

Magda quickly went about her business, gathering armour and weapons, carrying them to an awaiting cart while her mistress slipped on a tunic and made for Quintus' carriage. On the way there Magda made one more attempt to tell her mistress of the furtive goings on she'd seen, but Africanus' head was too full of the coming combat to listen and silenced her with another resounding slap.

"Who are they?" Magda asked, watching as a cart load of boisterous women unloaded at the villa entrance.

"Prostitutes," Africanus informed disgustedly, getting out of the carriage and making her way into the atrium

Quintus was already there, and came forward to greet her. "Your combatant is Valda," he informed at once.

"Another savage," Africanus said flatly.

"But a good fighter," he added quickly. "You will not be wearing armour, only a skirt and boots. You will be bare breasted and will be armed with batons."

"It sounds more like a brawl," she snorted.

Quintus reddened, almost too embarrassed to admit the

166

truth that was exactly what it would be; two near naked women beating the shit out of each with no holds barred. But he was being well paid to stage the event, and a display of wobbling breasts and buttocks would go down well, especially when the wine was flowing, not to mention a pack of ribald whores doing their stuff.

Africanus went off to change her clothes, although there was very little to change into. She might as well have been completely naked for all the use a single skirt and boots would be. Magda accompanied her into the changing room and was about to raise the subject of the priestess again, but thought better of it. A slap from her mistress was no light thing and the side of her face still smarted from the previous blow.

Africanus buckled on the skirt which was made of thick, dark green leather, liberally decorated with bronze studs. It was longer than she anticipated reaching to about mid thigh. But it was the boots which held her fascinated. They reached just below the knees, the toes forming into an apex were protected with bronze points, and at the heels were spurs, huge wheels with long spikes projecting from them. It didn't take much imagination to realise the fearful damage they could inflict on a pair of bare buttocks. There was other protection of sorts; thick leather arm bands with more studs protruding from them, and a leather collar decorated with bronze motifs. The baton was a stout length of highly polished mahogany about as thick as her wrist. A golden head band held her hair in place.

"You look wonderful, mistress," Magda chirped, her eyes wide with adoration. Her voice dropped to a conspiratorial whisper. "Are you going to fuck me again afterwards with that thing?"

Africanus rolled her eyes. "Depends if any of the male guests want me for fucking. Got up like this I wouldn't be a bit surprised. If they don't, I'll be fucking you, you little piglet."

She went to the banquet and seated herself out of sight, helping herself to wine and sweetmeats. The whores were there, stark naked and waiting on the guests, having their buttocks pinched as they passed by, or their breasts fondled. Soon the contest between the gladiatrices would be staged and afterwards the whores would be on their backs and legs spread wide, taking as many of the guests still sober enough to get an erection.

It wasn't long before the master of ceremonies called the combatants to take the floor and Africanus arose from her seat, then suddenly her head went into a spin. She fell against a column and for a few seconds thought she was going to faint. But it cleared as quickly as it came and, putting it down to sour wine; she strode into the centre of the floor.

Valda came out from behind a curtain looking no less devastatingly attractive and just as deadly. Her skirt was made of long strips of thick leather which parted tantalisingly over her buttocks. She too wore knee length boots and at the heels was a single long spike glinting in the lamplight. Bronze and silver arm bands reached from wrist to elbow beautifully embossed with Celtic runes and symbols. Her hair was tied in bunches either side of her head. For a full minute both women stood appraising each other, getting the measure of their height and strength. They were fairly matched, even though Valda was a good head shorter than her opponent, but what she lacked in height she made up in muscle. Her limbs were not as powerful as Africanus, but more wiry and she could move fast. There was no doubting that.

A hush fell over the guests who leaned forward in their seats, goggling at the gladiatrix. One of the whores seated on the lap of a man closest to the combatants was rudely pushed to the floor. She got up rubbing her bruised bottom and swearing like a trooper. That could only be Amenia, cursing and spitting as usual. She went past Drusa, pausing for a moment to look at the shocked look on her face.

"You look as if you've just sucked off a horse," she said crudely, turning to see what had brought on such a startled expression.

Drusa quickly retreated into the shadows. "But I thought the gladiatrix were going to fight in the arena," she wondered aloud, staring at Africanus, stunned at seeing her right there not a few feet away.

"Not always," a man informed. "Lucius hires them now and then to liven up the proceedings." He smiled to himself. "And we get to fuck them afterwards."

"But they're only armed with sticks. How can they fight to the death with those?"

"It's not a fight to the death. But I imagine they're going to inflict some serious damage with those spurs."

Drusa knew the outcome even before the combat commenced. But the end result was not what she had hoped for. Trust these fucking Romans to foul up her plans. Muttering curses she retreated further into the shadows but was quickly grabbed by a male guest who seated her on his knees. She forced a smile as his hand went straight between her legs, parting her creamy thighs and fingering her cunt. Lucius caught her eye and she returned his gaze, recognising the man who had visited her at the brothel and was suddenly reminded of her earlier commitment. Already her jaws ached at the prospect of being simultaneously fucked. She smiled a weak smile and felt the man's hands on her hips, lifting and turning her over his knees. Her thighs parted and she straddled his cock, facing him whilst he tore open her gown, baring her breasts and teasing her nipples. Over her shoulder, she heard the first clashing of the batons as the gladiatrix locked in combat.

Valda kept out of range, swinging the baton in her hand, but slowly circling her opponent, her back bent and on her heels ready to spring. Africanus fixed her eyes on the Celt, watching and waiting for the first blow. Then suddenly they both moved at once, charging into one another, batons and arms flailing so fast they blurred. Valda went into a fast spin hoping to catch her assailant off guard, but the momentum lifted the tails of her skirt and in a trice Africanus sent her baton smacking into Valda's bare buttocks. She would have struck another blow but her aim was poor and she missed and went tumbling over the floor. Valda was there at once, returning the blow on Africanus' naked breasts. She raised her baton for a second strike but the black woman rolled over and lashed out, landing a smacking blow on the backs of Valda's thighs. Africanus was on her feet and winging her baton into Valda's rump. A hollow thump echoed around the hall as the wooden shaft sank deep into the soft fleshy globes. Already her pale buttock skin turned a livid red. She howled with pain and came quickly back, catching Africanus off guard and sending her baton smacking into her flank. But the black gladiatrix took a leap backwards and swung her weapon in a wide arc, landing directly between Valda's shoulder blades. She hit the floor and lay panting on her stomach. It would have been easy to have finished her then, her bare back presenting a splendid target for the wheeled spurs. But even Quintus could see something was wrong.

When Africanus lifted her boot to run the spiked wheel down the length of Valda's back, she hesitated, seemingly losing her balance. Valda rolled clear and got up, smacking her baton hard into Africanus' belly. They had only been combating each other for a few minutes, yet Africanus knew her strength was failing. A dull ache spread through her arms and thighs and her eyes went into double vision. But she just managed to parry the next blow, knocking Valda's baton clean out of her hand. Defenceless now, Valda retreated, expecting to be beaten senseless, but her opponent merely lashed out into thin air missing her by miles. Valda was quick to realise that Africanus could hardly stand and it took one swift kick at the back of her thighs to send her crashing over the mosaic.

She lay on the floor staring at the ceiling, an agonising pain going through her legs and arms. Try as she might, her arm refused to budge and Valda unhurriedly lifted the hem of the black woman's skirt and placed it neatly over the small of her back, baring her buttocks to the audience.

Angry beyond words, Quintus didn't have the patience to watch his most prized gladiatrix not lifting a finger in defence whilst the Celt lashed her buttocks until they throbbed. But Africanus felt no pain. The sounds of the baton smacking onto her numbed bottom grew fainter and she passed out cold. Valda, wrinkling her nose, tossed away her baton in disgust and, as a final insult, crouched over Africanus' back and speedily emptied her bladder. Magda watched in tears as a fast jet of yellow, steaming urine cascaded over her mistress' shoulders and hair. Valda squirted the last drops on Africanus' buttocks and stood up amid deafening cheering.

Then she marched off, but not before sending the toe of her boot hard into Africanus ribs. Somehow, she felt she'd been cheated.

# CHAPTER TEN

"I'm selling you," Quintus said with no trace of emotion. "You made me a laughing stock. You have cost me a great deal of money. I might recover a few sestertii putting you up for auction. Any gladiatrix who drinks before combat is worthless. You couldn't even stand."

Africanus lay on her cot, her head thumping so hard tears streamed down her face.

"Please, master," she muttered. "I only had one goblet."

Magda came forward, bowing low. "Please, master, I have something to tell you. When my mistress was in the temple I…"

Quintus silenced her with a slap on the jaw. "Have this thing taken out and flogged, and then sell her along with this useless piece of…"

He was so angry he couldn't readily think of an apt word.

"Give them both forty lashes," he said to the guard. "Then take them both to the slave market."

The guards lost no time in carrying out his instructions, dragging the still comatose black woman and her young slave to the whipping post.

"Forget the post," the captain of the guard suggested. "I have a better idea."

He whispered to his comrade who instantly bust into a peal of laughter.

And he went off to fetch some shackles and chains

"Spread your legs," he told Africanus, gathering up the shackles.

She did as she was told; shuffling her feet over the sand until her legs were widely parted. Still in a daze after all that had happened, she stared blankly into the distance, hardly noticing her young slave standing in front of her, mirroring her actions.

The guard shackled their ankles, pushing the younger woman tightly against the gladiatrix. A length of chain was wrapped around their knees and another more tightly at mid thigh. A longer length passed neatly around the waists and pulled so tight both women uttered a gasp.

He paused, admiring the way their breasts squashed into each other and their bellies flattened as the chain was locked into place. He took the remaining shackles and secured them to their wrists. Face to face, breast to breast, belly to belly, the two women rested their heads on their shoulders, wondering what else their tormentor had in mind.

"Now let me see you kiss," the guard chortled.

Shackled and chained together it was useless to argue. They looked each other in the eyes and pursed their lips, giving each other a quick, half-hearted peck. They might well enjoy a long lingering kiss in the privacy of their rooms, but never in public and in full view of these animals.

"Not good enough!" the guard barked, cracking his whip across Magda's naked rump. "Open your mouths and get your tongues down your throats."

He watched closely, so closely they could smell his beer-laden breath. Out of the corner of her eye, Africanus saw his cock stirring as they opened their mouths wide and crushed their lips together. Magda just dumbly obeyed, forcing her wiggling tongue into the throat of her mistress, whilst she in turn remained passive, letting her tongue submit to her young slave's advances.

Dimly, she recalled Magda trying to tell her something had taken place in the temple which she ought to have known, and now she began to wonder if her lost combat with Valda had some connection with it. But the thought was driven abruptly from her mind as Magda's body jolted against her.

The whip had landed perfectly across her bottom cheeks, smacking into her ripe buttocks with full force. The pain going through Africanus' veins came not from the whip, but from Magda's teeth biting into her tongue. Now she understood why the guard wanted them open mouthed and kissing each other. Every lash on their bare buttocks and backs brought an instant reaction, grinding their teeth and biting on their tongues, trying to stave off the red hot pain blazing into their naked flesh. Another lash descended, this time across Africanus' more prominent buttocks.

"See how these two love each other," the guard mocked, watching the two shackled women writhing and squirming against each naked body.

It was a curious mixture of pain and pleasure which had their nipples erect and bellies quivering, that and the added sensation of being naked and chained body to body.

"I want to see them both come," the guard's companion leered, eyeing Magda's twitching buttocks.

"That can be easily arranged," his friend grated, coiling the whip.

He took careful aim, raising his arm high over his head and letting it fall in a rapid, sweeping arc. Magda's tongue shot from Africanus' throat and she emitted a deafening howl. Neither was the searing pain lost on her mistress as the whip sailed into their open sex. For several mind numbing seconds their buttocks and hips jolted and danced and the guard's throat went dry with despair. He'd whipped dozens of shackled slaves; some fettered back to back, others chained only at the wrists, many chained at the ankles and prostrated over benches, but none had exhibited such a cock throbbing display as the two now writhing in agony only an arm's length away.

The second lash came a lot faster and harder than the first, cutting deep into their gaping sex, going so far under their legs the tail end licked into Magda's arse crease. At a signal from the guard, his companion hurried across the yard and came back carrying another whip. The men stood either side of the shackled women, positioning themselves behind them,

174

a little to the left so that their right arms had full rein to send the whips whistling into the proffered buttocks. Magda held her breath waiting for the next lash, filling her lungs and thrusting out her chest. Then it came; both men lashed at once, striking both pairs of buttocks, bringing the whips in a whistling upward cut. The shriek of pain paled into insignificance compared with their jolting bodies. Only their hips and shoulders had freedom to move and both squirmed and writhed from the welts now forming in the whips' wake.

The guards knew exactly where to send the whips, striking at the backs of the women's knees, and moving steadily upwards, concentrating on the backs of their thighs, lashing so hard the long lengths of leather coiled all the way around their fettered legs. But it was when the whips bit hard into the buttock halves the women broke into wild hip twisting dances. It was just what the guards wanted, watching hips and buttocks rolling and separating from the deep creases, coming back together so tightly the buttocks went into deep hollows. The women couldn't help but press against each other, struggling to avoid the next onslaught, the whips biting like firebrands into their naked rumps. The guards couldn't fail to see the way the huge breasts suddenly squashed, nipple to nipple, swelling into gorgeous rolls of flesh; their bellies slapping and wobbling, but most rewarding was the sight of their hips now gyrating so fast they thrust outwards, going into a circular motion. Magda's eyes began to mist, the eyelids getting heavier, her breath coming in faster rising pants. The guards knew at once what was happening. The ferocity of the whips had the women pressing their sex mounds together, the friction from the black slave's pubic bush slowly bringing them to orgasm.

The second guard almost dropped his whip at the sight of both naked women, legs widely spread, long lengths of splendid curving calves and muscular thighs creasing at the buttocks splitting open and revealing the tantalising tufts of hair beneath. It was too much to resist and, dropping his whip, he came forward and passed the palm of his hand under their legs, rubbing it hard into the now soaking slits.

The women had no choice but to submit to the groping palm rubbing back and forth against their sex pouches. Neither could they help the juice trickling from their slits, nor did one look at their faces tell the guards what they wanted to know. They were there at once, dropping their breeches and gripping their throbbing cocks. It took only one thrust to penetrate the fettered slaves.

"Let's hear you grunt," the guard slamming into Africanus commanded, filling her to the hilt.

He slapped her flanks and thighs, treating her like an animal. Magda was almost on her toes her body lifted from the juddering cock pounding inside her cunt. But it was the sensation of feeling Africanus' body that had her gasping for breath. Her mistress' nipples, much larger than her own had risen hard and poked into her tits, but it was her sex mound that really brought on Magda's orgasm, that and the erection stabbing inside her.

Africanus was grunting like a sow on heat, emitting deep-throated grunts, obeying her tormentor who was now slapping her so hard her skin stung. Her hips thumped into Magda, grinding the pubic hair until the skin rubbed sore.

"Now kiss," the guard ordered, knowing he was about come.

There was no faking the tongues worming inside their hot mouths, searching into their throats, kissing with full passion as they suddenly erupted their sex juices. The guards finished quickly and withdrew leaving the women still tightly shackled.

But the lashing was not over. The sex was only a brief respite and the guards sent the whips whistling into the soaking slits. They could hear the leather going deep into the parted sex now hot and dripping. The women, exhausted from their orgasms slumped into one another, held upright only by the shackles and chains. But the fresh onslaught of pain was real enough. Only when the final tally had been delivered did the lashing cease, and as soon as the shackles were released the women crashed to the ground, tumbling over each other and lying in a bruised and sexually satiated heap.

The guard kicked Magda's rump. "Best piece of fucking flesh I've had in a long while," he complimented, wondering if it was worth his while to give her another insertion of his pulsating erection.

But there was no time for that. Quintus had ordered them both sold, and he didn't care to whom.


"On your knees, bitch," Lucius Proximus had commanded, when the combat was ended.

Drusa dutifully knelt naked before him and his best friend, Eugenius. Both had a curious penchant for being sucked off together in the hot willing mouth of a woman.

"She's in good condition for an old cow," Eugenius observed, looking at her ample breasts.

"But she doesn't come cheap, so take your time. She's going to suck us both until her jaw aches."

There was no doubting that. Both men were fully erect and standing so close she could feel the heat rising from their cocks. Despite the beaming smile that seemed to send her lips almost half way around her face, there was rage in her breast. The poisonous concoction that she had prepared, and afterwards risked life and limb trespassing in the temple posing as a priestess to deliver it, had all been in vain. It was meant to slow the gladiatrix so that her opponent could finish her off once and for all. Now the bitch was still alive, bruised maybe, but still breathing. And that piqued Drusa.

"Open your mouth," Lucius Proximus ordered, looking down at her breasts.

Eugenius was not in such a hurry to have her mouth embracing his cock. He stood at her side admiring her thighs and bottom. For a savage her skin was remarkably pale, most were darker. Her nipples were large and a rich brown colour which the paler surrounding skin seemed to emphasize.

"How much cock have you had in your time, old woman?" he inquired.

"Plenty," she said, seeing little point in saying anything else.

"I've heard a tale that you satisfied a whole cohort. A hundred and fifty men one after the other and still begged for more."

Drusa reddened. She guessed that story would soon travel far and wide, but she certainly hadn't gone begging.

"I did have quite a few," she admitted, lowering her head in pretentious shame.

"Well let's see if your mouth works as hard as your cunt," Lucius Proximus broke in, teasing her lower lip with his cock plum.

Her hand closed mid way around his shaft and guided it into her mouth. It was as much as she could do to take that, let alone Eugenius' throbbing length. He patiently waited while she sucked at his host, taking her lips right into his pubic bush before sucking back to the plum. Her cheeks hollowed beautifully and her head bobbed fast, going up and down slicking his cock with saliva. She popped the shaft from her lips and sent her long tongue furling around the plum, taking great care to clean out the groove beneath.

It was too much for Eugenius, whose cock throbbed so much it ached.

He stood beside his best friend who angled his body sideways but still kept his cock deeply embedded in the whore's mouth. Eugenius came along side him, gently easing his cock plum along Lucius Proximus' shaft until the plum nudged her lips. Her mouth was already stuffed full and lips widely stretched, but she dropped her lower jaw and forced her lips to crease even wider. Slowly and carefully, Eugenius guided his cock into her mouth keeping it tight against Lucius Proximus' embedded shaft. He heard the whore gulp and a soft grunt shook her throat. Eugenius watched goggle eyed as she worked her stretched lips down both shafts, stretching them even wider as she took in both shiny plums. She used both hands to hold them, one on each, holding them rigid as her head very slowly moved up and down, taking in as much as she could.

"We're both going to come at once," Lucius Proximus advised. "So hold back until the time is right, and then we'll both fill her belly."

Eugenius felt like holding back all night if needs must. Many a slave, willing and unwilling had had his cock in her mouth, some were good, but this old whore surpassed them all. Her tongue flicked rapidly from one side of her mouth to the other, licking and teasing their silky-skinned plums, going into the eyes and around the base until the whole cock length tingled. With gargantuan effort she opened her mouth a little wider and started nibbling at both shafts already half in her throat.

Eugenius began to wonder exactly how much the bitch could take in that seemingly bottomless throat. He also had another idea.

"Fill the cow's mouth with aniseed," he suggested grinning like an ape. "That'll make our cocks tingle."

Lucius Proximus called for a slave and a young girl quickly answered his summons. He told her to fetch a jar of aniseed and she bolted from the room. One look at that old woman on her knees mouth stuffed with two men at once was enough to make her belly chill. She came back and handed her master the jar and then fled before it was her turn.

"Fill your face with this," he said coldly. "The whole jar."

Drusa let the cocks slip from her lips and upended the jar.

The liquid was bitter and burned over her tongue. Holding the liquid in her mouth she took the cocks in her hands and gulped them into her throat.

"The old sow's eating our cocks!" Eugenius said rudely, watching her mouth grinding and churning, swirling the aniseed round and round her teeth. But the effect was startling. Both men went wide-eyed at the sensation the aniseed was having on their cock plums. It both burned and chilled at the same time, one second hot, and the next turning cold as her mouth worked faster and faster.

Drusa closed her eyes, thinking only of the money she was earning and plotting her next move against the black gladiatrix. If poison had failed she would soon come up with another idea equally as terminal.

Her throat warbled as the aniseed began to trickle down her gullet. Now, Lucius Proximus reached forward clamping her head between his hands. He shot a sideways glance at Eugenius who immediately understood. Their loins broke in to a slow undulating motion and Drusa held her breath. Both shafts suddenly heated and trembled, a sure sign they were about to come. She saw their ball sacs grow tight and in the next instant both men let out a long groan and came cascading into her mouth.

"Keep still!" Lucius Proximus barked, clamping her head and forcing it downwards.

She felt a hot stream of spunk ejaculate all around her mouth, quickly followed by another. It seemed endless and she tried to draw back, holding her breath and keeping the fat globules of spunk sloshing against her teeth. But Lucius Proximus was wise to that old trick and slapped her hard between the shoulder blades. Her head shot forward and she almost choked on the male meat throbbing in her mouth, but the hard slap did its work and she swallowed every drop.

"You can get up now," Lucius Proximus laughed as streams of spunk dribbled from her chin.

"The old whore certainly knows how to use her jaws," Eugenius complimented, stroking his glistening shaft. "I know of a brothel in Rome that would pay at least a hundred denarii for her services."

"True, the old whore's wasted in a town like this. I wonder if she takes it up her arse as well as she does in her mouth?"

Drusa was on her feet, licking her lips and grinding her punished teeth. She had no intentions of going to Rome until at least she was revenged against the black woman.

True to his word, Lucius Proximus paid her the fifteen denarii's and sent her packing, but not before she was forced to use her mouth on all the other guests. Her belly churning and full of spunk and aniseed she went to the nearest fountain and drank a bucketful of cold refreshing water. She smiled ruefully, these Romans might treat women like mere pieces of fucking flesh but at least they paid well.

And she set off through the streets heading for her lodgings.

She passed the Forum where the traders were setting up their stalls and the military barracks where legionaries were drilling on the square. One or two yelled ribald comments inviting her to beat her own previous record, ignoring them she wandered through a warren of alleyways and backstreets and took a short cut through the slave market.

For a moment she thought it was the aniseed making her delirious seeing the black gladiatrix about to be sold. She stopped and rubbed her eyes, shaking her head and rubbing her eyes again. Then she marched into the courtyard tossing her long raven hair behind her.

There were about a hundred slaves on offer that morning, women and girls mostly, naked except for loin cloths and seated around the walls or huddled in nervous groups.

"The black woman, how much is she likely to fetch?" she asked the auctioneer.

He stroked his chin thoughtfully, appraising the woman in the blue cloak, guessing at how much she could likely afford.

"She's from good stock," he commenced. "Strong as a mare, and in good condition. No illnesses and young enough to breed. I couldn't let her go for less than twenty denarii's."

Drusa stroked her chin thoughtfully. "I'll have to look her over first. I mean thoroughly."

The auctioneer nodded his assent and took her over to where Africanus was standing. She recognized the former high priestess at once and both women gazed at each other with glazed hatred, made even worse because she had to stand stock still while the prospective purchaser began her inspection.

"Good breasts," she acknowledged, squeezing the ample globes, still unable to believe it really was her she was groping. "Responsive nipples too," she added, giving each teat a painful tweak.

She kept up the act, feeling and pinching her arms and thighs, lifting each foot, pinching her toes and heels. Inwardly cursing, Africanus turned and gritted her teeth as Drusa slapped her buttocks and backs of her thighs.

"Freshly whipped, I see," Drusa said loudly. "That tells me she's a trouble maker. Now bend over, I need to check your arse hole and cunt." ·

"Bend!" the auctioneer said sharply, already thinking he might get away with fifteen denarii's.

Africanus hissed through her teeth, suffering untold humiliation as she put her hands on her buttocks spreading her cheeks. Drusa put her forefinger up Africanus' bottom seemingly checking for any hidden disease, then she wormed her fingers into the open slit, sliding them back and forth. Nothing untoward there either. A flick of the auctioneer's whip on her bottom returned her upright.

"Now her teeth," Drusa said, stepping closer.

The auctioneer put his arm around Africanus' shoulder and the other fingers on her chin forcing open her jaw. Drusa couldn't help laughing as she put her fingers inside the black woman's mouth wiggling them over each tooth. Her fingers still smelt of anal and vaginal sweat which Drusa thought very funny. But Africanus wasn't laughing. She didn't think for one moment that the high priestess was serious in wanting to buy her.

"I'll offer five denarii's. Take it or leave it. She's rotten from head to foot."

It was true, the black slave did not look her best, having been recently flogged and fucked, and the after effects of the poison still hadn't quite worn off giving her eyes a dreamy, vacant look.

"Make it seven, and I'll throw in her slave," the auctioneer invited.

Drusa nearly choked. "You mean this thing has her own slave?" she asked agog.

"They came together, if you'll pardon the expression. The younger one is a savage but I daresay has her uses. Hitched to a plough they could both prove useful."

"I'll give you six, and no more," Drusa said flatly, poking Magda's bottom.

"Six it is, and what a bargain!"

Drusa ignored that. "I want them chained and weighted immediately."

She handed over part of her previous night's earnings and, folding her arms and tapping her foot, waited patiently while an assistant obeyed her instructions. He fitted iron collars to their necks and connected them with a single chain. Shackles were swiftly fitted to their wrists and the connecting chain linked to a heavy stone fitted with an iron ring. Both slaves struggled to carry it to an awaiting blacksmith who lifted each foot in turn and fastened a sturdier manacle to each ankle, then connected them with a length of chain, just long enough to allow them a tentative step.

Now what was Drusa to do? She had acted on impulse and could hardly take them back to her lodgings. But she had secured a bargain and the wonderful satisfaction that both slaves were now her legal property. Leaving them in the capable hands of the auctioneer, she rushed off to her lodgings and tipped over the bed, slicing open the mattress where the rest of her earnings were secreted. All in all about forty denarii's. Not bad for an old whore with a big mouth and cunt to match. And a strong stomach, she thought heading quickly into the city. She went straight to the nearest property agent, a greasy looking man with dark swept-back hair and eyes like a serpent.

It took less than ten minutes to secure the lease on a house by the military barracks; an equally rapid transaction obtained a licence to open a brothel. The auctioneer kindly delivered her newly acquired stock to the house she had leased, walking them through the city carrying the heavy stone and sweating like mules in the hot sunshine. At her request he left the wrist shackles and iron collars in place, but took away the remaining chains and the stone with the ring.

"You caused me a great deal of trouble," Drusa began, after her slaves were manacled to a cellar wall. "I had a good business at the stone circle until you ruined it. There was a fortune in that pond. Now it's all gone." But she wisely kept silent about the horde hidden under the sacrificial stone. "After you pissed on me and made off I was crucified and thrown into the river. But that's nothing compared with what I've got in store for you." She paused in her remonstrance, lifting a goblet of wine to her lips, drinking half of it then sending the rest hissing through her teeth all over Africanus' face. "By my reckoning, you owe me at least five thousand denarii's. So I'm going to set you and that little shit to work, day in and day out until your cunt's are so ravaged you won't even recognise them." She paused again, shooting her slaves a spiteful grin. "And when you've paid off the debt, you're going straight back to that mine. Your arms and legs will be in good condition, even if your arses are wrecked."

She turned to go, but came back again. "I forgot to mention that I shall be deducting the cost of your board and lodging from your earnings, so I think you and I are going to enjoy each others company for quite a long time."

And she went off, locking the cellar door behind her.

"Mistress, who the fuck was that?" Magda asked, settling her bottom on the bare stone floor.

"A savage, like you," Africanus replied unfairly. "Only she's a clever one. How the fuck did she ever find me, I wonder."

She twisted her neck, trying to get comfortable with the iron ring chaining her to the wall. She drew up her knees and closed her eyes, wondering at how rapidly her fortune had changed in the course of only a day.

# CHAPTER ELEVEN

It had all began with that strange sensation in her limbs when she was battling Valda, the peculiar numbness which quickly spread rendering her impotent. When it came to the final moments she couldn't even wield a sword. She knew it wasn't the wine. One goblet could hardly bring on those symptoms. It had to be something else. But what she wondered, shifting her cold bottom over the stone floor.

"Piglet," she whispered. "Are you asleep?"

Magda stirred and flicked a cockroach from her hair. "I'm awake," she muttered.

"You wanted to tell me about something you saw in the Temple of Nemesis. What was it?"

"Promise you won't slap me if I tell you."

"It's important," Africanus snapped irritably.

Magda recounted everything she saw and then shuffled out of arm's reach. She never knew how her mistress might react after telling her all that. But she remained passive; thinking hard. She believed every word of Magda's story and just when she thought she had the answer it fled from her mind like a ghost at cockcrow. She stared blankly at the wall, watching a spider weave her web. As far as she knew she had no enemies in the temple and no one could possibly disguise herself as a priestess and get past the guard. It just didn't make sense. The only thing she knew now was she had that fearful bitch Drusa to contend with.

"Piglet, listen to me," she whispered. "You know what's in store for us?"

"That woman's going to have us fucked rotten," Magda sobbed, thinking that her sex was becoming a receptacle for any man who wanted to empty his balls.

"That's not going to happen, my love. As soon as we're out of these chains we're going to run like hell. She can't watch us all the time. After a man's fucked a woman, the first thing he does is roll over and start snoring. When that happens, I'll get us out of here. Just be patient."

Magda smiled in return, but said nothing. Somehow she had a feeling that the clients' they were going to be servicing wouldn't be the kind that would just roll over and start snoring.

At sunrise, a hideous-looking man with a bulbous nose and wide glaring eyes came into the cell and unshackled the two women. He dragged them to their feet and kicked their backsides all the way along the passage, herding them forward like animals. They stumbled up a wooden staircase and along another passage. At the first door, he stopped, keyed the lock and sent Magda tumbling over the threshold. The door quickly slammed and he repeated the exercise at the next door, but managed to grope Africanus' breasts before kicking her across the room.

She quickly took in her surroundings; a small heavily barred window facing a dark, sunless courtyard; a bucket to shit in; a huge wooden bed with iron rings let in the head and foot boards; the ceiling cracked with more iron rings let into the joists; no other furnishing of any kind apart from a cupboard, barred and locked. Not even a stool to batter her client over the head if needs must. She seated herself on the bed and found it surprisingly robust and so large, more than enough room for herself and a client. Even when her legs and arms were fully stretched they still didn't touch the edges.

"Oh well, at least I'll be comfortable," she murmured, resting her head on the pillow.

A plan of escape loosely formed in her head. Get this troublesome business over and done with, fuck like a stoat, and when her client had lost the power of speech and was fast asleep, get the hell out, go directly into Magda's room, kick in the door if necessary, quickly deal with any unforeseen resistance, and then get clear of this stinking hole. She was a trained gladiatrix and could stand up against anything she might come across. Then she would go immediately to Quintus and repeat everything Magda had told her. She would soon be back in the arena and knocking out her opponents like flies.

What could be more complicated than that?

And she smiled and put her hands behind her head awaiting the first man stupid enough to cross the threshold.

It was some time before she heard footsteps coming along the passage and she sat up, crossing her legs and folding her hands in her lap, looking like the subservient and willing whore she was supposed to be.

A key grated in the lock and the door creaked open.

"Allow me to introduce you to your first customer," Drusa told her. She turned to the man coming into the room. "If you need any assistance, don't hesitate to summon my servant who will be only too willing to oblige."

And she locked the door and laughed so much her stomach ached.

Africanus wasn't laughing. And neither was her customer. He unlocked the cupboard and an avalanche of whips, chains, ropes, manacles and peculiar leather harnesses cascaded over the floor.

"You're a tall girl," he mused, running his eyes over her body. "We'll need something strong to take your weight."

Africanus' eyes rose to the iron hooks embedded in the ceiling, then at the pile of foreboding instruments.

"I'm a slave whore," she said, looking him steadily in the eye. "I'm not paid enough to go through this."

He was tall and dark with heavily set features, a man used to getting his way, neither was he slightly built, but she reckoned she could probably lay him out if she caught him off guard. She shifted her body, ready to spring.

"I thought you might be difficult," he mumbled. "The madam warned me about you," and he tugged on a rope dangling beside the cupboard.

The man with the bulging eyes was there in no time, letting himself into the room and locking the door behind him.

"I need assistance," the swarthy client said flatly.

Now there two of them to contend with, Africanus knew resistance were futile. She watched in simmering silence as her client selected a leather girdle and shackles. The whips he would choose at leisure.

The man with the bulging eyes took the girdle and fitted it to Africanus' waist, going about his business with amazing speed and precision. A length of leather passed under her legs and was connected back and front to a thicker waist band. At the sides of the band were rings and hasps through which he slipped lengths of rope. One dexterous sweep of his arm tossed the rope ends through the rings in the joists. Her client could hardly contain his longing when the man gave a sharp tug on the ropes. Africanus caught her breath as her feet left the floor and she was pulled upwards suspended by the girdle now cutting deep into her sex.

The man was quickly at her sides, shackling her wrists and tossing the connecting chains through more rings set much wider apart overhead. Africanus' body slowly lifted and as it went upwards her arms stretched wider and wider until her wrists crashed into the rings. She hung like one crucified, her body gently swaying in the girdle, her whole weight bearing on the leather strip going under her legs and up through her bottom crease. The man tugged again on the ropes and she felt her shoulders suddenly wrench.

"Beautiful," the client acknowledged, looking at the magnificent black woman swaying on the ropes.

It would have to be a peculiar man whose cock didn't harden at the sight of her long legs hanging limply, her belly heaving as the leather cut into her slit, her arms outstretched, lifting her breasts and making them wobble.

"Now you can flog the bitch to your heart's content," Bulging Eyes said, giving her rump a hard slap.

He left and went off muttering and cursing that he was getting fed up with these disobedient whores, and it was about time the madam taught them a lesson they would not forget.

Africanus had a pretty good idea that she was about to be taught a lesson she would not forget as her client kicked through the pile of whips and canes littering the floor.

He selected a plaited whip, long and supple, frayed and weighted at the end for maximum effect.

"Such a splendid arse," he whispered, prolonging the agony of waiting, smoothing his palms over her buttocks. "And long thighs too," he added, running his fingers from hip to knee.

For a moment he was distracted by a shriek of pain coming from a nearby room. Africanus recognised the shrill tones of Magda and heard the dull thump of a whip landing on her naked flesh. In the silence that followed Africanus' client stripped off his tunic and breeches and stood naked before her shimmering legs. His cock was rock hard at the sight of her and it was only a matter of time before she would be chained to the bed, legs spread and being ridden sore.

"I think I'll start with your arse," he said, flicking the end of the whip across her bottom. "A good place to start, don't you think?"

Africanus couldn't care less where he started. In her position there was nothing she could do to stop him from whipping anywhere he chose.

The whip sailed into her buttocks and Africanus' back arched from the sudden shock. He stood back and watched her legs thrash the air, her knees bending and calves splaying outwards. Before her body straightened itself he sent the whip cracking into the small of her back and again across her arse cheeks. Her hips suddenly rolled and she shot forward, her arms threatening to tear from their sockets as she swung back and forth. But it was the leather girdle that hurt most. It was her only means of support and as more lashes descended on her thighs and bottom the girdle seemed to tighten. She could feel the leather strip cutting deep into her sex and bottom crease and although she wriggled and squirmed the leather strip cut deeper. Dimly, she guessed what was happening. The girdle was not made from one piece of leather but a single strip designed to pass through the hasps in the waist band, and the more she wriggled the tighter the pressure on her sex and in her bottom.

She gritted her teeth and clenched her fists, awaiting the next lash, determined not to twitch a muscle. He sent the whip whistling under her buttocks, striking the fat of the overhang where each cheek creased into her thighs. He could see the agonised expression contorting her face; her body and mind battling against the fresh onslaught of pain darting through her spine.

"I can see you're used to this," he remarked with grudging admiration. "But there is one trick you haven't bargained for."

She saw him drop the whip and go to the pile of implements, selecting a long length of tightly woven rope. One end was wound around her ankles and the other passed through a ring at the back of the girdle. Slowly and deliberately, he pulled on the rope until the slack had been taken up. The rope tautened and she heard him grunt. Her legs suddenly bent at the knees and her calves smacked into the backs of her thighs. The loose end of the rope was swiftly knotted into place and he picked up the whip, flexing it in his hands.

"Now we'll see you dance," he rasped, going behind her.

Before she could utter a sound the whip thrashed over the soles of her feet and Africanus thought she'd been struck by a bolt of lightning. A tongue of flame seemed to pass through her calves and thighs and burn all the way around her bottom. She let out a scream and doubled at the hip, her body swung so far forward her knees almost bumped the wall. She swung back again and he struck the underside of her toes. Her body twisted from left to right and pain struck everywhere. The girdle was so tight it felt as if the leather strip under her legs was sawing its way through her body. Her bottom was splitting from the strip biting hard and deep into her arse crease, and through her feet and legs numbness spread leaving in its wake a dull pain.

"What about the front of your thighs," he said, coming around her. "Mustn't forget those."

"I've taken enough," she sobbed.

"Your mistress told me that the clients could do anything they pleased with you," he said flatly. "You and that other little whore along the passage. She even suggested I could piss all over you if I chose. But don't worry; I'm not going to do that. The whip is much more entertaining, and of course, you will be fucked later. It's all in the price."

He took careful aim and landed the whip over the front of her thighs, delivering six lashes in rapid succession. Her body jerked backwards and she heard her arm sockets crick from the strain. But the girdle had tightened to its fullest extent and the leather strip had all but completely vanished into her sex slit. But that did not stop her body from writhing and twisting, her hips, buttocks and breasts breaking into the agonising dance he told her would come.

Africanus had taken quite a few whippings in her time and had learnt to bear them. She had also suffered from any number of torments, both sexual and physical, but none that she could recall caused so much pain all at once.

He was much harder now, his cock throbbing so much it positively ached to get itself immersed in her hot, wet sex.

He went behind her and released the rope at the back of the waist band, his fingers moved fast at the girdle, unfastening the hasps and ropes. One sharp tug slipped the leather strips from her sex slit and bottom crease.

"You're so wet," he murmured, looking at the juice slicked strip. "You must be begging for it."

She couldn't deny that the sensation of the whip lashing into her buttocks and the girdle tightening into her sex had brought on a cataclysmic orgasm. It was also impossible to disguise the effect it had on her nipples now standing proud and erect. He worked faster, untying the chains that held her wrists and letting them run through the rings. She hit the floor with a resounding crash, hugging her knees and moaning from the pain still throbbing in her limbs.

Her client gathered her in his arms and carried her to the bed, dropping her on the centre of the mattress. Unresisting, unopposed, expected, he stretched out her arms, shackling the wrists to the rings in the head board. Equally unresisting, she allowed him to take her ankles and bend her long legs far over her head, parting the thighs and manacling her ankles to the rings in the bed posts. Her sex lay open and glistening, the lips quivering in anticipation ready to allow his throbbing cock to penetrate her. She knew that after being hung in the girdle and flogged, her arms almost wrenched from their sockets that his cock would eventually give her the real satisfaction she needed.

He knelt between her legs, not penetrating her as yet, but teasing her breasts and nipples, giving sharp bites of his teeth on the succulent dark buds. His tongue went all around the pimpled areolas making the nipple harden and crinkle with longing. When his fingers ran through the outer portals of her sex she finally succumbed.

"Please fuck me," she begged. "Don't play with me, just go on and give me your cock."

He chuckled at the desperation contorting her face and ran the shiny cock head over her nipples, only just allowing the tip to tease the aching buds.

"Put out your tongue," he whispered hoarsely, lying right over her.

His hands were on her thighs, smoothing the silky flanks and magnificent lengths of silken skin. She poked out her tongue and sobbed, wondering for how much longer he intended to make her suffer the agonies of waiting.

But he was in no hurry. It was all part of the treatment, flogging her to orgasm, letting her wait for the cock she now sucked into her throat, and prolonging the agony of riding her quivering cunt.

"Please, just give it to me," she wailed, rolling her head from side to side.

"Not yet," he whispered, wriggling off her and going to the heap of chains and shackles.

He came back with an iron ring as wide as his wrist and ran the edges over her soaking cunt lips. When it was thoroughly wetted he carefully positioned it at the entrance to her sex.

"You'll look much better ringed," he said seriously, and guided the ring between her lips, stretching them around the iron perimeter.

Africanus struggled against the shackles binding her wrists and ankles, desperately wanting to throw her arms and legs around him. One heave of her hips would have her cunt filled, but still he kept her waiting.

He began slapping her thighs and belly, hitting her in quick succession, going up and down her sweating skin. When she was sobbing and dripping, he concentrated on her breasts, cupping and lifting the wobbling dark globes and flicking his thumbs over her nipples. Her belly creased at the navel as she took in deep breaths and he paused then, listening to the rapid pants coming from her parted lips. She was on heat and almost at the point of orgasm. Only his cock would bring her off and he watched seemingly fascinated at the way her head and eyes rolled, her fingers and toes curling with desperation. Then without warning he thrust his cock hard into her sex.

"Oh, by all the Gods," she moaned, feeling at long last his naked cock riding her belly.

His arms encircled her thighs, hugging and stroking them where the skin was most sensitive, tickling the backs of her knees and running his fingertips under the sweep of her calves.

Pushed to the very limits of endurance it wasn't long before her orgasm erupted over the mattress, her juices flooding from her in a stream of pearly liquid.

"You came too quickly," he returned angrily. "You weren't supposed to do that."

Was he completely stupid, or what? Didn't he understand that she had been so aroused by the whip and his constant denial that she just couldn't help but climax?

"Now I'll have to punish you," he said angrily.

Again she was defenceless against the plaited whip sailing into her bottom. With her legs bent over her head and ankles securely manacled to the bed posts, he couldn't fail to land the whip across the whole expanse of her buttocks. Each lash brought fresh agonies of pain and arousal so much that her body went into spasms, shaking her breasts and belly until she cried out for it to stop.

"You're mouth is too loud," he complained, discarding the whip and fetching a short length of rope. "I ought to have gagged you from the start."

And he wound the rope around her head, forcing it into her mouth and silencing her.

Only muffled grunts escaped her lips as he continued the flogging, lashing her buttocks and then aiming it into her sex. There was no need to whip hard; just a touch of the plaited leather against her sex had her writhing in agony. When he knew she was coming he stopped and guided his hand through the iron ring. Quick movements of his wrist brought on her second orgasm as it twisted from side to side, going steadily deeper with every thrust.

"Now suck your own come," he grunted, taking his fingers from her soaking cunt and pushing them into her mouth.

He watched in silence as she sucked them dry, swallowing her juice and tasting its powerful musky aroma.

"Now you can stay there," he told her, reaching for his tunic. "A woman always looks her best with her legs open and her cunt ringed."

He tugged on the rope and Bulging Eyes duly arrived and keyed the door.

"I have no further use for this whore," the client said, heading into the passage.

"If you don't, I have," Drusa said, coming into the room. "I can see my customer has had a merry time with you," she smirked, folding her arms over her breasts. "And as you are already in that position it would be a shame to waste all the effort getting you there again."

Bulging Eyes gathered up the pile of ropes and shackles and put them back in the cupboard and stood leering into Africanus' open legs. But whatever he had in mind for the splendid black woman lying on her back with her legs spread was quickly dispelled when his formidable mistress returned, leading a gang of men behind her.

"You may have her," she said, standing aside, allowing the gang full view of Africanus' long legs and quivering slit. "There is time before her next client arrives so you'll have six minutes each to slake your lust. And if I were you I'd leave that ring in place. Her cunt looks all the better for it."

She went off to see how Magda was fairing, leaving the gang to form an orderly queue while the first lunged over Africanus' belly. They were common labourers working on the newly built Forum and word would soon spread that in the House of Figs there was a magnificent whore with a cunt like a mare. Drusa reckoned it was worth giving them a free fuck to save the cost of advertising. And while they rode her, she let herself into Magda's room and quietly locked the door.

Magda had had her fair share of punishment and sat sobbing on her bed.

"What's the matter with you?" Drusa enquired coldly.

"They whipped me," Magda said, hugging her breasts.

"That's what you're here for," Drusa snorted, casting a casual eye at an array of whips littering the floor. "Did any of them fuck you?"

"No, mistress," she sniffed, wiping her eyes with the back of her hand.

"What a waste, and such a pretty cunt ripe for the taking. I just don't know what these men are thinking of some times. Still, the night is young and there are plenty of customers waiting. I wonder how you would look dressed as a priestess of Nemesis, with your face chalked and your cunt shaven."

She went off, but did not take long to come back armed with a razor and bowl of white chalk powder and black face paint. To thwart any resistance, another woman accompanied her, slender and wiry, a face that brooked no nonsense.

"Shave this whore, then plaster her face with powder, paint her eyebrows black and dress her in this robe," Drusa quickly commanded. "If she argues, beat her."

"Yes, ma'am," the woman obeyed, throwing off her tunic.

Wearing nothing but a knowing smile, the woman stropped the razor, honing its edge and testing it with her thumb.

"Get on your back and put that cushion under your arse," the woman said, whipping up a pot of lather.

"I can see you've had a good seeing to," she added, throwing open Magda's legs.

"He made me hold my breasts while he whipped them," she uttered, settling her bum onto the cushion.

"You've got a nice pair," the woman acknowledged, whirling the brush into Magda's cunt. "And such a size for a girl of your age. I suppose they're hand reared?"

"I don't know what you mean," Magda said, knitting her brow.

"A girl's tits get bigger when they're fondled, especially when she's young."

"I didn't let anybody feel my tits," she lied, wondering what on earth it had to do with her.

The woman dropped the brush and picked up the razor, angling it skilfully into Magda's thigh crease.

"Keep still or I might end up slicing through your clit," she said crudely, neatly shaving around the labia.

Magda held her breath whilst the woman swept her wrist back and forth, humming quietly as she shaved her cunt naked.

"Now lie on your front and keep the cushion under your belly," she smiled, patting Magda's thigh.

A fresh dollop of lather plopped on her bottom hole and under her legs. The woman held her steady by resting her hand on the right buttock, giving little pinches and squeezes as the razor shaved away the last few remaining hairs and fluff growing around Magda's bottom.

"All done," she said gaily, slapping the shaven girl's buttocks.

But when she tried to get up the woman held her tight to the mattress and swung her leg over Magda's thighs. "There's a little bit of hair growing between your shoulder blades," she whispered, leaning over and spreading her legs.

Magda lay dead still as the woman wiped the blade through her shoulder blades. Her slender body was in motion now, moving stealthily across her raised bottom, gently rubbing her own shaven cunt into the soft, wobbling globes.

She finished shaving and Magda heard the razor rattle to the floor.

"Can I get up now, mistress?" she asked, pained at the way her whipped breasts crushed into the aged mattress.

"Call me, Carla," she whispered close. "And no, you can't get up yet. Does this feel good?" she asked, rubbing her sex harder over Magda's naked bottom.

She dug her knees into the mattress and, using them as supports, began riding her faster and faster. Her arms went out and she grabbed Magda's shoulders, gripping the collar bones tight. Magda winced as her fingers bit into the hollows.

"Please stop, you're hurting me," she wailed.

"It'll hurt a lot more if you don't stop squealing," she snapped, lifting her body then thumping her arse hard onto Magda's bottom.

Magda reached out and grabbed the bed rails, curling her fingers and biting her tongue as Carla's sex juddered and slapped into her bottom crease. Then suddenly the biting pain in her shoulders stopped and she felt Carla's hands slithering under her chest.

"Your tits are like pumpkins," she complimented, now lying fully over her.

Her small, pert breasts pressed hard onto Magda's bare back while she carefully laid the full length of her legs on the back of Magda's. Her tiny hands groped and squeezed each breast, rolling them around and around. Magda jolted when her fingers pinched on the nipples.

"If only I could have you as my slave," she whispered, blasting hot breath on the back of Magda's neck. "You'd like that, wouldn't you? Being ridden by me instead of those horrible men."

Magda froze like a corpse. She didn't know which was worse, being whipped on her tits or fucked by this half starved harridan. Then Carla stopped riding her and lifted her hips, sliding her hand under her legs and stroking her cunt until her fingers were thoroughly wet. She slipped sideways and inserted her soaking fingers deep into Magda's cunt, forcing them in to the knuckle.

"Come," she whispered. "Come all over my fingers, and afterwards you shall suck them."

Magda nodded her consent. All through her body tiny spasms started to prick and she felt her skin goose bump.

Her nipples were throbbing and between her legs a tingling sensation chilled her sex. A strong smell of female essence began to drift from Magda's sex and Carla angled her head on the pillow, flicking her tongue into Magda's ear.

"Shall I suck your cunt?" she breathed, nibbling the lobe.

Magda's lips parted with longing. "Yes," she muttered. "Suck my cunt."

Carla was off her quickly and rolling her over on her back. Like a weasel, her slender body slithered down the mattress and her head dived between Magda's thighs. Her long tongue lapped at the foaming sex lips, licking at the creaming juice pouring from the labia. Her hand went over Magda's plump belly, smoothing and poking around the navel, pressing hard where she knew the arousal was fiercest.

Magda threw back her head and let out a high-pitched howl, loud enough to echo along the passage and attract the attention of Drusa heading towards the door.

"Just as I thought," she hissed, lashing her cane hard onto Carla's back. "I ought to whip the pair of you for this. On your feet both of you."

Still in a sexual coma, Magda struggled to her feet, juice running from her sex, whilst Carla blushed furiously.

"Stand front to front and put your arms around your shoulders," Drusa ordered, flexing the cane.

When both women were pressed hard against each other, she lashed each one in turn, swinging her arm left and right, striking their naked buttocks, not stopping until she had delivered a dozen strokes.

"That's what you get for taking advantage of my whore," she hissed at Carla, whistling the cane into her pert bottom. "And this is what you get for encouraging her in the first place," she said to Magda, smacking the cane hard on her rump.

Magda might have said that she hadn't encouraged anything, but held her tongue as Drusa delivered the punishment. The final lashes came from the full strength of her arm, the cane almost splitting as it bounced off the welted cheeks.

"Now get the bitch dressed and painted," she seethed. "And if I catch you riding her again, I'll sell you as bait in the arena."

She went off mouthing curses, lashing at a harmless serving girl doing nothing more offensive than showing a prospective client into Africanus' room.

"I'm sorry I got you a flogging," Carla apologised, shaking out the robe and rubbing Magda's bottom.

"It was my fault, I shouldn't've made such a din," Magda offered, lifting her arms as Carla dropped it over her head. "Why do I have to wear all this stuff anyway?"

"Any man would pay a fortune to fuck a priestess from the Temple of Nemesis. That's why she's passing you off as one. Now sit down while I chalk your face."

"But what do I know about the Temple of Nemesis?"

"You don't have to know anything. All you have to do is fuck," she said flatly.

And she smeared a light coating of oil on Magda's face then applied the chalk powder, brushing it on with even strokes until she was covered. She dipped a brush in oil and soot and painted her eyebrows until they were finely arched.

"Now you look like a real priestess," Carla praised, standing back admiring her handiwork. Her voice lowered to a conspiratorial whisper as she gave Magda's breast an affectionate squeeze. "Thank you for not betraying me. That bitch would've thrashed me senseless if she knew I seduced you."

Magda looked in the darkened window at her reflection, her eyes like vacant moons. A thought flashed across her mind but was as speedily clouded when Drusa came in.

"You get out," she barked at Carla, sending her whip winging into her backside. "And you," she threatened, turning

201

to Magda, "will do what ever the client wants from you, because if you don't, I'll have you're arse throbbing for months. Got it?"

Magda nodded fast. "Yes, mistress," she said softly.

And Drusa beckoned him forward.

She looked up at her client and swallowed. He towered over her and was built like a statue his body a solid mass of rippling muscles and capable of crushing her skull with one hand. Scars from previous combats lined his torso and she guessed that he was either a gladiator, or had once been one.

He reached out and slammed the door in Drusa's face shaking the whole building. There was no need to lock it. No one would ever dare interrupt the former champion, Avitus and his whore.

Drusa had already informed him that Magda was a priestess from the Temple of Nemesis and although ready and willing to do his bidding was sworn to secrecy. He wasn't the slightest bit interested in the goings on inside the temple. On his last visit the Goddess had refused to answer the priestess' summons and he had lost in combat. Now the opportunity to avenge himself was too good to miss.

"Are you going to whip me?" she simpered, backing away from his gigantic frame.

"That's the very least you deserve," he grated, curling his lip. "But first I think we'll have a little sport. Take off that robe."

While she stripped herself naked, Avitus went to a cupboard and fetched a length of rope and two small jars of ointment.

"You're a fine-looking girl," he complimented, handing her one of the jars. "Now get on your knees and grease my cock."

Magda knelt, his cock hovering ominously at her lips. She scooped a finger of ointment and began oiling his shaft, going up and down his throbbing length, filling the groove and gently smearing the purple head. She took a generous dollop and filled her palm placing it under his balls and manipulating them in her hand. At first she thought it was no more than a thoughtful exercise, greasing his cock so it would slip easily inside her, but after a few moments she saw the real reason. His cock hardened and grew longer, and longer until the veins threatened to burst. His balls moved inside the sac, seemingly rotating against each other. The purple head shone like a polished plum and felt hot when he rubbed it against her cheek.

Instinctively she gripped the shaft and started tossing her hand, hoping he would come quickly, even if it did mean she might have to suck it, at least she would be spared having that thing pounding inside her cunt.

"Take your hand away from there," he said urgently, slapping the side of her head.

He grabbed her arms, forcing them behind her back. The rope went speedily around her wrists, binding them tightly and she saw the trailing end pass through a ring in the ceiling. His biceps flexed as he effortlessly pulled on the rope and Magda bent slowly forward, her shoulders and spine tearing at the sinews. Her face creased with pain as he lifted her by the wrists, and went on lifting until her body hung suspended and swaying.

"Open your legs," he rasped, slapping her buttocks.

Magda uttered a cry of pain and slowly spread her thighs. Her toes just touched the floor when her legs were fully open, but did nothing to alleviate the pain wrenching her back. For a moment nothing happened while he opened the other jar of ointment. She swallowed and blinked. The ointment was both cold and stinging when he generously worked it around her sex lips. He heard her grunt as his fingers went inside her, the greased tips covering her vaginal walls. He waited for a moment or two, going to the front of her and watching fascinated at the changing expressions crossing her face. She blushed from pale pink to scarlet and her lips visibly trembled at what was taking place inside her belly. At first it seemed no more than a mild tickling of her cunt, a curious sensation of needles and pins pricking her most intimate parts. But it was not long before the sensation increased to a desperate throbbing and she could feel her sex juices trickling from her lips. Her nipples enlarged and stood proud and erect from her thrusting breasts. All down the length of her outstretched legs the skin quivered and trembled. Her sex lips now swelled from a sudden inrush of blood and Avitus could see her cunt quivering and winking. Even the merest touch would have her screaming for sex. There was no denying it; the mistress of this seedy brothel certainly knew a trick or two when it came to having women on heat and begging for a good stiff cock. His own erection remained hard and long and it would be some time before the hardness abated, enough to satisfy the little whore, swaying and groaning on the rope.

"A splendid arse," she heard him mutter, as his fingertips roamed over the proffered cheeks, then slowly wormed into the crease smoothly stroking its tight silky depth.

Magda's legs shuddered and she turned her head in agony.

"Please master, fuck me," she begged, flexing her thighs.

He made no reply but nudged his cock between her quivering sex lips, only to withdraw and smooth it over her bottom.

Close to tears, Magda could only suffer his torments and the racking pain in her limbs. He moved around her, kneeling under her bent body and lifting his head to her breasts. His tongue flicked over her aching nipples teasing the buds and making them tingle until a flush reddened her sweating skin.

"You're like a cat on heat," he smiled, sucking on her nipples and biting them hard.

His arm went under her legs, raising her effortlessly. She hung suspended, her cunt rubbing into the crook of his arm. His fist clenched, gathering strength as he flexed his biceps then brought his forearm tight against her buttocks.

"Now squeeze your arse," he laughed derisively.

Magda wriggled her bottom wedged in the crook of his arm, gasping and moaning when her sex lips slithered against his bulging biceps. Again his lips sucked on her nipples, drawing them deep inside his mouth and then biting so hard she screamed.

"Why don't you just fuck me!" she sobbed, teetering on the edge of orgasm.

"Do you think you need fucking?" he asked, adding to her torments.

She nodded and sobbed, tears of anguished frustration streaming down her cheeks. "Please, I need it."

He lifted her higher, deftly balancing her weight on his arm. "Then I want to hear you beg."

"Please master, give me your cock," she complied, toppling over his head.

He dropped her and aimed his cock not where she so urgently needed it, but into her mouth.

"Now suck on that," he said bitterly, delighting in tormenting one of the priestesses who had contributed to his downfall in the arena.

Her mouth closed over the shining plum and with puckered lips she obediently obeyed. His hands went around the back of her head clamping it to his rippling torso. Her throat gurgled as he forced her head downwards, her mouth taking in as much as she could swallow. With her hands still tied behind her back there was little she could do to make him come except suck on the shaft almost choking her.

"That will do," he said at last, taking a tuft of her hair and pulling her head upright. "Now you've earned you reward."

He dropped her head and went behind her, kicking open her legs. Magda's cunt quivered at the sex lips in anticipation of being shafted with such a huge weapon, but anything was better than suffering anymore of this torment. It would have taken just the merest penetration to have her trembling in orgasm. Her breasts and nipples tingled and ached, a cold, clammy feeling stirred in her belly and she braced her hips ready to take him.

He was behind her now hands gripping her hips holding her steady. But then she saw his hand reach out for one of the jars.

"Now squirm," he said gruffly, slapping a handful of oil into her bottom crease.

He rubbed it in hard, gritting his teeth and moving his hand fast over her bottom, making sure the oil was worked well into her bottom hole. He emptied the jar over her sex lips until her pouting pink mound glistened. Even the movement of his palm against her sex had her mouth open and gasping.

"Now hold still," he told her, taking hold of his shaft and tickling the plum over her cheeks. Magda held her breath and waited…

The piercing shriek escaping her lips echoed through the brothel. Below in the tavern where more customers were gathered, Drusa's lips curled into a rueful smile. Above, Magda's arms were tearing from her shoulders as his cock juddered into her anus.

"Not there!" she wailed. "Please don't fuck me there."

It was too late and her pleas fell on deaf ears. His hands held her in a vice while his hips slammed against her arse cheeks. When she was fully impaled he released her hips and reached under her bent body savagely groping her breasts. Bent forward, her tits appeared much larger and more ripe than when she was standing upright and he feasted on her melons, rubbing them round and round, squeezing and squashing the globes against her chest, cupping and playing with each one in turn and all the while grinding his shaft deep into her bottom.

Drusa crept along the corridor like a spy, her face rigid and eyes glinting. A small hole in the wall allowed her to view the goings on and she saw framed in the hole, Magda rocking on her toes with the gladiator pumping her so hard his legs bowed.

"Serves the little shit right," she muttered, smiling at the thought that there were a dozen more clients ready and waiting to go where Avitus was at that moment. She moved on and peered through another hole conveniently situated at Africanus' door. The client she had just serviced lay on his back and she could only see the back of the black woman's head bobbing over his middle.

"I'm going to have you later," she thought aloud, trembling at the sight of Africanus' hips and bottom shining with sweat.

And she crept back to where Magda was now being properly fucked, her legs fully splayed and breasts jiggling from the pounding she was taking. Drusa stood up, her face screwed in thought. If the sight of watching Magda being well and truly fucked was enough to make her blood rush, it might have the same effect on her male clients. And she went downstairs to the tavern summoning Bulging Eyes who, when the brothel was closed for rest, would artfully enlarge the holes in the walls and then disguise them behind a shelf of bottles and goblets. There were plenty of men who would pay handsomely to watch her whores being whipped and fucked. She could probably squeeze a few extra denarii's if she threw in a girl slave to suck them off while they watched.

If she had thought of it earlier, whoever might have been watching would have seen Magda's arms straining at the rope while Avitus' cock rode her steadily, making her come time and time again.

"You're tight for a priestess used to her cock," he observed, slamming her hips back and forth.

Magda ground her teeth, thankful that he had unwittingly taken away the discomfort and pain of ravaging her freshly deflowered cunt. The combination of the oil and copious juice pouring from her sex allowed his shaft to ride her with the minimum of effort, and after a while she quickly learned to relax and let him penetrate her with long easy strokes. Only her arms and shoulders ached and, when at last he erupted into her, she breathed a sigh of relief and fell crashing to the floor.

"Now must come the whipping," he said, taking up a switch, long, supple and well-polished. "Where would you like it, on your bare arse, or on your thighs?"

"I don't want it anywhere," she wailed, hugging her knees.

His foot sailed into her ribs, turning her on her belly. "Spread your arms and legs," he said, swishing the switch through the foul air.

Magda struggled to obey, spreading her limbs until she formed an X shape.

"Now clench your cheeks, and keep them tight and I might give you less than you deserve." He paused, his arm in mid air. "Count the strokes," he commanded, and sent the switch cracking over her cheeks.

"One," she shrieked, writhing in agony, her hips and bottom twitching from the shock.

He saw her tiny hands form into fists and her breath held while she awaited the next blow.

"Two," she sobbed, clenching her cheeks so tightly they ached.

"A fine arse, and good hips too," he admitted, watching livid red welts manifesting across her pale skin.

"Thank you, master," she whispered, suddenly realizing that she could not count past ten.

He gave exactly that amount, lashing her buttocks with full strength, delighting in the hollow sound of the switch landing on naked flesh. She had the curious habit of wriggling her bottom when the switch lashed into the crease and he didn't need anymore oil to get another throbbing erection.

"Turn over," he said, tossing away the switch. "And get your legs in the air."

Magda rolled over and dutifully pointed her toes to the

ceiling. He was on her at once, penetrating her with a single thrust and riding her hard, grunting and groaning like a hog. Magda bucked her hips in time with his manic insertions and she came not in a flood but a gentle weeping. The juices dripped into her bottom crease, warm and comforting as he came in her with a gush.

They lay exhausted, his powerful arms under her shoulders holding her tight to his massive chest. Magda gazed absently at the wall, wondering how her mistress was fairing from the numerous men who had come and gone through her door.

But there was little time to dwell on that. As soon as Avitus had left, Drusa was in the room wrinkling her nose at the acrid smell of sex and sweat. Carla was quickly at her heels carrying a fresh supply of chalk powder and eyebrow paint.

"Scrub the bitch," Drusa ordered abruptly. "And rub some scent into her cunt. She stinks."

And Carla went about her trade fast and furious because in the corridor men were already getting into a queue, and Avitus was in the tavern telling everyone what a magnificent fuck the little priestess had been. And he booked her again, and again, and again.

# CHAPTER TWELVE

"Piglet! What are you doing in that get-up?" Africanus asked agog, when she came into Magda's room.

It was that time of the day when the whores were allowed to rest and regain their strength from the servicing of their clients, and were permitted to wander along the upper floors of the brothel.

"I'm supposed to be a priestess from the Temple of Nemesis," Magda informed, looking bedraggled and worn.

"I can see that," Africanus replied, staring at her young slave in amazement. "But where did you get that robe, and who painted your face?"

Magda told her everything and the black woman listened with growing astonishment. It seemed inconceivable that anyone outside the temple precinct could possibly pass themselves off as a priestess, let alone dress like one.

Then, as if some preternatural waves passed between them, both women stared at each other, going wide-eyed and open-mouthed. It was Magda who spoke first.

"It was her," she exclaimed. "She was the one who put that stuff in your goblet when you were in the temple."

"Drusa," muttered Africanus savagely. "The bitch passed herself off as a priestess and poisoned me. By all the Gods, I'm lucky to be alive. Oh sweet piglet," she burst out, hugging Magda close. "You tried to warn me and I was too stupid to listen."

"Yes mistress," Magda agreed, submitting to Africanus' fond embrace.

Africanus broke away and crashed her bottom on the sagging mattress. "I could've been killed if I had been fighting in the arena. The artful fucking cow. Wait 'til I get hold of her. I'll rip her head off."

The full implication of what might have happened now

sank in and it was several minutes before she regained composure. She stopped trembling and swearing and her face went into deep thought. Wanting to rip off Drusa's head was one thing. Doing it was quite another. And she had friends here, numerous and powerful. A woman like that didn't very often make mistakes, except one.

"If she hadn't dressed you in that robe I would never have guessed," Africanus said slowly, rising from the creaking bed. "But you do look the part," she laughed, cupping Magda's face and kissing her full on the lips.

"Men like fucking priestess'," Magda smiled slyly. "And did they give it me. You wouldn't believe the things they made me do."

Africanus shot her a dry look. "Oh yes I could," she said dully. "And I have a shrewd feeling that you enjoyed some of it."

Magda blushed, smiling at the remembrance of Avitus' massive cock punishing her virginal cunt, and Africanus playfully tweaked her nipple. Well, it had to happen sooner or later. But now there were more important things on her mind than piglet's deflowering.

"If you could get out of here," Africanus muttered, smoothing the robe and wiping her finger along the blackened eyebrows. "No one would dare touch you if they thought you were a real priestess. You must get to Quintus and tell him everything you know about Drusa and this fucking awful place. He'll know what to do."

She paced the room, looking out of the window and then quietly opened the door and peered along the passage. It was unusually dark and gloomy, and the silence that greeted her seemed peculiarly emphatic. She distinctly caught the clicking of door handles from somewhere in the shadows, and the very subdued whispering of harsh, uncouth voices. There was no doubt that all the whore's rooms were being stealthily watched by Drusa's myrmidons.

211

"Summon this woman, Carla," Africanus said softly, and Magda went along the corridor bawling her name.

It wasn't long before she arrived, semi naked, attired only in a piece of tattered cloth knotted around her waist.

"Are you a slave to Drusa?" Africanus asked, casting her eyes over the slender woman.

"She bought me from the fuller's," Carla admitted. "It was terrible there I can tell you. I had to stand knee deep in piss trampling over the clothes, and didn't I stink afterwards."

You don't smell too sweetly now, Africanus thought, but kept that thought silent. "Does Drusa flog you, or are you a whore like the rest of us?"

Carla turned and lifted the tattered cloth revealing a pair of tight, pert buttocks well crossed with whip welts, telling Africanus what she wanted to know.

"I know a man who would pay you handsomely to get us out of here," she said. "All you have to do is escort Magda to the house of Quintus Varus and let her do the rest."

"There's no way out of here except through the door that leads to the alley where I empty the shit buckets, and I'm the only one allowed to go there. And I'm watched every time by the guard."

Fuck, thought Africanus. It seemed that Drusa was always one step ahead. "Do you have sex with him?"

"I have it with everybody," she said sadly.

"And you are going to have it with him now," Africanus said bluntly. "Let him fuck you up against the wall and make sure his back is turned. You'll be well rewarded, I promise you."

Magda wrapped a blanket around the white robe to darken it and Carla picked up the shit bucket.

"Where do you think you're going?" the guard at the end of the passage asked Magda.

"She needs to shit and the bucket's full," Carla said quickly.

"Why can't she hang her arse out of the window?"

"If a turd caught one of the consuls you'd be for the arena," Carla replied.

He couldn't deny that. One never knew who would be passing in and out of the tavern below. He jerked his head and the two women descended the staircase.

At the bottom of the stairs Magda halted whilst Carla went about her duties emptying the bucket into a drain and coming back and accidentally catching the tattered cloth on the door jamb. She struggled and it conveniently ripped leaving her naked. She wasn't in bad condition for a brothel slave at the beck and call of anybody who wanted a casual fuck, and the guard looked at her with undisguised relish as she bent over to retrieve the cloth.

While they coupled, Carla artfully placing her back against the wall and positioning him neatly in front of her, Magda slipped through the door and into the street. Attired now as a priestess, she passed unmolested through the throng and made her way to Quintus' villa.

"You expect me to believe that!" Quintus sneered after Magda delivered her story. "A brothel keeper inveigled her way into the inner sanctum of the temple, passed herself off as a priestess and poisoned my best gladiatrix. Pooh, I've never heard such rubbish."

"But it's true, master!" Magda protested. "I saw her!"

Quintus eyed her with an air of ambiguity. Dimly he recalled her mentioning something about the temple, but that was before he had sold her so her story might have some credence after all.

"I shall report your story to the authorities and have this place raided," he said sternly. "But if you've lied to save your mistress, I'll have you both executed."

Magda swallowed hard. That was one thing she hadn't bargained for, and she went off to change hoping that Carla wouldn't lose her nerve under interrogation.

The magistrate moved fast. Violating a sacred temple was

a very serious matter and he was in the mood for raiding a brothel. As a rule prostitutes threatened with the death penalty would do anything to be acquitted and he hadn't had a decent shag in a long time.

There was no shortage of volunteers from the local garrison and captain Octavius led his men through the streets resplendent in gleaming armour and marching in perfect time.

"I wish to speak with the owner of this pit," he said, striding into the brothel tavern.

Drusa leaned over the balcony and almost discharged her bowels.

"Fuck," she swore, instantly recognizing Octavius, who in turn would just as quickly recognize the woman who had tried to pass herself off as a sister of a general who didn't even exist.

"I come by the authority of the People and Senate of Rome," he announced, casting his eyes over the frightened assembly. "On a charge that a whore from this dump was forced to impersonate a priestess from the temple of Nemesis. If that be true I shall arrest all those concerned."

"Can I help you?" Drusa asked innocently, coming down the stairs.

A look of total disgust came over his face. "Well, well," he said, placing his hands on his hips. "If it isn't the sister of General Felix."

Drusa ignored that jibe and motioned him to a chair. A slave quickly fetched a jug of wine and put it on the table.

"What is all this?" she asked, pouring him a drink. "One of my whores posing as a priestess. I've never heard the like of it."

"Bring the witness," he said dully, but finding it difficult to keep a straight face. She was as beautiful as he remembered. Not a hair out of place and her legs shining and shapely.

Magda was brought in and stood before Drusa who affected total surprise.

214

"Who is this woman?" she asked.

Octavius wasn't sure whether she was lying or telling the truth. Drusa leaned back in her seat casually ignoring the transparent dress stretching tightly over her thrusting breasts.

"I think someone is having a joke at your expense," she said seriously and folding her hands in her lap.

"Ask Carla," Magda panicked. "She was the woman who painted my face with chalk and blackened my…"

"Shut your mouth!" Octavius interrupted.

He looked Drusa hard in the face, watching for any signs of panic. But she remained perfectly composed and crossed her magnificent legs, letting the dress ride up her creamy thigh.

"Bring me this woman, Carla," he said, raising a goblet to his lips and eyeing her erect nipples over the rim.

Carla was fetched and instantly denied ever having set eyes on Magda. She was no longer wearing her usual rags but was attired in a blue linen dress, her face heavily painted whose layers of make up hid the bruises around her eyes.

"Ask my mistress, Africanus," Magda said, going weak at the knees.

"Who?" Drusa returned. "We have no woman here by that name."

Octavius crashed the goblet to the table. "Search the dump," he ordered, just as a plate brimming with fresh oysters and fish arrived.

"Please allow your men to refresh themselves. All on the house," Drusa offered, leaning forward, lowering her voice and letting her breasts squash on the table top. "And if there is anything you require captain, I'm sure you can be amply accommodated."

Under the table her knees nudged those of the captain, but she was careful not to overdo things and promptly sat upright. His men clattered down the stairs knocking over a table and a whore.

"Nothing," the sergeant said flatly. "No one here by that name. Or any black women either."

Octavius' face clouded. "Have the girl flogged for wasting public money and then hand her over to the magistrate."

"Ohhh," Drusa sighed sympathetically. "The girl is a simpleton, captain. Look at her; anyone can see she's deranged. Please don't punish her. I'm sure I can find her a place, you know, cleaning tables and scrubbing the floors. That sort of thing."

"You're very considerate," he said on a note of sarcasm. "But she deserves a flogging. Have her stripped and flogged immediately, then give her to this woman."

A bowl of fruit arrived and another bottle of good wine. Drusa excused herself and ordered everyone back to work, but not before the whores had paired off with the soldiers and each man presented with a bottle.

"You seem to have done well for yourself," Octavius complimented, when they were alone in Drusa's room.

"We are all on the wheel of fortune and make our way the best we can," she smiled, closing the window shutters. "Now, how can I help you?"

And she stripped off her robe and straddled his thighs, whilst in the courtyard below Magda was writhing in agony from a cat o' nine tails lashing into her back and buttocks.


"I might've guessed you'd try something like that," Drusa said, standing over Africanus.

She was bound and chained in the cellar, her face utterly crestfallen. Drusa had moved fast after Magda's escape and had narrowly avoided having her whole operation confiscated, not to mention being condemned to death.

"So I took the necessary precautions, and now that little farce is over it brings me back to you, and that other troublesome wretch. There is no doubt in my mind you will attempt the same thing again, which is why I'm selling you both, but not before you've earned me compensation for all the trouble you've caused."

She turned and saw Magda dragged into the cellar, naked and well-whipped. "Have them chained and taken to the Water Gate."

"I'm sorry, Piglet. It's all my fault," Africanus apologised, as they were hauled outside, tightly chained and manacled.

"It's all that bitch's doing," Magda said bravely. "She lied and then fucked the captain of the guard."

"Men are so weak," Africanus said disgustedly, unaware of Drusa's former encounter with Octavius, and the bag of gold she had presented him after he had fucked her sore.

They stood side by side whilst one of Drusa's henchmen placed a long wooden pole across their shoulders. He held it in place whilst the collars fitted around their necks were secured to the shaft. More chains linked their wrists and ankles, and when they were ready to make their journey to the Water Gate Drusa made her final appearance.

"Both of you have far too much to say for yourselves," she quipped, opening a leather pouch. "And so as a precaution I shall have you rendered dumb until you are safely on the river. Open your mouths."

Bulging Eyes was ready and waiting with two long sharp needles.

"Put out yer tongues," he grunted, rolling his horrible eyes.

He went to Africanus first, holding the tip of her tongue between a pair of pinchers whilst he shoved the pin through her tongue.

"Aroogh!" she grunted, recoiling backwards.

Magda's tongue fast disappeared inside her clamping jaws. Africanus' tongue still poked from her mouth speared with the needle. Saliva had already gathered at the corners of her mouth and dribbled over her chin.

"Open yer gob," Bulging Eyes snarled, watched by his evil grinning mistress.

"I'll keep my mouth shut, I promise," Magda shivered. "But please, don't put that thing through my tongue."

"You should've thought of that before you opened it in the first place," Drusa reminded her unsympathetically. "Now do as you're told."

She reached over and grabbed Magda's hair, twisting it until the young slave's neck almost snapped. In her agony she let out a scream and Bulging Eyes nipped the end of her tongue, pulling it from her mouth.

"Aaaraaagh, you furkig bidch," Magda managed, before her tongue was fully pierced.

"I wish you both a pleasant journey," Drusa said viciously and, as a farewell present sent the flat of her hand slapping into their breasts. "When you are clear of the city you may use them as you desire. These miserable offerings are of no further value," she said, turning to the boatman.

He affected a polite bow and herded them into the street, whipping their hinds towards the Water Gate and the barge that lay moored alongside the quay.

To their surprise, they were not the only passengers crowded in the fetid hold. A dozen other women, naked and chained sat in huddled groups; slaves who had outlived their usefulness, or who could no longer command a good price in the city slave market. Relieved of the needles, Africanus and Magda were seated in the stern and it didn't take them long to realize that they were in the company of the very dregs of womankind.

"Piglet," Africanus whispered, edging closer. "I sense a fight breaking out any moment. Just stay close and keep your head down. I'll handle these sows."

It happened much sooner than she thought. In the semi darkness a fist lashed out and struck the side of a face which howled in pain. As if acting on a signal the whole hold erupted in a melee of swinging arms and kicking legs. Hands clutched at tufts of hair and feet sailed into naked rumps. Still manacled at their wrists and ankles, Africanus and Magda got to their feet, keeping their backs to the hull while the fighting increased in its ferocity. The lengths of chain were used to full effect, wrapped deftly around unsuspecting necks and almost strangling the victim, whilst a thin, nubile redhead leapt onto the back of a more sturdy blonde and attempted to gouge out her eyes. A dark-skinned brunette headed straight for Magda but was swiftly averted by a savage kick in her cunt delivered by a tall shaven-headed woman. The brunette doubled up in pain and was felled with a fist cracking into her jaw. Through the gloom, Magda saw a closely-cropped woman crash to the floor and her pretty assailant leaping on top of her and biting her nipples with razor sharp teeth. When the nubile redhead came for Magda, Africanus, taking her weight on one leg delivered a blow directly between her legs and she lifted bodily and went sailing backwards against the hull. But fighting is exhausting work and one by one those who were left standing fell to their knees, bloodied and bruised, panting and snorting, wiping away trails of mucus dribbling from their mouths and nostrils. The fighting ceased almost as speedily as it had begun and an unnatural silence pervaded the darkened hold broken only by subdued groans and swearing.

"They must be mad," Magda whispered, surveying a scene of carnage.

"It's not madness, Piglet," replied Africanus, after a few moments of deep meditation. "It's lack of cock."

"What?" exclaimed Magda.

"Cock, Piglet," continued the black woman, with knowing emphasis. "It's lack of cock that makes women violent, and looking at these animals, I should say they haven't been fucked in a long while. I reckon they're criminals let out from prison and sold to the same place as we're headed."

Magda swallowed hard. She could see the women biting their lips and clenching their fists in frustration. One or two were blatantly fingering themselves and others were fondling the breasts and thighs of their neighbours. Only a slender girl with a thin face and extraordinarily wide mouth had not taken part in the affray, and now she sat alone, pressing her face to the timbers, peering through a hole and watching the passing scenery.

"What can you see?" Africanus whispered.

She took her head away and turned abruptly at the tall shaven-headed woman who was standing legs apart and gushing urine over the dazed brunette, much to the amusement of the other bruised women.

The slender girl watched the crude display for several moments then came over to where Africanus and Magda were seated. On her shoulder a number had been branded into her skin, a sure sign that she had been a convict.

"At a guess we're heading through the Gorge," she said, stretching out her legs.

Her breasts were small and pert but with huge dark areolas and large sprouting nipples. Without a word she took Africanus' hand and placed it on her sex mound, rubbing it gently back and forth. Africanus knew at once what she wanted and leaned over sucking on the girl's begging teats. She spread her legs wider allowing Africanus to slip her fingers inside her sex. Her head rolled against the hull, eyes closed and lips parting in ecstasy. Magda encouraged by Africanus' willingness to satisfy the girl, couldn't help but worm her hand under her mistress' bottom and finger the dark, scented sex.

The slender girl opened her eyes and stared Africanus in the face.

"Please, suck me," she pleaded softly.

How could Africanus deny the girl a few moments of pleasure not knowing where they were destined or to whom they might be sold?

The entrance to the slender girl's sex was unusually large,

whether it was natural or had been stretched from so much trafficking was not her concern. She wriggled between her legs and pressed her face into the quivering lips. Her tongue searched deep, flicking around the sex walls and tasting a strong musky scent oozing from her already hot and sweating cunt.

"Make me come," the girl sobbed, rolling her eyes.

Africanus' bottom jolted as Magda's fingers fluttered inside her. She took a quick look around the hold. Most of the women were either sleeping or foully cursing each other. One or two were pressing their naked bodies close together, going through the motions of feminine love making.

She rapidly flicked her tongue, so fast it blurred and at the same time pushed her face forward onto the girl's cunt. She opened her mouth embracing the girl's sex lips, hungrily feasting herself on the swelling, pouting labia. Several times she thought the girl would explode with climactic release. Her whole body trembled and quivered, but with amazing self control she held off, delaying her climax for as long as she could. Her breathing came in harsh, heavy pants through her wide-open mouth. Her skin shone with sweat and she reached out clinging at the chains hanging from the walls. Africanus sucked on the girl's love bud, nibbling and biting the tender flesh, but fully conscious of Magda's fingers fluttering delicately inside her. The slender girl bit hard on her lip and uttered a muffled grunt and then, with a sudden heave of her hips, poured a torrent of sex juice over Africanus' face. She gulped and swallowed and for a moment it seemed she was drowning in an endless river. The girl gave another heave of her hips and expelled a faster flowing stream which Africanus couldn't prevent cascading over her chin and trickling between her breasts. She made to remove her soaking face but the girl seized her head holding it fast.

"Leave it for a while," she whispered, raking her nails across Africanus' scalp.

221

Then Africanus uttered a subdued moan and, arching her back, reached her own climax.

The girl sighed and released her grip, going limp and exhausted.

"No one's done that in a long while," she breathed, her lips creasing into a happy, satisfied smile.

"The Gods have certainly favoured you," Africanus remarked tactfully.

"You mean, I have a big cunt," she replied humorously. "I was captured by a neighbouring tribe and given to a man with a large cock. I couldn't take it so they put a ring in me and after a while exchanged it for a bigger one, and kept on doing it until my cunt was as big as a goat's. Now I can't find a man to satisfy me."

"Poor girl," Africanus sympathised, remembering her encounter with Proteus and his outsized organ.

But even he would have been hard pressed to satisfy her.

The hull gave a sudden lurch and bumped against the bank. Overhead the urgent sound of footsteps ran back and forth, and the hatch was suddenly drawn back.

"On deck, you animals," the boatman bawled, turning pale from the stench rising from the sweat-grimed bodies.

"Fuck you," the shaven-headed one swore, bending over and displaying her buttocks.

"That just earned you a dozen lashes," the boatmen promised, shaking his whip over the hatchway.

The women went up the ladder in a procession of naked thighs and buttocks, prodded and stabbed by the stock of the whip. When the shaven-headed woman clambered onto the deck she was promptly seized and hurried to the mast. Her hands were taken around its girth and just as promptly tied.

The other women formed a semi-circle on the deck; some idly leaning against the gunwale, one or two casting their eyes upwards at the towering cliffs, and others watching disinterestedly as the whip sailed into the proffered buttocks.

A deep satisfying groan escaped the woman's lips as the lash descended on her broad buttocks. It would be unjust in describing her arse as fat, because although it was ample in its proportions, the buttock halves were strong and firm and easily capable of absorbing the cracking whip.

At the third stroke the woman slowly raised her left thigh and began rubbing it against the mast. The expression on her face changed from anguished pain to one of pure and contented pleasure.

"See, I told you these bitches haven't been fucked in a long while," Africanus observed, watching the woman pressing her body tighter into the mast. At every fresh stroke she writhed and squirmed, now forcing her belly and breasts on the smooth, weather-beaten wood, then rubbing her sex mound, spreading her legs and angling her cunt for maximum satisfaction. Her breasts, huge and globular wobbled and shook and, as Magda leaned forward for a closer view, the nipples rose to the size of baby's thumbs. Her face was flushed with ecstasy; her mouth open and panting, the eyelids drooping as if she were really embracing a cock deep in her sex.

Then, to the surprise of everyone aboard, she raised her right thigh and clung like a limpet, thrusting out her whole bottom.

"Give the dirty cow another dozen," one of the women jeered.

The boatman needed no second telling and, after taking a hefty pull from a wine bottle, resumed thrashing her willing rump. She bucked and jerked, working her pelvis faster and faster and it needed no imagination to see she was fast approaching her climax. But then the boatmen dropped his whip and his breeches. While she clung fast to the shaft, sobbing and moaning, his hands gripped her hips and lowered her expertly onto his hardened cock. She let out a long sigh and allowed her body to impale itself on the throbbing organ prodding inside her sex. Suddenly the hard insertions seemed to evaporate the pain scalding her whipped bottom and she returned his thrusting with a splendid rotating motion of her hips and buttocks.

"What an artful cow," one of the women hissed savagely. "She did that on purpose."

If raising her thighs and offering her bottom was an incitement to sex, she wasn't disappointed. The boatman rode her hard, thumping his thighs unceremoniously against her wobbling cheeks and just for sport, started slapping her ribs.

"Get used to this," Africanus muttered to Magda, listening to the woman's orgiastic howls and grunts. "Because wherever we're going, we're going to get a lot more."

"I hope so," the slender girl with the wide mouth added, her thighs already twitching at the prospect.

The boatman spurted into the woman with a grunt and staggered backwards grinning like an imbecile. The mate cut the ropes around the woman's wrists and she slumped into a blubbering heap, her legs falling open giving a wonderful display of her juice-drenched sex. He kicked her ribs and ordered her to stand and take her place with the other slaves now lining up at the gang plank.

They filed off and headed up a steep bank roped together and carrying large sacks on their heads like a line of draught animals. The boatman and his ugly crew were no longer jovial, but lashed their whips with gay abandon into the rumps of the heavily-burdened women, driving them ever upwards, seemingly towards the gaping mouth of a cavern high up in the cliff side. At intervals they passed skulls mounted on stakes which greeted them with macabre grins. Africanus was certain their progress was being steadily watched and followed by unseen furtive eyes, and the further the file progressed the more certain the feeling. Near the cave mouth they rounded a bend and halted, dropping their loads and wiping sweat from their stinging eyes.

"Hail Belgeron, King of the Regnentes," the boatman greeted, affecting a bow. "I bring you fresh slaves and sacks of grain."

The man standing at the cave mouth looked more like a creature from the underworld than an imperial ruler. He stood well over six feet in height and was clothed in animal skins. His face was hidden under a huge shaggy beard and an explosion of wild, unkempt hair. But his eyes were aglow with primitive, unbridled lust as he surveyed the file of naked slave women, now rigid and silent. Inside the gloomy cavern, Africanus caught sight of more sinister looking creatures passing stealthily to and fro. Ferocious looking dogs guarded the cave entrance and padded towards the naked women encircling their legs and sniffing at their cunts.

"Bring them inside," the King ordered, eyeing in particular the nubile redhead.

The cave entrance led into a chamber of much greater proportions, which went deeper into the cliff face and faded into total darkness. Piles of weapons lay in jumbled heaps against the walls and recently skinned carcasses hung from crude wooden frames. There was no furniture of any kind except upturned barrels which served as tables still littered with plates of bones and goblets. The occupants, it seemed slept on the earthen floor using an animal skin as a mattress. The tribe left their fires and gathered around the women, some almost naked, their skin painted with woad, others were more fully covered in skins and their hair had been fashioned into crudely-woven braids. Yet oddly, most of them wore golden rings and necklaces, and some had brooches attached to the braids. It did not take the women long to realize they were in the abode of bandits, outlaws and thieves who lived on the very edge of civilisation.

"You may keep them for as long as you like," the boatmen explained to the King. "But up until you sell them, their rightful owners expect payment in gold."

Africanus' throat went dry. She understood at once that the payment for keeping her and Magda was the compensation Drusa demanded, and she had a sinking feeling it would be a long time before these savages decided to part with any of the slaves.

"I accept," the King agreed, going off into the depths of the cavern.

He came back with a leather bag and tossed it at the boatman, who counted out the contents and seemed satisfied. This wasn't the first shipment of slaves he'd delivered to be used and then sold to whomsoever the King chose, and it certainly wouldn't be the last. He also brought useful information concerning Roman troop movements and baggage trains, not to mention wealthy travellers who could be easily waylaid and robbed, or if the rewards seemed worthwhile, taken as hostages.

"Pair them off," the King grunted, eyeing the slender, wide-mouthed girl. "And when you've had your fill, change them, if your cocks are up to it."

The whole band rushed forward grabbing the women and dragging them roughly by the arms to their awaiting beds. Africanus had no doubt that she would have at least half the band before they sold her on. She only hoped that Magda would survive being so thoroughly fucked. Mercifully there was no sign of whips, chains or any apparatus on which the women might be tormented or flogged, just a tribe of wild, unkempt savages bent on having equally savage sex.

The creature that had dragged Africanus to a darkened enclave stripped off his fur skins and stood naked before her. She knelt on his rude bed and looked up at his cock. Wordlessly she closed her hand around the shaft and began slowly stroking it.

"Hmm... good," he murmured, placing his hand on the back of her head.

Her tongue dropped from her mouth and she rested the

plum on her lower lip licking at the underside of his shaft. Her free hand embraced his balls, larger than normal and tight in the crinkled sac. Out of the corner of her eye she saw the wide-mouthed girl on all fours with the King pumping hard at her rump, whilst his kinsmen filled her mouth, an astonished look on his face as she easily swallowed his length. Soon, the cavern was filled with sounds of sex; grunting and heaving echoing from all corners, and the slapping of bellies and buttocks. Magda was on her back, her legs wrapped around her lover's back, seemingly enjoying the sensation of his grinding cock.

Africanus slipped the savage's cock from her mouth and rolled backwards, her legs spread and knees bent.

"Good thighs," he grunted, kneeling between them and kneading the flesh with his rough hands.

"You've got a nice body," she returned truthfully, squeezing his biceps.

He was strongly built with a body well-honed from combat and strenuous hunting in the forest. Neither was he as ugly as at first appeared with a powerful square jaw and eyes that were not cruel, just fierce and penetrating, eyes that some women find sexually attractive. Numerous braids had been woven in his hair and hung with gold pendants.

His hand went out, groping and squeezing each breast in turn, not crushing the soft orbs but gently savouring their full ripeness. He pinched each nipple, watching fascinated as the buds rose erect and throbbing. His cock had reached full length and he rested it on her pubic mound, rubbing it softly to and fro over the tight nest of curls. Whilst his hips moved over her thighs he put two fingers in her mouth and she sucked them in, moving her voluptuous lips up and down from tip to knuckle. His free hand delivered a hard slap on her thigh instantly filling her with longing. The sexual battering she had anticipated was not going to happen. She realized that now he was actually enjoying her, treating her as a delicious plaything, providing she was willing to do anything that was expected of her.

"I am a slave," she reminded herself. "And it is my duty to obey my master."

He placed the plum of his cock at the portals of her sex and filled her with a ferocious pelvic thrust.

"Oooh," she sucked her breath, holding it in her lungs as he thrust again, slamming his cock deep into her cunt.

Then, without warning, his arms went under her shoulders and rolled her over and she lay on top and astride him.

"Sit up," he commanded, his voice stern and brooking no resistance.

Africanus seated herself upright impaled on his shaft, and again its hardness caught her breath.

"Now ride, you dirty whore," he hissed, slapping her thigh so hard it numbed.

Her eyes blinked and stared in shock. The tenderness had evaporated and in its place a sudden longing for animal sex had filled his loins.

All right, she thought, if that's what you want, that's what you'll get.

She wriggled into position, settling her bottom over his cock, making sure she was well penetrated, then rocked her hips and buttocks.

"Faster!" he croaked, slapping her breasts.

He took a handful of her braids and dragged her head towards his chest. For a moment it seemed her hair would rip at the roots, but then the grip slackened and he kissed her full on the lips, driving his tongue deep in her throat. Months of pent up emotion broke like waters over a dam and he reached out, fumbling amongst the furs. He found what he wanted and Africanus' spine arched from the belt winging into her back.

"I'll beat you raw if you don't fuck," he rasped, lashing at her ribs.

Africanus reached out and closed her hands like talons around the loose flesh of his breast. He groaned as her nails pierced his skin and twisted it.

"I'll fuck you!" she shrieked, eyes blazing with anger.

He returned her painful squeezing with whistling lashes of the belt all around her pounding buttocks.

But as the scalding pain burnt deeper into her bottom and thighs, the desire for greater pain arose within her now soaking sex.

"Slap my tits!" she shrieked, sitting upright and thrusting them forward.

They were large, larger than any other pair he'd ever had the pleasure to own, and he wasted no time in fulfilling her demand. His hand sailed over each nipple, striking so hard the erect buds all but disappeared into the surrounding areolas. He hit them until they were sore and then placed both hands on the sides of the swinging globes and crushed them together. The crease seemed twice as deep and long stretching from chest to navel as she leaned forward, angling her hips for maximum penetration. He was harder now and she could feel the tip of his plum nudging the base of her womb. She flexed and squeezed her vaginal walls, gripping the length of his shaft in a wavering, fleshy glove.

"Good," he breathed, sitting up and hugging her body close.

An acrid smell of sweat arose from their joined bodies and they slithered together like mating serpents. Their hands went everywhere, nails raked into backs and thighs, fists pounded into ribs, and above all came the indescribable intoxicated feeling that only derives from deep penetrated sex.

His coarse hands gripped her buttocks and he uttered a deep-throated purr as he pulled apart the wobbling halves. His fingers wormed into the bottom crease exploring its dark valley of hot, sweating skin. Africanus raised her haunches allowing his fingers to penetrate her bottom hole. For a half wild savage existing on the fringes of civilisation he knew a great deal about the sensitive and secret places of women, and she jolted as he touched the rippling corrugations of her anus.

"How did you know where that is?" she asked, a cold thrill chilling her belly.

"A woman's arse is as good a fuck as her cunt," he said primitively, wiggling his fingers.

Her buttocks flexed tight holding his finger and he moved it slowly back and forth tickling the soft tissue within. Her arms went around his back savouring the sheer animal strength of his muscles, hard and solid. She lifted her bottom higher and brought her knees level with his chest.

"Keep still," she whispered, and unfolded her legs, aiming them straight over his shoulders until her whole weight bore down on his shaft. His hands were quickly away from her bottom and around her shoulders, supporting her while she balanced on his middle. His head twisted from side to side, tongue flicking rapidly over her silky skin.

Heart racing, Africanus reached out and snatched up the belt.

"Beat me," she rasped, hardly able to speak. "Please, beat me hard. Prove I'm your slave."

A little surprised, he took the belt and coiled it around his fist until only half its length remained but enough to give what she so desperately needed. A long, swift uppercut brought the leather cracking against the bare expanse of her naked back. A sharp burning dart shot up her protruding spine and she let out a long harsh groan.

"Harder," she muttered. "Belt the shit from me."

That was a language he could much more readily understand. He appreciated women who liked a beating when they were being fucked. And the belt resounded with a hollow thump against her ribs. At every stroke her arse jolted and bucked and he could feel the wetness rising inside her. His cock was harder than he could ever remember and with a long, shapely pair of glistening ebony legs resting over his shoulders he felt himself amongst the Gods. Her arse was equally as beautiful, the splendid dark buttocks bouncing joyfully both from the pain of the belt and the hardness of his cock had him wondering if the King would allow him to have her as his exclusive woman slave. Her breasts shook over his chest, the nipples just lightly grazing his skin, and he stopped beating her and reaching under her arms, grabbed both spheres and rolled them under his horny palms. It was the roughness of his hands that had her gasping. Each coarse squashing of her soft flesh sent ripples of pleasure through her belly, and when he crushed her nipples between his fingers and thumbs she went wild. Clinging like a limpet to his shoulders, she bounced her bottom, wriggling like a rabbit in a trap, making her hips writhe and dance, juddering her legs against his head. His hands went swiftly to her legs, stroking and kneading the long length of her powerful thighs, then going under the graceful curve of her calves.

Africanus released her grip and leaned backwards letting his cock glide against her clit. She threw back her head and gasped for air. All at once her whole body broke into a shining sweat.

"Pump your spunk," she shrieked, loud enough to send an echo resonating into the darkened depths.

The beautiful black slave reached her orgasm, her body alive with movement, twisting and writhing, legs as straight as arrows, breasts wobbling and slapping, the nipples so swollen they seemed to twitch. She uttered a howl and slipped her hands away from the bandit's neck, her back falling full length over his legs. For several minutes she kept his cock deep in her cunt and slammed her sex hard on its root. Then, with another grunt and heave of her hips, her orgasm reached its climax and she lay still, panting and gasping, her whole body limp from exhaustion.

For five long sex-crazed months, Africanus, Magda, and

the all the other women lived in the cave, waiting upon their savage Lords: cooking, skinning animals, fetching wood and berries from the forest, and then returning for night after night of wild, unrelenting sex, changing partners as the whim took them, fucking every man in the place. It was towards autumn when the first chill winds breezed into the cave that a party of Phoenician traders arrived.

"Who is she?" the Phoenician asked, watching the black woman sliding from her lover's cock.

The King shrugged. "A slave I've hired for the pleasure of my men," he informed, sensing a profitable interest.

"And the rest?"

"They are all for sale," he said quickly, motioning to his second in command.

The women, some still in the throes of orgasm were dragged into a ragged line, naked and wearing the fresh bloom of sex on their flushed faces.

"They're a sorry looking heap," the Phoenician remarked, running his eyes over the shaven-headed one.

He walked along the line inspecting each slave in turn, careful not to show much interest, but couldn't help pausing over the girl with the wide mouth and the tall black one with long thighs and more than generous breasts. The nubile redhead also caught his attention and all three were singled out for possible purchase.

"I've hired all of them," the King was quick to point out, and fell into a long preamble about how much he had to pay their owners before he could even consider selling them.

The Phoenician snapped his fingers and more traders entered the cave bearing wooden boxes and bolts of finely woven cloth. The King might have been a savage, but he had a keen eye for business and knew that the boxes of onyx and alabaster would fetch good prices, not to mention the gold. There was more than enough to pay off the contract on the slaves, plus the selling price would turn a handsome profit.

Both he and the Phoenician set to bargaining; the King pointing out the merits of the women, particularly Africanus' sexual resilience, and the sport to be had from the wide-mouthed girl. The redhead was an especially good fuck, he added.

The Phoenician expertly checked each slave, feeling their breasts and thighs, slapping their buttocks and haunches. They bent over and touched their toes whilst he fingered their intimate parts. He checked their teeth and tongues, and when it came to the wide-mouthed girl made a crude joke which rocked the entire assembly.

The price he offered was a fair one and the savage King knew he would not be budged.

All three women were closely chained to an awaiting sledge loaded with heavy bundles of tin, iron and animal skins. Magda watched her former mistress straining under the weight and waved her farewell.

"Goodbye, Piglet," Africanus called out, wishing that they could have at least embraced.

Magda shed a tear and turned directly to the bandit who had fucked her until her cunt was sore. She watched Africanus out of sight and fell into his arms, reaching for his cock. She hoped it would be a long time before she was sold, and the bandit carried her back to his bed and was instantly between her thighs.

At the river's edge, the boatman showed no surprise that three of the slaves had been singled out for sale. He had rightly guessed that the tall black woman and the redhead would be amongst them.

He packed the cargo and the women into the hold and set off for the estuary. The Phoenicians rode ahead and were waiting with their ship when he unloaded the cargo.

"Have the women chained," the trader said, going into his cabin.

Herded below, they were fitted with collars and chained to the hull. Manacles were fitted to their wrists and ankles and each woman was chained to the next. Large iron rings pierced their nipples and were in turn chained to the front of the collars.

"Sit your arses on this," a crewman said, tossing an old sack on the bare boards.

Africanus seated herself between the women and flexed her aching muscles.

"Any idea where we're headed?" she asked, listening to the sounds of the sea lapping against the hull.

"Wherever it is, it can't be worse than that stinking hole," the redhead grumbled.

"I liked it," the wide-mouthed one beamed. "You should've seen the size of some of those cocks. Phew!"

"With a cunt as big as yours, I wonder they didn't mate you with a bull," the redhead said spitefully, and shifted her arse over the prickling sack.

They were well out to sea before one of the crew arrived shoving bowls of porridge into their laps.

"Eat your fill," he said gruffly, unlocking the manacles and looking blatantly between the wide-mouthed girl's thighs.

He made a crude joke, comparing her sex with that of a camel, and went off laughing.

"What the fuck's a camel?" she asked.

No one answered and they went on spooning porridge into their hungry bellies, eating in silence until the crewman returned and collected the empty bowls. He released the collar chains and ordered the women on deck.

"The black one will go to my cabin," the captain said to the crewman. "The other two are for the use of the crew."

Africanus padded along the deck, too wrapped in her own thoughts to notice her nakedness. She was getting used to it by now. Not having any clothes to wear was becoming more and more regular, not to mention having sex with any man

234

who desired her. The captain was no exception and wasted no time in mounting her belly. Overhead the sails flapped in the freshening wind and the ship pitched on the frothing sea.

"Where are we going?" she asked, throwing her long legs over his swarthy back.

He was unlike any man she had ever met in this wild, barbaric country, and a strange, long forgotten similarity awakened visions of her homeland. The cabin smelt of spices she remembered as a child and she had seen the ornaments he wore on slaves captured in battle. His skin was dark and sunburned, a man unused to the colder climates of the Northern provinces.

"Guess," he said, not unkindly.

"Africa!" she said suddenly, jolting as his cock slammed into her.

He settled over her breasts, nibbling on her nipples.

"Good try," he smiled, licking all around her throbbing teats. "You're almost there."

She searched her memory and images of sun-baked deserts and palm trees came flooding into her mind. Her hands went to his buttocks, pulling him tighter.

He propped on his elbows and ran his tongue over her lips, savouring their sweetness. Again she asked the question and he whispered in her ear.

"Egypt!" she said aghast.

"You'll like it," he said. "Black women are highly-prized there, especially amongst the Roman rulers."

And the Phoenician plunged hard into her sex, riding her in time with the gentle swaying of the vessel, wondering how much she would fetch in the Lady Octavia's brothel.

Africanus is a beautiful North African girl enslaved by Rome from an early age and then given a chance to train at a 'ludus' for a career as a gladiatrix. Her owner's business affairs depend on her success in the arena but immediately she becomes the centre of a web of deceit.

The treacherous slave girl Nydia spies on her. The lady Octavia, wife of her owner is having a torrid affair with the games sponsor and the creditors are closing in on the ludus.

Filled with all the decadence, sex and danger of life in ancient Rome, the first instalment of Africanus' adventures is a headily erotic read in the best traditions of Silver Moon books.

The beautiful Nubian slave girl, Africanus, arrives in ancient Egypt. Soon she finds herself embroiled in the seedy brothels of Thebes. To escape she agrees to spy on the Roman governor by joining his harem. When her information leads to his being attacked, Africanus barely escapes with her life. She makes it to Alexandria and finds a ship to take her to safety... ...or so she thinks.

**Silver Moon**

## Trojan Slaves
### Syra Bond

The army of the Greeks is encamped outside the walls of Troy and the legendary war rages all around. So when Sappho and Chrysies, two beautiful Trojan girls are captured by their deadly enemies trying to flee the city, their situation is not a good one.

The question of who will possess and dominate the two slaves becomes the source of friction within the Greek camp and the two hapless captives can only pray that some miracle will help them escape from the cruel and warlike men into whose hands they have fallen.

ADULT FICTION
**Silver Moon**

# Trojan Whores

Syra Bond

As the great Trojan war moves towards its catastrophic end, the beautiful Trojan captives Sappho and Chryseis struggle to survive in the hostile camp of the Greeks. They are the helpless playthings of powerful men who fight each other for the spoils of war.

Praxis and Ajax, Achilles and Polydorus, slave traders and warriors alike want their share of the plunder from the ruins of Troy. The two girls are simply desirable flotsam to be exploited and used by whoever possesses them.

Trojan Whores provides more non-stop erotic action from the pen of Syra Bond.

There are over 100 stunningly erotic novels of domination and submission in the Silver Moon catalogue. You can see the full range, including Club and Illustrated editions by writing to:

Silver Moon Reader Services
Shadowline Publishing Ltd,
Box 101
City Business Centre
Station Rise
York
YO1 6HT

You will receive a copy of the latest issue of the Readers' Club magazine, with articles, features, reviews, adverts and news plus a full list of our publications and an order form.